# BRONTIDE

## T.D. CLOUD

To Jack,

Please enjoy (')

—J♀ ♀♂♀

Illustrated by AmbiSun

# BRONTIDE

## T.D. CLOUD

ISBN-13: 978-1537377223

ISBN-10: 1537377221

# Acknowledgements

There are so many people I owe thanks to for making this book a reality. Everyone who has sent their well wishes and encouragements deserves a place here, but I'd need an entirely new book just to name them all, so I'll just say thank you. Without you guys, I'd never have summoned the wherewithal to see this through.

Thanks goes to Daphne and Marz, for helping me with the impossible.

To Tess and Iza, for being so excited, and for letting me siphon that excitement to keep me going, even when I felt stagnant.

To JJM, Nico, and Linden, for being such careful, thoughtful editors, and for being brutally honest when I needed it most.

To Sun, for the beautiful art, the boundless energy, and the dedication to see another two books through with me.
Together, I know we can do it.

To all my friends who suffered through my frustrations and kept helping me, even when the way seemed blocked for good.

To my mom, who supported me through it all and remains to this day my number one fan.

To Yougei, my beloved, the one who inspires my all.

***Thank you for believing in me.***

# Contents

# CHAPTER 1

Corbet furrowed his brow and tried as hard as he could not to grimace at the man in front of him.

"Directions?" he repeated, speaking as slowly as possible, as if that would make the villagers better understand his foreign words. "I need directions?" The men stared at him in incomprehension and he sighed, rubbing tiredly at his eyes. Out of options, he gestured towards the forest nearby and mimed walking.

The man, a butcher by trade from the looks of his bloodstained apron, scratched at his head, hemming and hawing while he prattled to his apprentice in Gaelic. The two exchanged words and a few looks, and Corbet straightened his posture a bit, wishing he had

had the foresight to fix himself up a little better before approaching. When asking for help from strangers, it probably helped not to look quite so unfriendly.

He put on a smile that he hoped looked better than it felt and did his best to appear amicable. With his worn garb and tired, untrusting eyes, he probably appeared every bit of the vagabond he was. Given all the places he'd been and every winding road he'd walked, he'd yet to find a village that took kindly to those who passed through with no home of their own.

The butcher held up a hand to him and pushed at his apprentice, sending the boy off towards the center of the village. Corbet shifted on his feet, feeling more than a little awkward staring at the man who couldn't understand a single word of his French. The scent of sheep's blood rose off his clothing, the wagon of freshly slaughtered meat waiting nearby for the man's cleaver. He'd interrupted him at work, but the butcher seemed in no hurry to get back to his trade.

A few moments passed in silence, Corbet not knowing what else to do but wait. Eventually, and thankfully, the apprentice came back, an older woman in tow. Her garb placed her as someone of the Book, a religious pillar in the community no doubt. Corbet swallowed, wondering why on earth she was called. Did they think he asked for a blessing?

"Um, hello," he said, inclining his head politely. This felt like a mistake. Perhaps he should have just ignored

the town entirely and carried on with luck as his guide. "Can you understand me?"

"I am Sister Máiréad," she greeted, startling him a bit when he understood her. "You need help? You speak French? I learn some in my study. Can I help?"

Broken as it was, it was still unmistakably French. He sighed with relief and nodded. "Thank you," he said, doing his best to speak slow and use simple words. "Can you give me directions? I need to get through the forest and I see no path to take."

The nun smiled serenely and reached for his hand, clasping it in her own. "Fortunate you stop here before night," she replied a bit brokenly, only letting him go when she noticed how surprised he was at her touch. "The forest has much danger at dark. Best you stay night here."

Corbet's widened a bit and he shook his head emphatically. "No, no, I need to be on my way. I can't wait until the morning, and I don't want to inconvenience anyone. Just directions, please. I can handle the rest myself."

Her brow furrowed a bit and for a moment, he wondered if he had spoken too quickly for her. She turned to the butcher and rattled off something in Gaelic. The man frowned, shaking his head at Corbet and her, crossing his muscular arms with anything but acquiescence.

3

"What did he say?" he asked anyway, unsure of what would make the butcher want him to linger.

She turned back to him after a moment more of conversation. "He say that forest is dangerous. You must stay with him tonight." She broke off there, the corners of her lips turned down in what looked to be displeasure. Another exchange passed between him, the sister's disappointment in the butcher apparent.

Corbet raised a brow and she huffed, begrudgingly explaining the rest of what the butcher had said.

"The village here is, how you say, old-minded?" she tried, using her hands as she searched for the words she didn't know. "They believe in the Aos Sí, that they hold the forest beneath the Sidhe."

That didn't clear anything up for him at all.

"The what?" Corbet asked, looking at the butcher. "What is ash-shee?"

The butcher began to gesticulate, the Gaelic falling thick and fast in the warm summer air. Corbet looked to the nun, and she just looked disappointed.

"Old tales," she simply said, crossing her arms. "Old and not of the Book. Do not think of it. Forest is dangerous because it is large, unkind. It good to wait the night."

"In either case," he began, looking between the two sets of eyes, "I really can't stay the night here. Tell me

4

the path through, and I'll do my best to get to the other side before night falls." He tried a smile, winsome and as sincere as he could make it. "I'm used to traveling unkind land. I will be fine."

There was a pause while she pondered the words before she turned to the butcher, repeating what he had said. Corbet backed up a step when the man's voice rose, his expression exasperated. He threw up his hands and grabbed his apprentice by the shoulder, walking off with him towards the center of the village, the young boy struggling to catch the ass's reins to pull the wagon along with them.

"He wasn't happy about that, was he?" Corbet tried, finding the sister at least sympathetic to his plight. "Do you know the way?"

Sister Máiréad sighed and looked out to the forest. The boughs of the nearby trees waved gently in the breeze, the sound of birds a tranquil song to their swaying. Nothing about the forest looked dangerous, at least, not in this light. She looked back at Corbet, worrying her bottom lip between her teeth.

"Not safe at night," she began, but her tone spoke of acceptance, not denial. "Keep to the west," the sister said. "Short way is west. Long way is south, but no need to cross river."

Corbet cocked his head a bit. "A river? How deep is it? Can I ford it on my own?" He'd heard tell of the rapids near these parts. If he could mitigate his risks for the

price of a longer walk, he'd do so.

She didn't look optimistic. "Possible, but not safe. Only at bend," Sister Máiréad told. "Walk for two hours along river, then ford at bend."

"And the rest is just a straight path?"

"The rest is straight path," she confirmed.

That didn't seem too difficult. He glanced up at the sky to check where the sun lay, his hand over his eyes to protect them from the glare. "I travel fast," he said, putting it at perhaps mid afternoon. "Don't worry about me, I'll be through the forest before nightfall."

She didn't look like she believed him, but she at least didn't say it aloud. "See that you are," the sister said, crossing herself and then clasping her hands together at her breast. "May God bless you, traveler."

Corbet blushed a bit, unused to the sentiment. Most people he met didn't care much to bless him for anything, except a speedy departure. "Thank you, Sister," he gave, shifting the pack on his shoulder. "Thank you for the help." Religion may not weigh heavily on his list of priorities, but the consideration was still well met.

Movement caught his eye and he broke away from her calm expression to see the butcher stalking towards them, his stride intent and his fists clenched.

The sister caught him looking over her shoulder, and she turned too to look. "Don't let tales scare you," she

sighed, taking up his hand again to squeeze it. "Your journey will be safe and good."

"I hope so," he said, and she let go, walking back towards the town before the butcher reached them. She stopped him for a moment and said something in Gaelic, and from the looks of it, it was a warning not to continue on with his "old-minded" advice.

Corbet looked towards the woods, wondering if he could make it to the tree line before he had to hear more himself.

"Oi!" the man shouted, and he bit his lip, turning back. The sister was far from them now, nearly halfway back to the village proper. Corbet sighed and prepared for another dose of miming and hand gestures.

"I already got directions, so-" he began, but the butcher plowed on ahead, grabbing his hand like the sister had, only much more insistent.

The bit of metal was shoved into his hand, and no amount of pushing would make the butcher take it back. It was cold and heavy, rough-edged and sharp. "Is this a piece of a church fence?" he asked, knowing wrought iron when he saw it. He hadn't traveled far into town, but even from here he could see the imposing, barbed fence surrounding the largest structure the village could boast of.

Corbet fumbled it in his hand. This wouldn't make the Sister happy, he thought, shoving it in his bag when she

looked over her shoulder back at them. He was known to pick a few pockets now and again to pay for his daily bread, but defacing a church for a scrap of metal was something he couldn't say he was all that comfortable with.

The butcher said something incomprehensible and suitably somber, no doubt warning him again of the folly in his choice. He wished he had the capability to warn the man about the folly in his own. It was idiotic to allow superstition to guide one's actions, especially if said actions included stealing from the parish.

A large hand fell to his pack and rested over the pocket where he had stored the gift, breaking him from his concerned thoughts.

"Aos Sí," the man repeated, saying it slowly.

"Um, sure," Corbet replied, nodding his head and smiling, though he felt more confused than anything. "Thank you." It was probably some sort of talisman to the villagers here. If it made the man let him go, he'd accept it with grace aplenty and get out before the sister came after him for defacing the church.

They stared at each other for a few moments, but when the butcher made no other attempt at conversation, Corbet figured it was an appropriate time to take his leave.

It fell to him to turn away, the butcher watching him intently as he made for the forest. Corbet tried not to let

the heavy weight of the man's eyes on his shoulders get to him. Was he really that concerned for him? He couldn't imagine there being anything to worry about in a forest beyond the wild animals. It was far too removed an area to make bandits a concern.

Ducking into the tree line, Corbet shook off the man's sight and his worries. He'd been traveling alone far too long to be fearful of the things that lay in wait within a forest's depths.

First impressions granted him nothing to be concerned about. The village disappeared behind him in a wall of green foliage, the boughs of the trees and natural growth springing back to envelope him in the wilderness's embrace. Corbet picked up his feet and moved carefully through the thorns and thistle, breathing in the crisp scent of wood and decay.

There was no path to speak of, even as the trees evened out and some of the denser underbrush began to thin. Corbet took to the deer trails, following the winding paths that navigated him through the rugged terrain. Birds called out above his head as he traveled, chirping intermittently as they hopped from branch to branch.

He watched them flit to and fro as he stepped over a fallen log, taking in the brilliant spectrum of colors hidden in their wings. When the sunlight hit them, they seemed to shimmer like gems. A smile graced his lips and he listened to their songs, using his hands to climb up a rocky hill. Below the music of nature, he was beginning

9

to hear what sounded like running water.

Corbet brushed the dirt from his hands at the top of the hill, looking around at the view it afforded him. The skin on the back of his neck began to prickle, almost like he was being watched by unseen eyes, but he paid it no mind, chalking it up to the breeze cooling the sweat on his skin. The aforementioned river lay below, winding and cutting across the landscape like a fraying ribbon. He'd found his guide. All that was left was to find the bend and cross.

He smiled to himself and began carefully to skid down the incline, making his way towards the water. They had all been so concerned that he'd be stranded in the forest, but with the progress he was making, he couldn't imagine it taking more than another couple hours to reach the other side.

Shale and loose earth clattered to the rocky base below when he jumped the last few feet, landing gracefully on a flattish outcropping. The river was visible through the trees, and he moved towards it, ignoring the uncomfortable feeling that he was somehow being observed. There was no one around for leagues, he told himself, pushing aside some wayward branches blocking his path. It was just his imagination.

The air near the river was cool and flecked with moisture, clinging to his flushed cheeks in a cooling mist. Corbet looked in either direction, craning his neck to see whether the river bent nearby. It curved gently behind the tree line and he sighed, slipping his pack to the ground to dig for his canteen.

The day was far from done so he figured it would be prudent to fill up now, in case the bend came faster than expected. Another shiver ran down his spine, like a clammy finger tracing down his vertebrae. Biting his lip, Corbet unscrewed the cap and took one last look around. He'd do this quickly and then be on his way.

Kneeling by the river, he lowered his canteen into the cold rapids, filling it up to the top.

It was then that he heard it.

A loud crack sounded in the thick brush behind him, and Corbet startled, nearly losing his balance and toppling into the river. He braced himself and turned, every muscle posed to move should it prove to be some wild animal hungry for travelers.

Branches rattled and twigs snapped and Corbet hovered his hand over the knife hidden in his boot. Whatever it was, it didn't sound intimidated by the threat of him.

"Is someone there?" he called, stoppering the canteen and shoving it quickly into his bag. Did Ireland have bears? He didn't rightly know. Thoughts of the village rose into his mind unbidden, and, for a moment, he wondered if he had been followed by something more opportunistic than a bear or a wolf.

His paranoia increased with the snapping of more branches, a heavy, bestial breathing cutting through the undergrowth with all the weight of a physical blow. There was nowhere to run with the river at his back and Corbet tore his eyes away from the shaking brambles to see what his options were.

Grabbing his bag in his fist, he steeled himself for the worst.

The river was just as cold and vicious as he had expected, but as unpleasant as it felt, it was better than sharp teeth or murderous claws. Corbet didn't let himself look back. He scrambled for purchase on the slippery rocks, the current thrashing him around so hard he half thought he'd be washed away.

Over the roar of the water, he couldn't hear if he were being chased. Corbet threw out his hand and grabbed for the far bank, coughing as his head bobbed beneath the raging water. Dirt and rock met his fingers and he clawed his way onto land. Adrenaline ran like hot iron through his veins. He forced himself to his feet and took off, looking to the trees for cover.

Darting past trees and logs and rocks, Corbet made himself as hard a target to track as possible. The natural landscape made the terrain hilly and rugged, costing him precious seconds with every step he took. White tinged the edges of his vision, but he kept going. Whatever that beast had been, he knew he was in no position to meet it face to face.

He didn't stop running until his lungs burned. There was no way to know for sure that he had outran the growling thing, but he swore he could still feel its hot, acrid breath on the back of his neck. A shudder ran down his spine, only partly from residual nerves. The wind chilling his soaked skin added to the shivering.

Leaning against a tree, Corbet wiped at his wet face, flicking the water away. He wrung out his shirt and shivered as another stiff breeze blew past, leaving gooseflesh in its place. He was soaked to his bones and far from the river's guiding path. This was certainly not how he had expected his day to go.

A quick glance skywards told him that at some point, in his haste, he had begun traveling north.

There was a certain anxiety associated with losing one's sense of direction that Corbet felt didn't mesh quite well with the serenity of the forest around him. A stick snapped beneath his foot, the path long lost and buried beneath the undergrowth of the wilderness's depths.

He could hear the sister's warning echoing in his ears, but there wasn't much he could do at this point. The sun shone dully through the treetops and with only a few hours left before it grew dark, he just couldn't find it in himself to care all that much where he was or where he was meant to be going, so long as he didn't run into whatever beast he'd left behind him.

Corbet sighed and pushed past a particularly dense patch of brambles, wondering how he had let himself get

so far off the path. His clothes were cold and damp, his boots uncomfortably wet. The pack on his back seemed no worse for wear, but he could tell he was going to be in for an unpleasantly chilly night at this rate.

Perhaps he had been too hasty in turning down that offer for lodging. It might not have prevented him from getting lost when he finally did manage to be on his way, but it would have at least ensured that he'd have made it through the thick forest before nightfall came. The way the sunlight shone, he could tell that he only had a few hours left until the day grew dark.

Shuffling the pack on his back, he reached for his canteen of water and took a deep drink. Cold and crisp, it settled his thoughts in a numbing wave.

What did it really matter? If he kept walking he'd make it somewhere in the end. The sky was clear and the night promised nothing worse than anything he'd had in the past. If he managed to scrape together a small fire, there really would be no point in worrying.

That is, unless whatever the butcher had been warning him about came calling.

Corbet rubbed at his face and smacked his cheeks, willing them to warm up. It was stupid to think like that, he told himself. He wasn't the type to let superstition guide his actions or let a stint of bad luck tarnish his mood any more than it already had. The nun had said it was nothing to worry about, so why was it weighing so heavy on him?

A clearing opened up further ahead and it looked as good a place as any to take a short break from his thoughts. The grass was soft and inviting, the small flowers dotting the ground like colorful flecks of paint on a green backdrop. The petals danced in the light breeze and filled the air with their gentle perfume. Somewhere beyond his sight lay a brook, humming and singing its own melodic composition to the rhythm of the forest. In a place this beautiful, it would be hard to let fear pollute his reason.

He sat down in a round circle of grass, a darker shade than the rest surrounding it, and set himself to sipping his water and basking in the natural beauty around him.

It wasn't often he found himself immersed so fully by wilderness. Most of his travels saw him on the open road, traversing cities and fields and conditions far less hospitable than this. Near his foot was a small mushroom, speckled like a bird's egg. It made him think of the illustrations in children's books, the ones where tiny creatures used the caps as tables for their meals. If he wasn't sitting in it, he might not have believed a place like this existed outside of idyllic art.

"You must be new here," a voice crooned behind him, close enough for warm breath to tickle Corbet's neck.

Startled, Corbet dropped his canteen, the water spilling across the grass. He turned sharply and looked up at the sudden company smiling brightly down at him. Slowly, his heart ceased its incessant and panicked

pounding, his body growing used to the stress this day was bringing.

It was just a man, just a fellow traveler wandering through the woods, and one who spoke French at that. He hadn't heard him approach at all.

What a coincidence, he thought, unable to shake the distrust in his gut.

"Why do you say that?" he asked warily, putting some space between them. There was a knife in his boot and he held himself carefully to keep it close, just in case.

"Your charming accent, for one," he said, his own accent tinged with the cadence of the Celts. "The state of your clothes, for another. You look as if you've taken quite the tumble." The man knelt down and picked up his fallen canteen, screwing the lid back on before holding it out to him with a disarming smile on his face. "Run afoul of some tricky paths, have you?"

Corbet felt his cheeks flush with indignity, but with his garb still damp and his hair still wet, there was no point in lying to save face. "I had to cross the river suddenly," he said instead, staring at the proffered water. He didn't trust this politeness. "This forest isn't very kind to strangers."

"Oh, it can be very perilous to those who tramp and stomp without care. For example, you're sitting in a faerie circle." His brilliant red hair glinted crimson in the sunlight, accentuating the paleness of his skin, the golden

hue of his eyes. He was colored like the height of fall, rich and deep. "No one from these parts would be so brazen."

If his coloring wasn't eye-catching enough, his height certainly made it so. He had to be a head or so taller than Corbet, his shoulders far broader than his own. Corbet wasn't the type to feel self-conscious, but compared to this stranger, he couldn't help but feel a bit dull. His own dark hair and eyes were certainly nowhere near as interesting to look at.

With careful hands, he reached out to take back his bottle, noting that it had been emptied of a good portion of its contents in the fumble. "You don't say," he murmured, putting it back in his bag to be refilled later.

Something of his confusion must have shown on his face and the stranger tilted his head, settling down into a comfortable sprawl just outside of Corbet's personal space. The air filled with the sound of the man's tinkling earrings whenever he moved, singing along to the forest's song. Corbet felt a stab of want, seeing how much nicer they were compared to his own simple studs.

"It's really quite a rude thing to do," he went on, gesturing towards the patch of dark, curly grass Corbet had settled atop. "It's said that faeries revel here under the moonlight. It's considered bad manners to enter the ring. The Aos Sí don't take well to rudeness."

Corbet ran his hand through the soft foliage, taking it in with new interest. There was that phrase again, the one the butcher had used and the sister had disregarded.

"Oh really? I hadn't heard tell of that. What happens to those who enter?" he asked, looking up with a smile at the man watching him. "Am I going to die?"

It shouldn't have surprised him so much to hear the man's laugh, low and pleasant as it rang through the clearing. The sound was as disarming as his smile, like a glass of wine on a quiet night. The sharp distrust almost softened at the sound, but Corbet was too on edge to lower his defenses just yet.

"Oh no, nothing so dire," his new companion answered, plucking a violet from outside the ring to twirl between his fingers. "But you may find yourself the object of the fae's displeasure. They can sense it, you know. When a mortal wanders into their territory."

It was Corbet's turn to laugh, this man obviously some bored villager with enough command of his language to think it fun to tease him. The fae? He'd heard stories of them, tales of small sprites and mischievous goblins that liked to play jokes on the unsuspecting. These Aos Sí must be the Celtic version, and he felt himself the furthest thing from intimidated by the warning.

"I'm already lost," he chuckled ruefully, "and wet and cold. I don't think my situation can get much worse than what it already is. Unless you're planning on killing me, that is."

There was a new light in the man's eyes, something not quite benevolent. Corbet watched him carefully but didn't move when his cheek was cupped and cradled in a

startlingly warm hand. His own hand inched towards his hidden knife.

"You shouldn't say such things so easily. Talking like that will only draw them all the quicker. The fae love foundlings, even more than they love misleading the lost."

He didn't hear a no, or anything resembling one. His hand palmed the handle of the blade. "You seem awfully knowledgeable," Corbet observed, staring into golden eyes as a reverent thumb traced the bone of his cheek. What an odd man, to touch strangers so casually.

The man smiled and leaned closer as if telling a secret. "It helps that I'm one of them."

Corbet huffed out a laugh and broke away from the touch to look past the man's shoulder and into the trees. "It's not kind to lie to strangers. You tell me you're a faerie but not your name. Am I expected to believe you sought me out for this transgression as well?" he asked, his brow lifting. "Did you sense me here, sitting in the ring?"

"Oh, but I am! I'm even a king," the stranger went on, eyes dancing as he fell into the role. "King of the Seelie Court. A king's duties are vast and varied."

He let the man have his attention again, if only so he could watch his performance. "I can't say I'm familiar with the terms. Your name might do me better," Corbet tried, determined to get the man to tell him. "It's hard to imagine a king wandering around the forest, informing

travelers of the faux pas they commit."

"Maybe I made an exception since you're so beautiful," he replied, smile a razor's edge.

"Maybe I'd believe you if you gave me your name," Corbet shot back, his own sharper. Beautiful? He'd be the first to admit that he wasn't rugged or large like the stranger before him, but he was hardly a waif deserving of such a flowery descriptor. A wet, half-drowned cat would be more apt.

A shadow passed over the man's face, the clouds above rolling in quickly enough to cast the clearing into relative darkness. "Names hold power, my lost one. You have to give me something in exchange. Nothing in this world comes without a cost."

Corbet shifted to his knees and looked towards the sky, taking in how far the sun had dropped since he had first sat down. There wouldn't be much time left of daylight, if he were judging correctly. His brow furrowed. He could have sworn he still had a few more hours.

At this rate, there was no chance he'd find his way through the forest before darkness obscured his way. One way or another, he would need to come up with a plan for how he was spending the night. Was it worth the risk to ask this stranger for lodging?

Corbet bit his lip and looked into the unfamiliar forest depths. He could leave now and try to find the path or perhaps even some shelter of his own, then settle up for

the night and try his hand at finding his way out of the forest come morning. There had been more nights than he'd care to recall where he had camped out in the open or up in a tree. It wouldn't be amiss for him to do so again.

The stranger watched him with appraising eyes, his every muscle a dare begging to be realized. With every moment he wasted with the man, the time for finding a safe bed was wasted as well.

"What would you want for it?" Corbet asked, too curious to just let the unspoken challenge die. "What would I have to pay to learn your name?"

His companion quirked a brow and took him in, golden eyes near hungry. "Now that entirely depends on what you're willing to give. Fae are greedy sorts, kings even more so. If you're not careful, you'll find yourself giving more than you intended." As he spoke his hands spun the flower between his fingers, making it disappear with a magician's skill.

"Perhaps you're right," Corbet said after a moment of silence, lifting himself to his feet and shouldering his pack. "Maybe I shouldn't risk it. You're obviously far too dangerous for me to play with so lackadaisically."

He made as if to leave and the man jolted as if slapped, scrambling to his feet to snatch Corbet's hand before he could move more than a step. Eyes wide and emotions plainly written across his face, he was all too easy to read. Just like a child about to lose a new toy.

21

Corbet eyed the hand holding his own, noting how small his looked in such a large hand. He waited pointedly, masking his smile with an expectant stare. "It's going to get dark soon," he said gently, tugging at his hand. "If you're not going to tell me I should just be on my way."

White teeth sunk into the man's bottom lip as he worried the flesh, thinking. It was plain to see that he didn't want Corbet to leave so soon.

"Tell me your name," he finally said, tugging Corbet closer and out of the faerie ring, into his space.

"Oh, are you sure that's a good idea? Names hold power you know," Corbet teased, letting the man pull him around, even following when he began leading them out of the clearing and back into the forest proper. "I wouldn't want to be taken advantage of by a faerie king with less than noble intentions," he said, scanning the man for any sign of weapons.

Though their clothing was similar, he could almost sense that there was something hidden on him. He too wore worn trousers, leather boots, and a shirt that had long since seen better days. While his cloak was a muted red, matching his hair, it was fastened with an expensive looking clasp that belied the simple traveler he presented as. A shiny leather satchel hung from his side by a strap, heavy with something unseen. Wealth or weapons, he couldn't tell, but he itched to find out.

"Noble intent is for the noble alone, my lost one. Tell

me your name and I'll tell you mine. Consider it a deal. We fae always honor our deals."

The forest closed in on them the further in they walked, morphing into something not quite right in Corbet's mind. The trees, flowers, and undergrowth hadn't changed, but the light took on an ominous glint, the air an inhuman weight.

Unease bloomed in his chest like a rose. Corbet felt his skin prickle and he drew closer to his jovial companion. He didn't feel welcome, like some force was pushing against his chest, telling him to turn around and leave. A glance at his companion told him that he alone felt the insistent pressure, and they continued to go deeper. He let the knife slip into his hand from his sleeve and angled it towards the man.

His mind told him to strike while instinct screamed to run.

"I'm Corbet," he answered distractedly, his eyes roving the unseen path his companion seemed to know intimately. "Something feels off. Where are we going?"

The man let out a breath and laughed a little, looking at him with new interest and intent. "What a strange name for a strange mortal. You are very far from home, aren't you?" His autumn coloring darkened with the sky, the warm colors flickering with some hidden decay. "Call me Ruari. And we're already here."

Beneath his feet the ground seemed to churn, the

mound before them roiling like an angry sea. Corbet shuddered, the unease and discontent rising into an unbearable din. He looked down at their joined hands and lagged a step behind. If he was quick, he could gut the man.

The pressure in the air stole the breath from his lungs and Corbet tossed aside his curiosity for the instinctual fear of what he felt coming. He was too accustomed to the taste to ignore it any longer.

A hand as strong as iron caught his as he swung the blade, self-preservation striking nothing but empty, charged air. With both his hands trapped, Corbet had no way left to defend himself.

"Wait," he tried to cry, but it was already too late.

Warm hands held him tight, his vision growing dark as the earth swallowed them whole.

# CHAPTER 2

Corbet came back to himself slowly to the feeling of a warm hand stroking his hair, a low voice talking incessantly somewhere above him.

Soft cotton brushed his cheek as he shuffled and shifted, the seductive call of sleep beckoning him back like an old friend after a long absence. He longed to follow but the voice kept going, prattling on and on, pulling him back from the edge just when he thought he would drift off. He let his hand swipe blindly at the source of the chatter, hoping to silence it like swatting at an annoying fly .

The fingers in his hair stopped to snatch up his lazy smack, yanking him fully from the embrace of slumber.

Corbet blinked blearily and tried to tug himself free, only stopping once he realized who had grabbed him. The unfamiliar surroundings coalesced around the stranger's smile, growing all the more tangible the longer he stared.

Through the layer of sleep still clouding his vision he took in the sumptuous environment, the bright tapestries lining the walls and the chandeliers lighting the space. They hung dripping with crystal, twinkling gently in the wake of their candlewick flames. An undercurrent of energy seemed to hum on the edge of perception, warm and transient like a heat haze.

They were alone in the room but it didn't feel like it. Corbet's heart thudded painfully in his chest.

Somewhere, out of sight but certainly not out of mind, lurked countless curious eyes watching his every move. He lay on some sort of soft couch, his head resting on something warm. Like this, there was hardly a place to hide from whatever watched with avid attention.

At least he was no longer wet, he thought frantically while he scrambled to piece together the waking dream around him.

"Ruari..." he managed, staring at the walls as if they threatened to open up around him. He pushed himself upright and off the man's knee where his head had been resting. "Ruari, where are we?"

"I love how you say my name," he answered, laughing a little at his accent. The man cupped his cheek and

26

smiled so brightly that it put the crystal to shame. "Welcome to my Court, my lost one. I hope your rest was kind and your dreams light."

He too had changed in the time Corbet had been unconscious. Where before he wore simple, rugged garb, not dissimilar to his own, now he was clothed like the monarch Ruari claimed to be. A crown rested upon his brow, silver like moonlight and organic like woven ivy. He swallowed and turned his sight downwards, ignoring the evidence that proved this stranger was a king.

Of his clothing, everything was colorful and sheer, iridescent like the wings of dragonflies. He let his fingers trail down the brilliant crimson fabric, something telling him it couldn't be real. What sort of dye could give such a pure color? The air itself doubled in weight under a dreamlike element, flickering in the corners of his eyes like a mirage.

Something almost like fear gripped him in a vice and Corbet stared at the smiling man, finally seeing for himself that his claims hadn't been in jest. He shoved at him in a bid for space, noticing only then that his knife had been taken from him.

Could he win, he wondered, if he went for the eyes? Ruari was far larger than him, in both height and stature. The hand holding his wrist gripped him tight, reeling him back in as easily as a child pulling on an unraveling thread.

Ruari smiled patronizingly and boldly kissed his

cheek, his hand sliding down to rest on Corbet's neck. "You really didn't believe me before, did you? For once I told the complete truth. Funny how that works," he mused to himself, enjoying the confliction on Corbet's face. "I can't believe you tried to kill me. What a dangerous one I've found."

He pressed a kiss next to Corbet's mouth, something quick and not quite chaste. "But it's of no consequence now. You're here and I couldn't be happier."

Corbet swallowed and pulled away from the casual, proprietary touch, searching for his pack, an exit, his knife, for anything that could give him some sort of stability upon which to ground himself. There was no telling where he was or how long he had been asleep. Ruari kissed his head this time, and Corbet wrinkled his nose, wondering just how hard he'd have to hit to phase the creature holding him.

Fighting wouldn't get him out of here though. The room was lit so brightly and there were no windows to account for the illumination. He knew from that alone that the candles weren't the sole force at work here. Some energy tingled against his bare skin, some sort of magic or something that he didn't have a name for. He bit his lip and felt a hand smooth down his spine, the man nuzzling him as if it were his right.

It was grating how Ruari watched him flounder for support, smiling like someone watching a new pet acquaint itself with an unfamiliar home. Corbet wasn't used to admitting that he was powerless, but with the situation as it was, he had little to rely on if not for the supposed king fawning over him.

"You need to take me back right now," Corbet stated, staring squarely into Ruari's laughing eyes while he ignored the sensation of being watched. "I appreciate you wanting to show me your Court, but I need to go."

Ruari's face broke out into a childish moue, his hands brushing an errant lock of hair back behind Corbet's pierced ear. "I don't think you understand. I told you what happens when you enter a faerie circle. You broke the rules so now you're mine." His smile became luminous, shining like dew on spider silk. "This is your new home. Or will be, soon enough."

There was no time to retort or resist. All at once the room exploded into movement. Corbet startled horribly and found himself wrapped up in strong arms, Ruari nearly cradling him as colors and figures scrambled through the hall in blurs of motion. It was so sudden, the silence and solitude replaced with a raucous party in the span of Corbet blinking.

"What..." he began as he took in the plethora of strange creatures darting to and fro, carrying all manner of things above their heads. Ruari lifted him to his feet from the chaise they had been resting on just before it too was whisked away in the flurry of activity. There was no thought to resist the contact, his vision dominated by the fantasy playing out before him.

Corbet couldn't tear his eyes from the sight of a diminutive figure balancing a steaming teapot on its head, its pointed shoes dancing and clicking to the music lilting through the air. Purple and orange hair hid its face from view but a long nose cut through the air like a fin guiding a fish through a current.

He had absolutely no idea what he was seeing before him if not the impossible.

"It's rude to stare," Ruari whispered in his ear and Corbet looked away, a blush staining his face before he remembered to be angry.

"What is this?" Corbet hissed back, plastering himself to the king's hip while he was guided through the hall. On all sides, similar creatures scrambled about. Some were humanoid, tall and graceful like Ruari. Others were completely foreign, more akin to storybook characters than anything found in reality. "Ruari, what the hell is going on?"

The world spun again when Ruari took him by the hands and twirled him in a dance, laughing when he yelped in surprise. "It's a feast, of course. Your first of many, so let's have some fun," he entreated, pulling him close to kiss his cheek again.

He had no choice but go along with it, letting Ruari guide him along to the front of the hall and through the roving mass of faeries bustling around. It was hard to tell with the amount of people flooding in, but Corbet swore the dimensions of the room had changed, elongating

somehow. There was no way the simple, quiet room from before could hold all of this without bursting at the seams.

Corbet stopped in his tracks when they reached the end of the hall, Ruari smiling down at him knowingly. "Impressive, isn't it?" the faerie asked, settling into his seat at the head of the table.

The table before them seemed to almost buckle under the weight of the feast resting atop it. Whole birds sat elegantly on platters, large bowls overflowing with delicacies of all types both known and unknown. Gold and silver plates and gem encrusted goblets lined the edges, the wealth almost as tempting as the food itself. Corbet stared in awe, suddenly ravenous as the plates and dishes were paraded past his eyes. He had never in his life seen so much food in one place. The scent of it all was like a physical blow.

A hurried tug pulled him into the seat at Ruari's side, their thighs touching beneath the edge of the table. The rest of the fae took their seats only once they had settled in, though several seemed to bustle about, serving the others as if they were servants. A rainbow of colored faces turned towards him the longer he stared.

Corbet didn't know where to look, certainly not at the creatures before him, and so he settled on the king at his side, the golden eyes so warm and pleased to have him there. With a careless wave of his hand, the feast began, everyone digging in and the conversation swelling into a

low din. Corbet let his plate be filled and stared at it all, unsure of where to begin.

"It can be a bit daunting," Ruari whispered in his ear, his soft lips just brushing the sensitive shell, tingling when they lingered on his silver piercings.

Corbet leaned into him a little, feeling entirely too much like a timid child thrown into the wild of a party meant only for adults. "This is unbelievable," he breathed. "I don't know what to try first."

"Why not this?"

Ruari held out a beautiful morsel of fruit, the ripe, vivid dark of a blackberry as perfect as those seen in paintings. Even before thinking, Corbet leaned closer, wanting nothing more than to taste the treat offered to him.

The king smiled, pressing it to Corbet's lips. It was cool and smooth but Corbet didn't open his mouth despite the delicious scent filling his nose. There was something off about Ruari's grin, something far too victorious and expectant for the situation. He flicked his gaze to the faeries gathered around the table, realizing in that moment that it had grown quiet.

There were so many eyes on him all of a sudden, all trying to maintain the guise of disinterest even though their excitement was palpable.

This is your new home. Or will be, soon enough.

32

The words echoed in his ears and Corbet pushed the hand away. He didn't know anything about this so-called fae culture. He had never grown up with the legends and tales told to him in cautionary whispers. But despite all of his ignorance, Corbet knew a trick when he saw it and they were far too focused on him eating for it not to be the last nail hammered in his coffin.

"Do you not like these, my lost one?" Ruari asked, faux concern painting his expression human. "Tell me what you like and I'll get it for you."

"I'll be trapped here if I eat or drink, is that how it is?" Corbet asked, his eyes sharp and his mouth watering despite himself. He could still feel the cool kiss of the fruit against his lips and he ached to lick them, to chase the phantom taste.

He knew he had it right when Ruari smiled at him as if he had just agreed to marry him on the spot. The king's eyes narrowed, his grin lovingly proud. "Now who told you that?" he asked, his tone not even trying to deny it. "Here I was, thinking you were unfamiliar with our customs."

Corbet rolled his eyes and tamped down on the flicker of pleasure the praise still incited somewhere deep in his stomach. It was a close save, and a good guess.

"It didn't take a genius to figure it out, especially when everyone in this room is watching to see if I take a bite. You're a lot of things, Ruari." He pushed the full plate away, determined to hide his hunger and thirst. "Subtle

isn't one of them."

"Ah, you see right through me," and Ruari threw his palm over his face, playing coy. He peeked through his fingers and rested his head on his hand, taking him in with new interest. "What am I going to do with you? You just keep on surprising me. Won't you please eat something? Stay with me forever, Corbet, I beg you."

Shifting in his seat, Corbet found it hard to meet the man's eye. "A king shouldn't beg, Ruari. It's embarrassing for the both of us."

His eyes went wide when Ruari snatched up his hands, forcing his attention back to him and him alone.

"What's there to be embarrassed about? I want you to be mine," Ruari declared with not even a hint of shame to be found.

Without his permission, his face flushed brightly, and he again had to avert his eyes. "You really don't waste time, do you?" he managed, growing steadily overwhelmed with the whole situation. "I tried to kill you. Do you not even care?"

"You couldn't have killed me even if you tried." Ruari popped a berry into his mouth and chewed with delight, his eyes dancing. "I may live for an eternity but you certainly won't, not like this at any rate. I don't want to waste any of our time together, no matter how this story may end."

Corbet watched him eat and he wrapped his arms around his stomach, holding himself tightly to keep his hunger silent. His head spun with the scent of the food, the words, and the boundless intent. Mouth dry, ears ringing, he forced himself to breathe in through his mouth, then out through his nose.

There was no way any of this could be real.

"I need some air," he managed to choke out, pushing away from the table and darting away without a single look back. The hall was massive and honeycombed with hallways that had to lead somewhere. He could feel the collective weight of a feast-worth of eyes on him, but he kept walking, his mind focused only on his breathing and keeping calm.

With his eyes locked onto the intricate mosaic beneath his feet, there was no way to avoid the collision before it was too late.

Corbet yelped when he walked right into the unflinching figure, bouncing off. He would have fallen to the floor had it not been for the quick reflexes of the hand that shot out to grab him. He fumbled for balance and felt himself be righted by two strong hands on his shoulders. Red and gold greeted him like an overzealous suitor and Corbet grimaced, now that much closer to panicking.

"You certainly left in a hurry," Ruari groused, holding him tightly to keep him in place. "I know you probably won't eat anything, but you could have told me if you wanted to leave. I would have shown you around."

35

Corbet ached to tell him he couldn't just teleport like that, but he knew there would be no point.

It was hard to look him in the eye, but somehow Corbet managed to anyway. "I need some air. Can you take me somewhere..." he looked around, gesturing weakly at the opulence and noise around them. There may not be an escape from Ruari but he could at least do without the crowds of fae staring at his every move. "Somewhere that's not here?"

Ruari took him in for a moment and seemed to sense some of his distress. "Of course, come this way. You would get lost if I tried to give you directions, so I hope you're able to suffer my company for a bit longer."

Smiling weakly despite himself, Corbet let his hand be taken in Ruari's, following him as he led the way through the labyrinthine palace. He lost himself in the shifting of Ruari's cloak, the fabric as fine and shimmery as spider silk. For all he knew, it could have been woven from a web.

"Right through here," Ruari said gently, guiding him through an arched doorway and into a room that was dimly lit and smelled of cool earth. "This is where I go when I need some space. Or well, where I go when I don't just venture aboveground to frolic with you mortals."

Corbet would have replied by saying some pithy little thing about kidnapping and marriage proposals and the likelihood of them occurring on his jaunts, but his breath was stolen in a way completely unrelated to his panic

from before.

He stared straight up at the pseudo-ceiling and gaped at the lights dripping from what looked to be willow branches. Like phosphorescent tears, they ran down the melancholic trees, casting the space into a soft glow. Dots of similar light speckled the ground, popping up between the stems of flowers. Though they proved the only source of light in the space, the air was lit with a low glow, like the pale blue of a moonlit night. The garden seemed without end. He stood transfixed, taking it all in, until a gentle tug on his hand had Corbet moving.

Ruari took him deeper, his golden eyes dancing in the dim light as he watched Corbet's wonderment grow. "They're called faerie lights," he said quietly, answering the unspoken question in Corbet's eyes. "Above they mislead travelers, making them stray from the path with their light. But down here..."

He trailed off and sat down on a convenient bench, coaxing Corbet to join him. "Down here...?" Corbet prompted in an awed whisper, mystified at how the pale blue lights painted Ruari ethereal.

"Down here, they dance, bringing a little bit of light to this dark place."

It was obvious he wasn't talking about a literal darkness. The hall from before had been so bright, so alive with joy and mirth. Corbet flinched a little when Ruari wrapped an arm around him, pulling him flush to his side. Any closer and he would be in the king's lap.

And of course Ruari noticed.

"You're very beautiful, Corbet," he said quietly, his voice dipping and swirling like the lights around them. "I would be very pleased if you would stay with me forever."

Corbet's face flushed and then paled, both hopefully hidden in the darkness. "You don't even know me," he whispered, turning his eyes to the delicate ivy crawling up the bench. It glowed an earthy blue and seemed to dance to some music unheard.

He felt more than saw Ruari's shrug. "I know I'd enjoy spending an eternity getting to know you. There's so much to tell you, so many things to share." Ruari unwound his arm and leaned towards the ground, snatching up one of the near lights and cupping it in his hand. "I've never had a mortal try to stick a knife in me before. You're certainly full of surprises of your own for me to discover."

The soft light was guided towards him and Corbet couldn't even feign disinterest, his curiosity more than piqued. He held up his own hands when prompted and gasped softly when the light was passed into his cupped palms, Ruari's holding them still and stable.

It was akin to holding ice but lacking the bite that came with such cold. The contrast between the light and Ruari's warm hands was jarring, like touching snow while being cradled in sunlight. He could feel the ball of bright move, bouncing against his fingers as if disliking the confinement. Up close, like this, he could see past the

dim corona.

Through the glowing light, he found that the small creature was more than just a ball of illuminated air. There was a shape to it, like tiny flower petals draped over a stem. With every flutter of movement it made, the petals lifted and contracted, propelling the light through the air like a sea creature through an ocean current. The more he observed, the more he saw past the glimmer. The garden was filled with the minute flowers, transforming the space into an underwater seascape.

Maybe that was why he was finding it so difficult to breathe.

Corbet looked to Ruari but saw nothing but an encouraging smile. He opened his hands and watched as the light rose, hovering near his cheek to examine him in return.

"It tickles a bit," he said quietly as the light brushed coolly along his skin.

"I think it likes you," Ruari chuckled.

Corbet bit his lip but he couldn't hold back his smile when the petals of light shivered in glee, darting back towards his hands, asking to play. "I like it too," he laughed, letting it chase his touch and nuzzle into his fingertips.

Ruari rested his head on Corbet's shoulder, watching his hands dance through the air after the pale glow.

"You're good with them," he observed, something like pride in his voice. "They usually don't like mortals. That's why they like tricking them so much, leaving them lost as they revel in the chaos that ensues."

His thoughts went back to that moment of fear in the forest, of the cold river and the snarling thing in the undergrowth. He was beginning to think that it hadn't been an animal.

"Are you like that?" he asked, turning to look at the fae leaning on his shoulder. "Do you enjoy misleading mortals like me?"

"Oh, I'm fairly certain there are no mortals like you, my lost one," Ruari crooned, tucking a strand of hair behind Corbet's ear. "You were already lost when I found you. I didn't need to mislead you to have you here. You followed me, hand in hand. Your knife at the ready, even."

His voice was so low and warm in Corbet's ear and he barely held back the shiver that longed to echo down his spine. The faerie light fluttered off, sensing the shift in mood, and with its cold light gone, he began to feel uncomfortably warm.

"But you still took me," he breathed, only just realizing how close their lips were in the darkness. Something like excitement churned in his stomach. Corbet's eyes flicked up from the inviting mouth, seeing heat in golden eyes. "You're still trying to take me, even now."

Ruari smiled close enough to feel and blinked lazily,

knowing all too well what he was doing to Corbet. "I don't think I'll need to take you," he admitted, drawing nearer to kiss him softly. "You'll fall into my arms all on your own."

The kiss was chaste and electric and Corbet pulled away slower than he knew he should have, bringing his fingers up to cover his tingling lips. "I won't eat the food," he managed, so breathless despite it being such a small thing. "I'll find another way. I won't eat it. You can't just have me."

The lights danced faster around them, their movements dizzying and mesmerizing. Weariness collected like a puddle in his limbs. He leaned heavily against the faerie king. Corbet let himself be coaxed into Ruari's arms, enjoying the warmth, comfortable and soothing were it not for the cocky grin on the fae's face.

He wrote the lethargy up to yet another display of magic. If he closed his eyes, he could pretend the acceptance was part of the spell as well.

"I look forward to it," Ruari replied, pressing another kiss to his cheek. "You're so clever that I'm sure you'll figure out an alternative in no time."

Corbet bit his lip and watched the lights dance, too tired to fight the comfortable embrace or the patronizing tone. He tightened his hands in the fabric of Ruari's shirt, his eyes struggling to stay open. There was something about the dazzling darkness and the scent of forest that clung to the fae holding him. He struggled to gather his

thoughts.

It was so quiet, the sound of his own breathing the loudest thing in his ear. Confusion rose though he knew not why. It took a moment to realize what was missing.

"Ruari," he mumbled, leaning more fully against his solid chest, curious.

"What is it, my lost one?"

"Do you have a heart? I don't hear it."

A hand stroked through his hair so very gently. "A beating heart is a luxury for those susceptible to time's touch. I have one, but it is silent, asleep." A kiss fell to his head. "You make it feel alive."

Were he not so tired, Corbet was sure he'd be embarrassed by that declaration. Instead though, he was only curious. "Tell me about you," Corbet said, his voice already beginning to fade. "I want to know everything."

Ruari laughed quietly and tilted his chin up for another breath-stealing kiss. "As you wish," he promised, his hand resting against Corbet's flushed cheek.

The last thing Corbet registered was the feeling of being held, gentle fingers carding through his hair while a low voice lilted in the dark.

# CHAPTER 3

Corbet awoke slowly in an unfamiliar bed.

He stretched against the soft, downy mattress, yawning luxuriously without an ounce of worry for his current location. When the bed was as sumptuous as this, it was fairly difficult to care.

Everything around him was a far cry from the way he usually spent his nights, which was almost always under the open sky and on the unforgiving ground. The strange shirt felt like satin against his skin and he blinked at the pale green sleeve. This was definitely one of the better ways he had awoken on his travels, all things considered.

At least there was no one lying next to him.

It was almost surprising in that regard. Ruari hadn't seemed like the type to let him sleep alone.

Piercing gold eyes filled his sight when he closed his own, every blink bringing back the man in question. The cool sheets did little to calm his pounding heart. He could remember all too clearly the night before, the easy affection shared in the garden. He didn't even know the man and yet he had already fallen asleep in his arms, as trusting as any lamb.

Stupid, he thought. Stupid and naive.

"You make it feel alive," Ruari crooned, no heartbeat to be found.

The warm voice echoed in his thoughts, and, for a moment, Corbet recalled the sensation of soft lips against his ear. He turned his face to the pillow, but there was no drowning out the memories.

"Why would a king want me?" he had asked, lulled into a light doze by the dark, the scent of forest that clung to Ruari like the ivy to the bench. "Why would you want me?"

"Why wouldn't I? You're very lovely and just so clever," Ruari murmured, holding him closer. "You're going to fit in so well here. You see right through us. I can't wait to teach you everything. You'll dazzle us all."

Corbet managed a small noise, barely more than a sigh as he buried his face in the fae's soft shirt. There

was no point in replying. Ruari seemed so happy at the thought. Sleep teased him like a breeze and his eyes fell shut, the dark as comforting as the arms around him.

A hand trailed through his hair and rested on his neck, a thumb skimming his pulse point. "What's the point of power if you're alone?" and Corbet was certain the words weren't meant to be heard. Ruari sighed and kissed his head, laughing quietly to himself. "Maybe you're not the only one who is lost."

Corbet scrubbed furiously at his face and tried to school his expression. Could it have been a dream? He didn't remember anything after that, his thoughts muddling like fog along a path.

In either case, he didn't have time to ruminate. His stomach growled painfully, bringing back the severity of his situation to him far faster than the fine sheets or fancy room.

When had he last eaten? A day? Two? He struggled to remember, casting off the diaphanous sheets. The last thing he recalled having had been a mouthful of water right before Ruari found him in the forest.

He had far more pressing things to worry about than the fae who was intent on his hand. He wouldn't last long if he didn't address the burning thirst and the aching hunger first and foremost.

A goal in mind, he wasted no more time ruminating on thoughts of the faerie king. His travel clothes

had been stripped off him, replaced with some soft, expensive outfit that flowed like water and sang across his skin. Corbet ran his hand along the sleeve, feeling for himself how much luxury was being wasted on him. They certainly treated their guests well here, minus the kidnapping.

There was no sign of his old garments, and Corbet worried his lip between his teeth. It was a bit odd to think someone had changed him while he slept. Disquieting really, if he were being honest with himself. A change of clothes sat on a chair near the door and he slipped them on without complaint, his earrings resting on top of the pile.

He felt like a prince while dressed in such finery, and that, if nothing else, suited his tastes just fine.

The boots nestled near the foot of the bed were similar to those he had worn before and he pulled them on, fixing his hair the best he could sans a comb or mirror. His fingers caught in the strands, uncommonly large tangles barring his way.

Distractedly, Corbet tugged and worked at the knots until they loosened, taking in the way the golden light filtered in through the ceiling itself and through the walls as if lit from some internal source. For a moment, Corbet turned his face towards it, basking in the warmth.

The room was a good reflection of what he had experienced the night before. The bed frame was carved oak, smooth and polished to appear like a growing mass

of roots. Its organic shape and low build made it look more like a nest than a traditional bed, the piled, messy bedding only adding to the illusion.

He wondered if all the fae slept in such contraptions, or if this were simply another luxury Ruari sought to bestow upon him. The thought made him shift. Corbet tugged at the sheets to try and smooth it out. It felt rude to leave it a mess, even if it hadn't been intended as a sort of gift.

Once that was done, there really wasn't much else in the room to occupy him. It only held the bed, a few chairs, and what looked to be a wardrobe and desk off to the side. A small door was situated near the desk, and a cursory peer inside proved it to be a small washroom. Decorations were plentiful but understated, something telling him that it was a room meant to be tasteful to all, but bare of personal touches; a guest room more than a permanent residence.

Corbet wrinkled his nose, flushing a little. He hoped Ruari didn't intend his own room to be the final destination. Barren though it may be, Corbet couldn't see himself being so desperate for personality that he came running to the king's bed.

His stomach chose that moment to growl, cutting through his introspection and bringing him back to the task at hand. He needed his things more than he needed thoughts of the king clouding his head. A quick look around proved there to be no sign of his pack or the food

he had stored inside.

If he was going to last without succumbing to the fae food, he was going to need to find it and fast. There was no telling whether the water available in the washroom was safe to drink without being bound to the realm, so his safest bet stood in finding the provisions he'd brought with him from above. With his appearance as good as he was going to get it, Corbet didn't see any other option than to explore.

He should have expected there to be guards right outside his room.

He should have, but he was still surprised. The two faeries snapped to attention the moment he swung open the door. Their musical language cut off abruptly when they turned sharply on their heels, facing him properly. Corbet smiled politely at them, not missing how curiously they took him in.

"Um, hello," he greeted, hoping they knew his language as well as their own. "Do you speak French?" he asked. "Have you seen the king anywhere?"

The taller of the two, which wasn't saying much given they both barely came up to Corbet's chest, scratched at her autumn colored head. For a moment, he feared she hadn't understood the question.

"The king is busy," she said in an accented voice, a little curt, "and we speak all languages." He could tell that she took her duty seriously, but since they were there

and understood him, he wasn't going to leave them be until he had some answers.

"With what? Don't tell me he's bored of me already," he huffed. It would figure that he'd only managed to be a day's worth of entertainment for the flighty creature. Corbet tried not to frown at the idea.

The short one scoffed and turned from his stalwart stance to glare up at him, his small hands gone tight around the stalk of the bow. "He is a king," the fae spelled out, looking far from impressed. "The Solstice is nearing and he works tirelessly to prepare."

He could tell from the fae's tone that this was a subject of some great deal of importance, but to Corbet, it just sounded like noise. "And what is that?" he probed, eyeing the weapons in their hands and the distance between them. Could he dart past them? They had such short legs, they would probably fall behind if it came down to him making a run for it.

The two shared a look and it didn't take a genius to gather that they thought him an idiot. The weapons were resettled, barring the way even more. Corbet narrowed his eyes and crossed his arms, reluctantly giving up on his idea to run.

"The Solstice is important," the female fae said, when she saw that her companion wasn't going to answer. "It maintains the balance between the Courts and keeps the equilibrium."

"That doesn't explain much," Corbet admitted, fiddling with the hem of his new shirt. "What does Ruari have to do with that?"

The taller fae gave him a look and rubbed tiredly at her eyes. "He hasn't told you much about us, has he?" she muttered.

Corbet gave her a commiserating smile. "I think he likes watching me stumble around in the dark until I find the light."

"That definitely sounds like the king," the short one sighed. "The king is a nexus. All decisions, power, and the like travel through him. Preparations take weeks, even months sometimes. If you see him today, consider it a gift on his part."

If it were a gift, Corbet could do without it.

The leafy haired fae huffed and pushed at her companion a bit. "Don't be so dreary about it, you oaf." She looked up at Corbet, her eyes partially obscured. "Tis just a ritual the king must prepare for. The feast encompasses both Courts, so you can imagine that the work is endless. You came at both an auspicious, and rather busy time. Don't think ill of him for being preoccupied."

He chewed the inside of his cheek and let out a breath through his nose. It figures that he would attract the attention of a duty-driven king. If it were indeed the case that he were as busy as they said, then he could at

least operate under the assumption that he wouldn't be accosted by the overly-affectionate fae while hunting for the exit.

"Do you know where my belongings were taken when I was brought here?" he asked, leaning against the frame a little. "If I'm to be left on my lonesome, I'd like to have the books I brought with me at the very least."

The loose hair rattled like dried leaves, a precursor to her reply. "The entrance hall?" she guessed, looking at her fellow guard for support. "It's been an awfully long time since we've had guests."

"The sprites might have taken it," the other piped up, leaning on his staff. He looked like a ruddy faced child, round and youthful, so long as he wasn't glaring. "They love rifling through things not theirs."

Corbet's eyes widened. "I hope that's not the case. I really need my belongings back. Could one of you check for me?" he asked, putting on his most winsome smile. These fae seemed far less tricky than Ruari. In comparison, they were almost helpful.

Both winced and shuffled on their feet.

"The king told us not to leave this spot," the female explained, apologetic.

That wouldn't do, he thought, his opinion of them souring. "Did he say that I wasn't to leave this spot?" Corbet posed.

The male furrowed his brow and frowned. "I believe he told us that you weren't to wander about, lest you get lost. Or, well," he hedged, a grin spreading across his face, "more lost than you already are, so he said."

They shared a laugh, as if being lost were the funniest possible thing that could happen to a person. He suspected it to be a jab, but he didn't take it personally. Instead, Corbet watched them, turning the words over in his head.

The guards couldn't leave and he wasn't to wander. He bit his lip. It wouldn't do to wait for Ruari to come to him and take him himself. His empty stomach and the alleged precocious sprites didn't allow for any more delays. No, waiting wouldn't do at all.

From what he could tell, the fae were tricksters. Ruari seemed to love his wordplay. He didn't know the rules, but there was no harm in probing loopholes.

"If you give me directions, I could just go check myself," he offered slowly, watching their faces for any sign of success. "That way you won't be abandoning your post and I won't be wandering around. I can't get lost if I know where I'm going."

They shared a look and, to Corbet's surprise, grinned toothily. Maybe he had said something right.

"A clever one, isn't he?" the female remarked.

"No wonder his majesty is so smitten," the male

snickered. He turned back to Corbet and bowed, his hand in a loose fist over his heart. The female mirrored the position on the other side. "It's our pleasure to serve you. Take care you handle our king well. He is the best of us."

Corbet coughed awkwardly, a bit flustered by the display. Did they think he was some bride, whisked away to marry their king? He didn't think he could bear it if every fae he encountered treated him like a suitor in need of blessings.

"The directions, please?" he prompted, trying to get them both to ease up.

Apparently it was common knowledge that their king was trying to woo him.

He could still hear them giggling when he finally made his way down the hall, his ears a furious red and his cheeks hot. From the sound of it, it was only a forgone conclusion that he was to remain with them, the king's newest distraction. Corbet increased his pace and counted the halls as he passed, looking for the one with the rose and aster archway.

Without his pack, he might as well just give in to the supposed inevitable. The idea rankled, so he walked faster, wandering through the halls, ignoring the chatter that broke out when he passed clusters of meandering fae.

Though he had left with directions, his promise not to get lost wasn't holding up well. It really didn't help his

search to find that all of the archways were decorated in some sort of floral motif. He wasn't a faerie with some preternatural knowledge of plant life. They all looked the same to him, but he did his best to parse out the details from where he stood.

A few curious, sharp-toothed fae asked him if he needed help, but Corbet simply smiled and said that he was fine. Playing with a faerie got him into this situation, and he wasn't eager to repeat the experience just to dig himself deeper.

When he thought he spotted thorns, he turned into the open hall, the entire thing looking far different from what it had been the night before. The changes only cemented his growing assumption that magic held more sway here than logic.

Gone were the long tables, the boisterous crowds, and the heaps upon heaps of food; the revelry and decorations were absent as if they had never existed to begin with. Corbet let out a breath he hadn't known he had been holding and quietly made his way through the space, eyes peeled for any sign of his bag or Ruari.

Here, too, were scattered fae, walking and chatting and flitting to and fro on wings like those of a dragonfly. Corbet kept his eyes to himself, remembering Ruari's admonishment about staring. They watched him go but didn't try to talk to him, saving their words for those closest to them as they gossipped.

There was plenty else to distract him from it. The

ceiling rose so high above his head that he felt he had to look at the floor lest he risk getting dizzy. It was mind-boggling to imagine how deep underground they must be allow for such heights, to imagine the weight of the earth piled on top of their heads. One faltering beam could send the whole place caving in and Corbet breathed a sigh of relief that there were forces at work beyond simple manmade supports. He couldn't imagine sleeping confidently without the hum of magic infusing the beams and tiles and stones.

Corbet let his eyes drink in the tiles decorating the floor, recalling how they seemed to dance in the light the night before. He wandered along the perimeter until he came to the end of the hall, spying a dark mass tucked into a corner behind a heavy tapestry depicting some sort of scene from antiquity.

A rush of relief passed through him when he made out the familiar shape of his knapsack, the worn straps folded neatly over the pack as if it had been moved out of the way of the partygoers by a conscientious servant. He took it by the strap slowly, still a bit distracted by the image before him.

The tapestry hung massively from the wall, far taller than Corbet and even longer along its width. His brow furrowed when he took in the image along its woven surface. Dozens of figures littered the scene, the inhuman characteristics proving them to be fae. A king stood at the center of it all, red and victorious. At the far left, nearly lost in the foreground, crawled a despondent

female, her back bowed and eyes hidden behind a wash of blonde curls.

Corbet cocked his head and tried to recall if he'd ever heard any stories that fit the scene before him. The center figure was probably Ruari, if the red coloring and crown were any indication. Could it be a tale of some great battle he'd fought?

The woman in the corner looked so sad. He wondered who she was.

The fae around him began to chatter and gossip louder, and Corbet turned his face from the massive tapestry, looking instead to the pack he had yet to look through. If the sprites had touched his belongings, there would be hell to pay.

He plopped down on the tiled floor with his back to the colorful wool and began to dig through the bag hungrily. His lips parted in a sigh, his mood calming when he looked down onto his untouched possessions.

Books, clothes, his canteen, that hunk of a broken fence that had done little to prevent this situation from happening: everything seemed to be there. He dug to the bottom and felt around for the parcel of food he had stored away, knowing where his priorities currently lay.

He hadn't bothered to enter the village properly when he stopped for directions, but the last one before it had yielded a decent supply of food. Quick fingers had taken up the cause when his meager money had run out, and

he lifted up his books, eager to see what still remained. He knew it wouldn't be much. That village had been days behind him.

At most, there might be a few blocks of granola, and even some strips of jerky if he hadn't already eaten it somewhere along the way.

When he finally located it, he was disappointed to find only granola, no meat left to give him some protein. The canteen was maybe half full, perhaps a little less. He allowed himself a single mouthful, just enough to soothe the burn in his throat. As long as he had water he could make it through. It was when it ran out that he needed to start worrying.

His stomach let out a rather loud growl and he frowned, taking a bite of granola to settle the angry rumbling. It wouldn't do to alert the entire Court to his whereabouts just because he couldn't quiet his empty stomach.

Ruefully, he chewed, longing for something more filling than a few mouthfuls of oats and a sip of water. He was in for a rather unpleasant stay at this rate.

Hissssssss

Corbet stopped chewing.

Hisssssssssssss

He narrowed his eyes, glancing around at the nearly empty hall. "Is someone there?" he called out in a

whisper, none of the fae near enough to hear. Corbet reached for his bag and the knife he hoped was still inside.

It was either reassuring that he felt the handle meet his hand or insulting, as Ruari would have been the one to put it there. Either the king liked the thrill of Corbet armed or he didn't consider him a threat at all even with it. He wasn't sure which he preferred.

A small shuffling, snuffling noise responded, followed by a light nudge to his thigh. Corbet jumped and looked down, ready to attack with the knife drawn.

Beady, black eyes stared up at him, completely unafraid and almost judging. The hedgehog sniffed at his thigh and then fearlessly at the blade hovering an inch above its nose before waddling around to climb his knee and stare at him with the new angle.

"Hello there," Corbet said quietly, his heart still pounding at the sudden shock. He lowered the knife and shoved it back into his bag, almost embarrassed to have been seen so startled by such a small animal. If any of the gathered fae noticed, he couldn't tell.

Carefully, he held out a finger to the snuffling nose, curious if the spines were as sharp as they looked. "Aren't you an unexpected surprise," he remarked, smiling as the little hedgehog let him stroke his back.

The creature made a dismissive noise and waddled towards the bundle of food resting at Corbet's side,

his restless nose prodding and curious. Looking up at Corbet, the hedgehog made an imploring bid for his only food.

"Are you hungry?" Corbet asked, breaking off a corner of his granola without a second thought. He never could resist a cute face or the camaraderie born from shared misery. "You poor thing. You and me both."

Snuffling his fingers, the hedgehog happily munched on the proffered food, nibbling the oats and nuts with evident glee. Corbet smiled gently and played with his spines, even getting away with lifting a tiny foot onto his finger as if shaking hands with his new friend.

"I can trust you, can't I?" he asked, utterly charmed. "You look like you're far more honest than all these fae." The small hedgehog looked up at him and chuffed, as if to say that he were leagues above the creatures milling around them.

He jumped a little when a flutter of wings sounded from behind, a few song birds appearing from on high to land a few feet from his makeshift picnic, their colorful plumage brilliant in the bright hall. "Are these some friends of yours?" he directed to the hedgehog, the small creature only giving him a look before going back to his munching.

The birds hopped closer, approaching slowly once Corbet crumbled some more granola, holding it out in his palm like an invitation. Yellow, black, and gold, their feathers all glistened as they preened.

Corbet giggled as their beaks tickled his hand, the beautiful trio of birds pecking gently at the bits of food. He quickly crumbled up some more to refill the depleting supply, not even surprised at the other animals beginning to wander over to him from their hiding places. He'd never had pets before and with all the traveling he did, he had always held a fascination for wildlife. Getting to hold and feed them like this was something he had only daydreamed about.

A large hare bounded fearlessly up to him, his butterscotch fur smooth and his dark eyes assessing. With a headbutt, he got Corbet's attention, pawing at his pant leg for his share of food. Corbet's heart fluttered and he bit his lip, eager to see how soft he was.

"You all must be really hungry," he said quietly, moving his filled palm to the rabbit's whiskered mouth. "This stuff really isn't that tasty. I can't imagine what your normal food is like if you think this is good." The soft ears flicked against his fingers when he stroked the rabbit's head, delighting in the soft fur.

Before long, he found himself buried in wildlife, the animals ranging from the first hedgehog to what looked to be a groundhog. He sighed with a smile on his face as the last of his granola was consumed by eager snouts and beaks, the animals all nipping and licking his fingers for the remaining traces. On his knee rested the hedgehog, his tired black eyes closing slowly as he succumbed to his full belly and warm perch.

Try as he might, he couldn't begrudge them all for eating his only food. At least he had water, he thought, running his hand down the back of the lumbering groundhog. One of the birds, the butter yellow canary, had burrowed into the creature's fur for its own nap.

He was tempted to follow their lead and take a little nap himself, nestled between their warm bodies as he was, but the sound of approaching footsteps kept him alert. Corbet pointedly kept his eyes down, pretending he hadn't heard.

He took the moments he had before they arrived to shuffle his knife beneath his thigh, keeping it handy if it proved to be something a little less kind than another hungry animal looking for a snack.

On his knee, the hedgehog opened his bleary eyes, his spines rattling and prickling in discontent.

"Well, would you look at this," a musical voice sang as two strange fae broke from the ranks of those gathered, coming right up to him. "I thought I smelled something sweet. If it isn't the new mortal, all on its lonesome."

Corbet threw on a kind smile and tried to make it reach his eyes. "Pleasure to meet you," he gave back, shuffling his pack closer to his side. They didn't look all that strong, but from the displays of magic he had already witnessed since arriving, he really didn't feel confident judging based on looks alone. The others watched curiously out of the corners of their eyes, but none made a move to intervene.

The taller and human-looking one, the one that had spoken, grinned and knelt down to his level, folding himself into a patronizing crouch. "What a pretty one our king has found, Avery," he purred to his companion, leaning closer to get a better look. "A pretty lost one all on its own."

Avery barked out a laugh that sounded inhuman coming from his sharp-toothed mouth. His head was oblong, flattened around the edges like a watermelon. The green tint to his skin only added to the illusion. Corbet doubted if he'd ever get used to the myriad appearances the fae seemed to take.

"Wonder what it has in its bag," Avery grunted, spitting the words out from between his fangs, his shock of indigo hair shifting like a cock's comb. "Wonder if it wants to play a game with us."

The animals around him bristled before he could react, the birds flapping their wings as they shrieked. Beneath it, he could just make out the uneasy whispers of the gathered fae, their foreign tongue lilting like rain patter.

Corbet hushed the animals at least and tightened his grip on his concealed knife, never letting his smile fall. Magic though they were, they'd have a hard time evading him if he decided to attack. He'd had too much practice, especially when it came to fighting with uneven odds.

"You'll have to excuse my friends," he apologized, giving the creatures a pointed look to calm down. "What

did you have in mind? I am awfully bored here, all on my lonesome. Not many of you seem brave enough to come this close."

The two fae shared a look and shot him a sugar-sweet smile, cloyingly malicious. "It wants to play, it does," crooned Avery. "It was lonely, it was."

"What a treat for us," the other replied before blinking slowly, like a snake. "The rules are simple, child. Just riddle with us. You answer right and we give you pretty things." His tongue hissed through his teeth, forked and long.

"And what do I give if I answer wrong?" Corbet asked, shifting a little to nudge the smaller animals behind him. Out of the corner of his eye, he watched as the smallest bird took to the air, flying away startled.

"Tell it what happens, Blisk." Avery inched closer, nearly reaching out to touch Corbet's ankle with a wickedly clawed hand.

The human-looking one, Blisk, loomed close and smiled a jagged smile, something imperceptible slipping away to reveal the fae beneath. "We get what we want," he answered, green eyes nearly glowing. "Whatever we want."

Corbet chewed the inside of his cheek and looked between the two fae, trying to figure out their angle. Hadn't Ruari proposed to him? He wasn't aware of how ownership was settled in this place, but one would think

that the king's plaything wouldn't be poached by his subjects. The others at the very least seemed hesitant, almost uneasy at the way this was progressing.

His eyes widened. Perhaps these two weren't aware that Ruari had already staked his claim. How cruel of the others, not to clue them in.

He smiled with renewed energy, determined to put these fae in their place. It wouldn't do to let them think they could push him around, regardless of whether Ruari's protection kept him off limits or not. They'd picked on the wrong mortal.

"Alright," Corbet agreed, loosening his hold on the knife. "I love riddles."

"Splendid. What always runs but never walks, often murmurs, never talks, has a bed but never sleeps, has a mouth but never eats?" Blisk posed, rocking on his heels with a cocky grin slashing his handsome face.

Corbet could've laughed at how prideful they looked, thinking they had stumped him on the first riddle. "You'll have to do better than that," he complained, leaning back into the wall. "The answer is a river."

Their grinning faces crumpled into ones of vicious anger, snapping at each other in their faerie tongue. Behind them, the crowd of fae laughed, a few even gasping as if surprised. He rolled his eyes. As if he couldn't solve a childish riddle. He'd be in dire straights if he couldn't manage at least that.

Corbet let them argue for a few moments before clearing his throat, gesturing emphatically at their persons.

"I believe you have to pay up?" he prompted, crossing his arms.

Avery punched Blisk's arm and Blisk grumbled, conjuring a handful of shiny trinkets and interesting wood figures, tossing them down towards Corbet's pack. "A lucky guess," he groused, some of his confidence curbed. They only just seemed to realize they had amassed a rapt audience. "Now for the next."

"What is greater than God, more evil than the devil, the poor have it, the rich need it, and if you eat it, you'll die?"

Corbet couldn't quite hide his puzzlement and immediately the fae began to gloat, looking to each other as they babbled in their language. The rest seemed to murmur as well, a low hum of anticipation. The hedgehog bristled at the sound and Corbet petted along the spines, soothing him as he thought.

"Is it stumped?" crowed Avery, looming closer to look at him with a newly appraising eye, as if sizing up what part he wanted to eat first. "Me thinks it's stumped!"

Glaring, Corbet pushed the fae's face back and furrowed his brow. Greater than God? More evil than the devil? There was nothing coming to mind.

Absolutely nothing.

Eyes widening, Corbet looked up at the gloating faces with a smile that spoke of anything but loss. "It's nothing," he said. "The answer is nothing."

Silence prevailed through the hall and another handful of treasure joined the first, the fae gnashing their teeth angrily as he won again. Glee washed over him in a wave and it was his turn to grin, looking past their shoulders to stare down the fae watching. Corbet gathered the winnings up and let the animals sniff at it, determined to take as much from these bullies as he could.

By the time Ruari finally stumbled upon them, the tiny blackbird perched on his shoulder and nipping at his earring, Corbet had the two fae on their last legs, their belongings strewn around him in a victorious heap. Those watching parted like the proverbial seas, making way for the king who looked anything but pleased.

"Oh, hello there," Corbet greeted brightly, dragging the various baubles he had won into his lap. The animals were busy playing with the other trappings he had taken from the fuming fae, yipping and chirping happily as their friend flew down to rejoin them. "We're just finishing up here."

Ruari looked back and forth between the fae avoiding eye contact and the pile of winnings Corbet held between his crossed legs. He shot another look at the tapestry behind him, closing the distance between them to run his proprietary fingers through Corbet's dark hair.

"Shetna here tells me you challenged him to a game?" he asked his subjects, the rumble of anger barely discernable past his smile or the flutter of the blackbird's wings. It was interesting to note that he addressed it loud enough for the rest to hear, the gathered fae flinching back a bit, as if they too were guilty of picking on him.

Avery began to sweat and nudged his companion, floundering.

"We were just welcoming it—" Blisk began, nearly swallowing his tongue when Ruari leveled him with an acidic glare. The feathers on his head crumpled, no longer coming off quite so cocky.

"You were what," he hissed, the question falling flat like a statement.

Avery paled to a sickly green and started where his friend had left off, his voice wavering like a leaf in a storm. "Welcoming him," he corrected. "With a game. A harmless game. Low stakes, nothing serious."

Ruari didn't seem to buy it and he pulled Corbet to his feet by the shoulders, lifting him bodily from the floor before folding him into his arms. "Was it now?" he asked lightly, his breath dancing past Corbet's pierced ear. "Did it feel harmless to you, my lost one?"

Corbet laid his hands over top of the king's, flushing a bit at the show of ownership he knew was playing out

right now. "I handled myself just fine," he gave back, trying not to fidget too much as Ruari explored his skin. "And it wasn't as if I were alone. I had plenty of back up."

"I'm sure Tailan was fantastic support," he chuckled, eyeing the hedgehog glaring up at him. "I think you could do with better competition," Ruari crooned in his ear, cradling him close against his chest. "Perhaps you should play with me sometime. We can find a game that actually challenges you."

With a commanding glare leveled at the fae, Ruari had them scampering off, their bodies shaking as they fled the hall without a single glance back. The room cleared just as quickly, none wanting to test the king's temper. "I'd hate to leave you bored enough to play with the scavengers."

Corbet tried to ignore how the animals were watching them, the hedgehog, Tailan evidently, particularly rankled. "I don't have much to bet," he gave, biting his lip when he felt a soft mouth nipping along his throat.

Ruari glanced pointedly down at the pile of valuables he had amassed from the fae, his grin only growing when he spotted the gold and gems peeking out from behind the knife and wildlife.

"I think we can make it a good game, until you run out."

It didn't come off comforting, not when the hands tracing down his body gave rise to thoughts of what could

be up for grabs should he run out of material things to wager. Despite it all, Corbet wasn't intimidated. He'd already proven to plenty that he could handle himself.

"If you think you can bear the shame of losing to a mortal, I'd say you have a deal," Corbet decided, looking into golden eyes the best he could with the position they were in.

"Oh, I knew I was right to want you. Such fearlessness." Ruari kissed him properly this time and Corbet found himself kissing back, helpless to the skill exhibited by the king.

He only hoped he'd fare better in their next game, because he wasn't giving a good showing in the one they were playing now.

# CHAPTER 4

The game piece clicked against the board with all of the conclusiveness of a thunderclap and Corbet smiled victoriously, leaning back in the seat to gloat at the king and his losing army.

"Are you sure you've played this before?" he asked cockily, snatching up the myriad baubles Ruari had put up for wager before they began. "Here you were, telling me I'd probably lose to your experience. It's been, what? Four games? And you've yet to display anything resembling skill to me. It's not kind to lie to guests, Ruari."

Raising a brow, the king looked anything but

impressed by his success. "So I see that what they say of mortals is true," he grumbled.

"What do they say of mortals?" Corbet asked, savoring the look of juvenile defeat on his opponent's face.

"You lose with petulant fury and win with even littler grace," Ruari complained. "You should be careful who you offend with that behavior. If you find yourself up against a true challenge, you may regret it."

Corbet laughed, enjoying himself fully for the first time since he'd arrived. "Maybe I'd have more of a challenge playing Tailan. I'm sure he'd be able to move the pieces with more skill, even with his tiny paws."

The hedgehog held little love for the king, but he'd been attached to Corbet at the hip since their meeting in the grand hall. If he asked, he was sure the creature would deign to indulge him with a game, so long as it meant annoying Ruari.

Ruari grumbled and sulked in his own seat, crossing his arms and resetting the three-tiered board with whatever magic he seemed to wield. "It's not my fault you're cheating somehow. There's really no other explanation for you being this good at a game created almost a millennia before your conception."

Corbet rolled his eyes and slipped on one of the rings from the pile, taking in how the blood red gem seemed to soak in the light around them. "It's not that hard to understand Ruari. You said you teach this to your

children, to train them for war? Am I not as smart as a child?" The gem was so brilliantly crimson, burning with the same intensity Ruari always seemed to command.

It was a bit embarrassing, but no matter the finger he tried, the ring still felt loose. Ruari said nothing as he watched him twist and play with it. He reached across the table to take his hand in his own. Cool magic brushed over his skin and the ring tightened on his right index finger, the band shrinking until it fit him perfectly.

"Oh, you're as smart as a child, but that certainly doesn't explain you beating me," Ruari shot back, pouting like a child himself as he let go and sank into his chair. His eyes were hot where they fell on his hands, staring intently at the ring fitted to his finger. Corbet could tell that the sight pleased him. "I think you've tricked me somehow."

"Tricked you," Corbet deadpanned, raising a brow in judgement. "If you're such a sore loser at a game, I can't imagine you faring well in a real war."

"I've fared very well, else I wouldn't be here before you." Golden eyes flicked up to meet his, an undercurrent of something slipping through the cracks of the mask Corbet was only just beginning to see for what it truly was: some sort of magical veneer, hiding the inhuman from him by way of a pretty face. "I've survived war, calamity, and horrors you couldn't even comprehend, my lost one. I've fought brutally to maintain what I've won from conflict."

For a minute, Corbet was almost tempted to ask.

"But enough of me," Ruari went on, spinning a pawn on the tip of a finger in a show of his strange magic. "What of you?

Corbet blinked. "What of me?" he asked, a bit defensively. The trinkets rattled in his lap when he shifted.

"You say I must be a poor general with my showing, so you must be something rather splendid up above. Tell me," he said, leaning forward, "do you command the hearts of those you meet as well as what you've displayed here?"

Corbet rolled his eyes and rested his elbows on the table, bringing them closer, as if to tell a secret. "If I do, would you treat me like a threat?" he asked, raising a brow.

"Thinking of taking my throne from me?"

"It'd be one way out of my current situation."

"You speak like you've many ideas."

Corbet grinned. "There's also me killing you. Haven't quite worked out the details yet, but I don't envision it being that difficult. You leave yourself awfully open around me."

Ruari didn't look angry, or even threatened for that matter. "What a dangerous mortal I've found. You'd need

some special tools to harm me. That knife in your boot won't help much the way it is now," he said helpfully, smiling as Corbet shifted his leg. "You'd need something a little colder to cut me."

He hadn't thought it was that obvious where he had it hidden, and he didn't appreciate the teasing.

"You're giving me advice on how to kill you?" Corbet asked. "You don't take me seriously at all. Am I entertaining you?"

"You intrigue me," Ruari sighed, watching him with a small, unreadable smile quirking his lips. "Most by now are so adamant that their loved ones are looking for them, that they'll be gone in no time at all once they're found missing. You've said nothing of the sort. Instead you talk of staging a coup. Of assassinating me."

"That's probably because I have no one to miss me," Corbet said, and it didn't even sting when he said it.

Any he might have called family had long been left back in France, and he knew he was better for it. That left only the butcher and the nun, and he hardly thought he'd made enough of an impression on them for any search party to come calling. He'd grown too used to the solitude for it to smart anymore.

He tapped his finger against the flower pattern on the board, tracing along the organic lines that made up the battlefield. "If I want something, I'm used to getting it myself," he murmured. "You can't count on anyone else

saving you when it comes down to it." Call it cynical, but one had to have loved ones to depend on if there was truly any other stance to take.

Ruari's eyes widened a little and he leaned forward, latching onto the information with abject interest. "No one at all?" he asked. "Not even a mortal lover? I find it hard to believe you haven't captivated all who stumble upon you like you did me. You're quite intoxicating."

Corbet scoffed to hide his blush and kept his attention on the jewels in his hands, watching the gold there instead of that in the king's eyes. "I think you're the only one to hold that opinion. I spend my time on the road, traveling. I don't come across many people. I rarely bother getting acquainted with any I do happen to meet."

The more he thought about it, the more he realized that this captivity might have been the longest he'd ever spent in the same place. He couldn't remember the last time he'd had a conversation that didn't revolve around bartering, directions, or the occasional distractions he took when he felt in the mood for them.

A thief and vagrant didn't have much time for companionship. Notoriety didn't exactly aid in keeping a low profile.

Something settled in his stomach, warm and worrisome, when he looked back up at the fae. He was probably the closest thing he had to a friend, even given the circumstances.

"Their loss," Ruari said with complete sincerity.

"Must be," Corbet managed. "But what about you?" he pressed, determined to take the heat off him. "Were you just capitalizing on what everyone else couldn't see? You couldn't have seen much from our brief introduction."

For a change, it seemed he had finally knocked the fae off balance. He shifted in his seat and looked as if Corbet had put him on the spot. "Oh, well, there's plenty of thought that goes into my choices," he blustered, obviously buying himself time to think.

Corbet grinned. "Oh? Like what? Are you in the habit of kidnapping random mortals in hopes of them being interesting?" he probed, loving the tables being turned for a change. "That seems like an awfully dangerous way to go about it. What if you happen upon a mortal determined to fight back?"

Ruari laughed and covered his face with his hand. "This is what I like about you," he admitted, resting his head on his hand. "You aren't afraid to tell me what you think. You like to play with me, and I certainly do love to play."

Brushing his hair behind his ear, Corbet smiled. "That must not happen often, given your station," he said, looking into eyes as warm as molten honey.

"It doesn't, which is why I turn to you mortals when I find myself with the time or excuse to go above." Ruari took another sip of his wine, and Corbet wondered how

sweet it tasted. "I could tell right away that you were different, and that you'd be the dose of levity I sorely needed."

Corbet huffed out a laugh. "Maybe I should be more boring so you'll let me go," he sighed.

"Maybe you should give up," Ruari grinned, "since I'm hardly the type to lose interest. Would you like some wine?"

Corbet looked at the proffered glass, and for some reason, he felt his cheeks flush. He pushed the hand away gently. "It's not that easy to get me to stay," he said quietly.

Ruari raised a brow and the glass disappeared into thin air, his empty hand wrapping around Corbet's wrist. "It could be," the fae smiled. "But you make me crave the challenge."

He held the gaze for one unshared heartbeat, then another, before looking away quickly. A kiss was pressed to his wrist before he managed to tug his hand back. He began shoving the gems and baubles into his bag. This wasn't what he had come for, he told himself. There were more pressing things to see to than Ruari's entertainment.

Once all the spoils had found their way into his pack, he set his nearly depleted canteen on the table next. It hadn't lasted him long at all, barely even three days. He was fortunate Ruari made time for him now, before he

truly ran out. One could only explore a magical palace filled with delicacies for so long before they began to wonder how bad giving in could really be.

"How about another game? And what do you say we raise the stakes this time," he offered, clearing his throat as the mood quickly shifted with his tone.

It certainly got Ruari's attention.

The fae sat up straight and leaned forward, his chin balanced on his propped up fist. "Feeling that cocky, are we? What did you have in mind? I probably should warn you of the dangers of gambling with the fae, but you seem entirely too confident to listen," he said breezily, letting the subject change without comment. "Especially considering how your last experience went."

"How about," Corbet began, completely ignoring Ruari's posturing, "if I win again, you have to give me food and water that won't bind me to this place. I'll still be able to leave once I've had my fill of fun here." He rattled his depleted canteen to illustrate the wager. If this didn't work, he wouldn't have any choice soon anyway. "Or killed you, whichever comes first."

Ruari nodded, smiling slightly. "What if I win, then? What will you give me?"

Corbet smiled widely.

"I'll let you decide. Anything you want."

To show his resolution, he unscrewed the cap and

drained his canteen in one pull, setting the empty vessel back on the table. Turning away now would only be postponing the inevitable. There was no way out but forward.

"Oh, Corbet," Ruari crooned, his eyes ravenous and completely inhuman. "You really should know better. I accept."

Just as Corbet knew he would.

He wasted no time in taking the first move, fitting since he had won the last game and all the ones before it. Corbet seized his...well, in his head he had called it a rook, since it moved like a rook. Ruari had thrown a fit each time he had used the chess terms when describing the pieces, but the fae name for them had escaped his mind the moment they had been spoken. The language was near incomprehensible to him, like trying to catch water in a sieve.

The piece snapped against the tiered board, resounding like the sealing of a contract. No matter their names, Corbet knew they'd bring him victory just as they had before.

"You must be very desperate to give me such control over my own reward, my lovely lost one," Ruari pointed out, making conversation as he moved his own piece to the top tier, using his knight to take a pawn. "It's the height of folly to tell me I can have anything."

Corbet narrowed his eyes in concentration, worrying

his lip between his teeth as he stuck with moving his rook across the board. "How about we call it confidence, since I'm fairly sure I'll win. You haven't had a very good showing so far, if your treasury in my pack is any indication," he replied, flicking his gaze up to take in his opponent.

The king sat relaxed, sipping on his re-summoned flute of wine in all his finery. Like this, he truly did look a monarch, the simple chair transformed into a throne just from his presence alone. The opulent crown completed the image, though his moves were anything but kingly. He commanded his bishop with slobbish care, opening up his ranks for Corbet to move his own knight in to take the enemy rook with ease.

Even as his pieces steadily began to pile up on Corbet's side of the board, Ruari kept on smiling.

"What do you think I would demand if I won?" Ruari posed, wincing through his grin as another one of his bishops was cleanly dispatched.

"I don't think you're going to win," Corbet answered, a cocky smile slicing across his lips. "It's not kind to force you to think on a future that's not meant to be."

Laughing, Ruari drummed his fingers on the arm of the chair and watched him carefully consider his next move. "Humor me. Hypothetically, in a perfect world where I won, what do you think I would demand of you?"

Corbet looked up and met his eye, cocking his head. "I

would assume you'd force me to eat, or just flat out make me stay here," he figured, wasting a moment to take in the unaffected way Ruari sat, how entertained he seemed through his losing war. Corbet grinned ruefully. "Maybe you'd just ask for me."

"You say that like you aren't a worthy prize."

Another piece met its death, but this time it was one of Corbet's, a knight that he had left unguarded.

Blowing his bangs from his eyes, Corbet snorted. "Maybe to you, but I could think of better things to ask for, given the situation." He drew his attention to his queen, taking her wooden form in hand to mow a path through Ruari's ranks.

"I don't think you see yourself the way I do," Ruari chuckled, completely ignoring his own queen to move his king one space at a time. "There's nothing more I think I want than you for all eternity."

Corbet, having at least grown somewhat used to this sort of talk, didn't blush. "You really do lay it on thick. Have you considered at all that this overwhelming affection you so readily proclaim is what makes me doubt your sincerity?" Another pawn met its demise, but Corbet paid it no mind, moving steadily onward with his queen.

"Oh? How so?"

One of Corbet's rooks fell, but again, he paid it no mind. "There has to be something else you'd rather have,

is all. I'm not much of anything. And normal people don't just admit to things like that. It's just not done," he explained, biting his lip as he watched Ruari make another slow move with his king.

"Well, perhaps they should. If you love someone, you should tell them, especially in your case," he gave, eyeing how close Corbet's queen had gotten. "You mortals live such short lives. Gone in a flash, really. You should love as deeply and wholly as you're able."

There wasn't really any way to respond to that, and Corbet shifted in his seat, ignoring it for the game. He brought his queen as close as he could to Ruari's king, lining it up to be taken in the next move. He knew this would be an easy win, the king's distracting conversation be damned.

Ruari rested his cheek on his closed fist, smiling lovingly at him from across the board. "You look so confident. I almost feel bad about this," he admitted, catching Corbet's attention.

"About what?" he asked, but Ruari was already taking his turn.

Incomprehensibly, Ruari moved his king six spaces forward and six to the right, a bastardization of the knight's traditional movements.

"That's....cheating," Corbet managed, staring at the board in shock as his queen was cleanly dispatched, putting his king in a straight line for Ruari's. The piece

fell and Ruari waved his finger, the king toppling right after it.

Disbelief was the first to greet him, followed swiftly by anger. He stood fast enough to knock over his chair, glaring at the laughing king. "That's cheating Ruari," he grated. "A king can't move like that."

To his chagrin, Ruari rolled his eyes.

"How many times do I have to tell you? This isn't chess. The piece can move quite easily like this. It's not my fault if you thought we were playing by mortal rules." His grin was luminous and dripped with pride at his trick. To add insult to injury, he righted the fallen chair with another display of his magic.

Corbet stared at the board and pointedly refused to sit back down, struck by his own stupidity. How could he have forgotten something like that? He thought back to when Ruari had explained the rules, his eyes growing wide when he realized he had never heard of that rule to begin with.

"You didn't tell me it could move like that," he said quietly, threateningly. "Ruari, you cheated."

Ruari raised a brow and crossed his arms, looking far too pleased with himself. "Oh, didn't I? Well, I'm afraid that doesn't change how the game is played. You still lost to me according to the rules, thus making me the winner of the bet. I did warn you about gambling with the fae, Corbet. This really isn't my fault."

To that, Corbet could only sit back down in his seat and glare.

"What do you want then?" he asked, his anger morphing into cold acceptance quickly enough. This wasn't that surprising. Not really. He had been cocky enough to make the bet and assume he knew enough to win.

Ruari had the gall to look as if he were thinking carefully about the question. "What do I want? Oh, many things, Corbet. I think first though, I want you to be mine tonight. Share my bed with me," he decided, grinning when he saw the look of annoyance on Corbet's face at the pronouncement.

"What—" Corbet began, only to be stopped by Ruari leaning across the board to cover his mouth with his fingertips.

"Oh, I'm not done. You said I could have anything. That also means I can have as many things as I want," he laughed, stroking down the side of Corbet's cheek when he saw the flicker of fear pass over him. "You really should learn to shape your speech better to avoid these sorts of incidents."

Corbet almost shook, the weight of his mistake collecting in the pit of his stomach. "What else do you want?" he asked, knocking aside Ruari's fingers so he could speak.

Ruari huffed out a breath and stood, crossing the

space between them to kneel at Corbet's side. His smile softened and his hand stroked through dark hair, almost as if he were trying to soothe away the fear he knew he had caused. Corbet watched as he took his hand and brought it to his lips, kissing the blood red ring on his finger like a vassal honoring his monarch.

"Just look at you, looking so resigned. I think I prefer you thinking about killing me." Golden eyes met his own with a smile. "The other thing I want is for you to have your free meal. Eat your fill, you won't be compelled to stay."

The words didn't process immediately, ringing in his head as if they had been spoken in the faerie tongue.

"A queen is powerful, but remember, Corbet," Ruari began, pressing his lips to Corbet's in a quick gesture of apology. "So is a king. I'll have a servant send you to my room later tonight."

Corbet watched him leave, melting into his chair feeling like he'd been knocked down a peg. A plate of food appeared before him, taking the place of the game board. A curious shake showed his canteen to be full. His stomach ached with hunger and he gave in, filling his mouth with cheese and bread.

This had definitely been a lesson in something. A lesson in what exactly could wait until after he ate.

-----

And just like he had been told, a knock on his door came later that night, just as exhaustion began to weigh down his limbs and sleep tease his eyes. He shared a look with his newfound friends, the animals making themselves more than at home on his bed. They had been waiting for him once he had finished with Ruari's game, somehow managing to sneak into his room despite the door being firmly closed and guarded while he was gone.

"Now who do you suppose that could be for?" he asked them, rolling his eyes. "One of you, I hope."

The birds twittered, laughing at him, but Tailan the hedgehog prickled his spikes, looking fearsome and ready to fight. He laughed a little and stroked them back down. "No sense in keeping the inevitable waiting," he murmured, carefully freeing himself from the pile of fur and feathers.

Corbet moved towards the door, opening it to see a tall fae waiting for him outside. He sighed.

As much as he knew it was coming, he still wished that it had been anything else.

"Good evening," he greeted politely, craning his neck to take in the servant. It was hard to keep his expression neutral. The creature looked for all the world like a grasshopper made human. Green and shiny with legs that tapered into thin feet, the servant ducked to meet his eye. "Can I help you?" Corbet asked, leaning back a little.

They stared down at him, their black, mirrored eyes

intent. "The king wishes for me to bring you to him," the fae chirped, bright and crisp like a cricket. In their thin hands they carried a folded parcel, holding it out to him.

Corbet raised a brow, staring at the sheer bundle. "What is this?" he asked, taking it when it was pressed into his arms.

If he weren't mistaken, he read something like pity in the creature's face. "The king wishes for you to wear this for the evening," they sighed, turning around to rest against the wall outside. "I will wait here for you to change."

Something like dread settled in his stomach and Corbet bit his lip, closing the door to take the outfit to the bed. He untied it in his hands, resting the package on the sheets to pull the garments out one by one. The animals stared up at him, pawing at the fabric when he set it down. At least they were eager and curious to see what the king had gifted him.

He trailed his fingers over the material and bit his lip. From it alone he could tell that it was nothing like the outfits he was used to awakening to. Holding up the top, he grimaced. He could see through the lacy garment, the cut resembling a woman's camisole more than any sort of shirt meant for sleeping.

"He isn't serious, is he?" he asked the animals, and Tailan hissed, cementing his fears. The hare nuzzled the other piece to the outfit, the soft material catching on his long ears. Corbet looked at it in horror. Were

those undergarments? Was he really that hellbent on embarrassing him?

A soft knock sounded on the door and Corbet jumped, realizing that he was in fact keeping someone waiting while he panicked. "Give me a minute, please," he called over his shoulder, looking back to the council of animals staring sympathetically up at him. "I really have to wear this stuff, don't I?"

Tailan bristled his spikes, telling him vehemently that no, he didn't, but Corbet wasn't so dishonorable that he would defy the terms of a bet, no matter how humiliating it may be. Taking the top in hand, he slipped off his own, closing his eyes when the soft, liquid fabric swam down his skin. It didn't cover much, but it felt nice, he admitted to himself begrudgingly.

"How do I look?" he asked his friends, untangling the bottoms from the rabbit to examine them. The birds chirped and flitted around his head, nipping his earrings, as if to tell him they approved.

Turning away from the watching eyes, he shucked his leggings and pulled on the undergarments. They ended just shy of the top's hem, which was entirely too short in his opinion. Rubbing at his eyes, he groaned into his hands. "This is going to be a miserable night," he muttered, dragging his hands down his face to reach for his discarded boots.

On a whim, he snatched up his current book from the stack on the desk before he made his way back to the

door. If nothing else, he could ignore the king while he enjoyed his victory. "Wish me luck, everyone," he called out to the animals nestled on the bed, their assortment of encouraging sounds making him wish he could stay with them.

Turning the handle on the door, he opened it up, the servant waiting dutifully at the wall. "I'm ready to go now," Corbet sighed, thankful that the fae didn't stare for more than a second or so. "Please lead the way."

"Follow me," they chittered, rustling like the wings of a grasshopper as they walked. "It's a bit of a walk, so try to keep up."

Corbet furrowed his brow but found out quite quickly that the advice wasn't for show. Their long legs yielded long strides, their one making up Corbet's three. The walk turned brisk for him, and he found himself almost jogging to keep up.

"Is this something you're used to doing?" he forced himself to ask, putting on a burst of speed to walk abreast of the fae. "Bringing the king his pets for the evening?"

Black eyes turned to look at him, the fae's head cocking. "I can't say that it is," they replied, bringing a hand behind Corbet's back to pull him closer to their hip as a flock of fae walked past them. "The king has been alone for quite awhile." Every eye turned to watch Corbet, taking in his bare legs and shoulders, and he found himself grateful for the guide letting him hide behind

them.

Frowning, he kept his eyes on the tiled floor at his feet. "I find that hard to believe," he muttered, a draft carrying through the hall. He wrapped his arms around his middle, cradling the book to his chest for warmth. "He seems like he's got this whole courtship planned out to the letter."

"Oh, I wouldn't say that. You definitely vex him too much for him to make anything predictable," his guide chuckled, turning them down a side hall where the foot traffic decreased substantially. "You didn't expect him to do this, did you?"

They gestured at the outfit and Corbet flushed, looking away. "I should've," he muttered. "He certainly seems like the type to pull out this sort of surprise." They turned another corner and Corbet looked up, finding them in front of a single door situated at the end of a long, empty hall.

"We're here," his guide informed, looking down at him with what he thought was a kind expression. "Would you like me to announce you?"

Corbet grimaced. "No, I think I'll just announce myself. Thank you for taking me here," he said, wrapping his arms around himself a little tighter. "I hope your evening goes better than mine."

The fae laughed softly, like leaves on the wind, and bowed to him. "Don't let the king intimidate you," they

advised, their thin, insect-like hands gesturing as they spoke. "He's very kind to those he likes."

Corbet blinked and the fae turned, leaving with a smile on their pale green face. Chilled as he was, he didn't waste time in ruminating before he opened the king's door.

"I'm here, as ordered," he called out, entering before another passing fae got an eyeful of him and began to spread more rumors. They'd all know he spent the night but he didn't have to stomach the idea of Ruari's little ownership taunt lying down. "I hate you and your sense of humor."

"And good evening to you as well," Ruari laughed. The king was, of course, in his bed, waiting ostensibly for him to arrive. "I think you haven't had a chance to really enjoy it or me just yet. Come over here so I can admire you properly." Corbet flushed and Ruari's golden eyes weighed heavily on him as he entered. "It's such a treat to finally have you in my bed."

"Don't stare like that or I'll leave," Corbet said, throwing his book towards the bed while he toed off his shoes. It struck Ruari in the chest and it was simple to pretend that it had been an accident, though it obviously wasn't.

Ruari huffed out a laugh and dutifully averted his eyes, but it was apparent that he wasn't worried about him actually leaving. "I don't think you can blame me for staring a little, Corbet. You look ravishing," he defended,

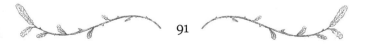

taking the sheets in hand to beckon Corbet beneath.

The sheets, like the rest of the room, smacked of luxury. Ruari's private rooms were a far cry above his own, though that wasn't to say his weren't nice in their own way. It was the personal touches that really brought the room to the height of excess, something that both suited Ruari and gave away a lot of his personality.

The walls were covered in frescos of trees, spots of natural growth intermingling with the paint to make it feel as if the viewer were nestled in the heart of a forest and not buried underground.

As he looked through the faux treetops, he caught glimpses of faerie lights. It made him think of that first night and of Ruari's melancholic expression as he spoke of escaping, running to the surface to be alone with his thoughts. He wondered if Ruari's room was an escape too, or at least as much of one as he could make it. The lights seemed to twinkle the more he stared and, for the life of him, he couldn't tell if they were real or just another display of fae magic at work.

Ruari made an expectant noise, breaking him from his thoughts. Sighing, Corbet went without a fight, focusing on the feel of the gossamer-soft bedding against his bare skin and not on the hot eyes devouring his every move.

The bed held none of the quaint charm of his own pillow-laden nest. It was large and looked as intimidating as the bed of a king should look, he supposed.

"I can blame you since you're the one who made me wear this," Corbet said, melting into the downy mattress. At least the bed was warm and the covers thick. He had no idea how he'd make it through the night otherwise. The provided sleepwear didn't grant him much in the way of coverage at any rate, and it had been chilly enough simply walking here.

The blankets enveloped him in a bundle of warmth and Ruari inched closer to him, his fingertips tracing gently down his exposed shoulder, falling to his hip. The heat of his hand burned through the sheer satin, making Corbet shiver a little. Corbet picked up his book and pointedly ignored the cursory touching. It was harder to ignore the bare chest so close to his back.

"This color looks beautiful on you," came a warm whisper, Ruari's breath tickling his ear. "Am I safe in assuming you didn't bring your knife to bed with you?" He brought his hand beneath the loose top, tugging it up to expose his midriff to his touch.

"If I had known you would be this handsy, I would have."

Ruari laughed low and warm in his ear, only touching him more. "I can't help it," he said, burying his face in Corbet's hair. "I'm just so pleased to have you in my arms."

Corbet held back another shiver as Ruari stroked a path up his stomach, his ribs, teasing at the thin satin hiding his chest from view. The deep purple did look

nice, he thought frantically, trying to ignore the heat rising to his cheeks. The color contrasted well with his pale skin.

Even in the candlelight, he could make out the thin strands of silver thread dancing within the fabric. Ruari traced the threads like one would lines on a map, following them down to the ones woven into the waistband of the small undergarments that made up the lower half of his outfit.

"You're awfully talkative for it being bedtime," Corbet replied, struggling to focus on his reading. "And this is awfully fast for a courtship, even if you fae are forward as can be." He turned another page and felt lips against his neck. They moved like a silent promise of there being no more talking from his bedmate.

The moment he felt teeth nip at his pulse point, Corbet realized he wasn't going to get any reading done that night.

He tossed aside his book and rolled himself to pin the king to the mattress, dutifully ignoring the interested hardness poking his thigh through Ruari's thin sleep pants.

If this was going to happen, Corbet intended it to be on his own terms.

"You're being distracting, Ruari," Corbet said, letting the man pull him down so they were pressed chest to chest. "Some of us are trying to concentrate."

"I could say the same of you," he replied breathlessly, his hands smoothing down Corbet's shoulders, basking in the softness of his skin, the muscles of his arms. Ruari tilted his head up and connected their lips in a chaste kiss.

Corbet didn't fight it. He watched even when Ruari's eyes slid shut, the king melting into the kiss as if it could be his last. Sweet, warm, and cloyingly earnest: Corbet's eyes fell to half-mast when gentle hands moved to cup his face.

He was surprised when Ruari broke away first.

The fae's eyes were dark and heavy. "I want you so much, Corbet," he whispered, near begging against Corbet's lips. His hands fell to Corbet's waist, holding and fondling and luxuriating against the smooth fabric over warm skin. "Do you want me?"

Corbet ran his hands through Ruari's hair and moved it from his eyes, slicking it back to how it was normally worn when the man wasn't half naked in bed, completely open and vulnerable to the object of his affections. Like this, no matter how aggravating he knew him to be, Corbet couldn't hold back the thought of how beautiful Ruari was. The room was filled with the scent of the forest, of Ruari.

His mind clouded with it and, for once, he couldn't begrudge the king for asking so forwardly.

Licking his lips, Corbet shifted in Ruari's lap, flushing

brightly when the patient stare grew hot. A thousand answers flooded his head, each at odds with the shiver of want teasing its way down his spine. He darted in for another kiss to buy time, his lips parting to deepen it into a wet press of tongue and heat.

Ruari kissed like he moved, confident and entitled. His tongue tangled with Corbet's and drew out another noise, though from whom was hard to tell. Sweet and hot, the world dulled into one singular point, one that wouldn't be enough to keep him sane.

Ruari's hands tightened on his waist, holding him so close that Corbet feared the fae might never want to let go.

It was when he felt fingertips teasing their way beneath the waistband of his undergarments that Corbet finally saw fit to discourage more of this. He pulled the hands from his skin and settled them on the pillow, framing Ruari's lovely face. Ruari stared at him, confused and waiting, his pupils blown.

Corbet bit his lip and lifted himself a little, putting some space between them. It was agony for the both of them, but he held strong.

"It's late, Ruari," he whispered, swallowing his own want as he threaded their fingers together. "We should go to sleep."

Ruari pouted, bringing their joined hands to his cheek. His eyes slowly skimmed down Corbet's body, like

he was taking one last look before it was denied to him. "If that's what you wish," he sighed, turning to press a kiss to Corbet's wrist, then another to the ring he still wore on his finger. "You don't need your knife to take me to pieces, Corbet. You've done it with just a touch."

For some reason, Corbet couldn't find his voice.

He managed a nod and gave Ruari back his hands, letting him pull Corbet down onto his chest. Like this, he could hear the silence of Ruari's heart in his ear, feel the warm movement of his chest as he breathed despite its absence. Strong hands settled on his lower back, stroking soothingly up and down his spine.

"I...do want you," Corbet whispered, breaking the quiet din. "I do but..."

Ruari chuckled and kissed his forehead, putting out the lights with a wave of his hand. "I know. I want you to be sure." The dark curled around them and it hid his face from sight, his expression unreadable but warm.

Corbet buried his face into Ruari's chest and let sleep slowly take him, imagining the silent heart beating in time to his own.

# CHAPTER 5

Whoever said the morning brought clarity had obviously never found themselves in a romantic entanglement with a faerie king.

Corbet awoke alone, burrowed in the soft blankets and lingering scent of the missing fae. A cursory check with his outstretched hand informed him that the bed beside him was cold, and Ruari long gone.

His first instinct was to frown, something thick and bitter like hurt rising up in his throat. It was stupid, he told himself, to feel so wounded by it. How many times had he been told, by both subject and king alike, that Ruari was a very busy individual? Of course he couldn't laze around in bed. The damned Solstice was approaching, so it was probably just duty calling like it always did.

Lifting himself up a bit, he looked for a note. The hurt became frustration when he found nothing. Not even a simple message of "See you later today," or "Had to do some work."

It figured, he thought ruefully. Groaning a little, Corbet buried his face in the soft sheets, loathe to leave the warmth of the bed, even if there was no sign of the one who had ordered him there. It probably wasn't worth his time to wait around for Ruari to return, if he returned at all.

The artificial light shone with all the intensity of a mid-morning sun. His stomach growled, but he ignored it.

What was he going to do? He hadn't anticipated on waking up without Ruari there. Given how fond the man was of touching him and smothering him with affection, it was almost jarring being dropped like this. Aggravated, Corbet rubbed his face into the sheets, wanting nothing more than to scream until his frustration left him.

If Ruari weren't here, he'd just have to entertain himself.

With his spite fueling him, Corbet lifted himself from the confines of the bedding. Come to think of it, he hadn't been alone in Ruari's room before. His perusal the night

before hadn't lasted long, given the king's insistence. Curiosity kindled in his stomach, drowning out the hunger for a blessed moment.

He felt a small smile quirk his lips, wondering what secrets a king could be hiding in his private chambers.

When he rose to check, he brought the topmost blanket with him. The room, though amply lit with light, was still chilly. He wrapped the sheet around his shoulders, moving towards the far wall where the wild looking mural crawled to the ceiling.

In the full light of day, it looked even more impressive than it had before. The gnarled boughs of the tree seemed to burst forth from the simple stone, the texture so artfully done that when he reached out his hand to touch, he fully expected to feel rough bark instead of smooth wall. Real vines were intertwined seamlessly, adding to the illusion of growth and movement.

The hand holding the sheet around him clenched in the fabric. It was daunting, this level of skill. He wondered who painted it. It had to be some artist of the Court. Wasn't that how these things were done? He didn't know, but of the books he had read of troubadours and chivalry, it seemed that royals always had artists at their beck and call. What an honor it must be to be responsible for the art in a king's bedroom.

Beyond the art, there were other oddities to look at. A large chest rested at the foot of the bed, unlocked though it held the tumblers and bolts necessary for security.

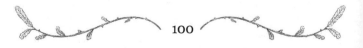

Kneeling, Corbet opened the lid.

He wasn't sure what he had been expecting, but it wasn't for the chest to be half-filled with sticks and leaves and forest bric a brac. Was this why it wasn't locked up? A small animal skull sat nestled in the corner of the chest, padded in a soft looking cloth to keep it safe. Nearby rested some more bones, small ones that looked to be from a rabbit, or was it a fox?

Reaching his hand in, he carefully prodded at the bones. They all were immaculate, surrounded on all sides by a collection of preserved leaves, flowers, and grass. On the edges of the chest, moss and lichen clung as naturally as if out in the wild. Slowly, Corbet realized that it wasn't a chest but a sort of terrarium.

Ruari really must miss the surface, he thought, closing the lid with far more care than he had used when opening it. He pushed himself to his feet, glancing around at what else there was to see.

Movement caught his attention and he turned, his own grey eyes reflected back at him in a bright, tall mirror. It hung over a shelf, high enough to be at eye level but low enough to remain unobtrusive around the wall's murals. Making a face, he walked to the vanity supporting it.

Corbet took in his expression and frowned, seeing how tangled his hair looked. He raked his fingers through the matted black mess, wincing when it pulled painfully. Did faeries have combs? He could do with one,

if this persisting affliction became his norm.

Glancing around at the vanity, all he could see were small trinkets and pieces of jewelry. A few gold earrings dangled from small inset hooks and he recognized them to be the ones Ruari had worn the first day they met. He touched them gently, just brushing them with his fingertips. They chimed softly, like a breeze through the treetops.

There really wasn't much else in Ruari's room. It wasn't spartan, but the personal touches were a bit lacking, given that this was his personal space and he had more than enough money to fill it with whatever he wanted. Corbet looked at his reflection again, wondering how he fit into the scope of Ruari's possessions.

He tapped at the surface of the vanity, drumming out a beat. There were leaves imbedded atop the wood, as smooth as glass when he touched. They were arranged in a line, the color shifting from springtime green to autumn brown in a facsimile of the changing seasons. Personal effects were sparse, but the ones that were there were understated and subtle.

A shelf of books stood off to the side, towering up to the ceiling. He walked to it, his fingers trailing over the wood the moment he was close enough to touch. The spines of the books were lined up neatly, rows upon rows upon rows of them weighing down the bookshelf. Some looked old, their covers ragged and rough from decades of handling. Others were newer, bound in leather and with pages as white as snow.

Corbet was as avid a reader as one could be when perpetually poor and on the move, and he tugged one of the older tomes free, eager to see the sort of books a fae king read.

He was immediately disappointed. The cover boasted no title and once flipped open, he found the pages incomprehensible. The writing on the parchment was entirely foreign, resembling nothing he'd ever seen in his years of traveling. Cramped yet fluid, the thick black ink danced along the white in curling loops and tight, condensed script.

So this was the fae tongue in its written form. He thumbed through a few more pages before shutting it and grabbing at another, only to find the same. Frowning, Corbet returned the books to their shelves.

Were they all in that language? He didn't fancy the idea of learning a new alphabet simply to learn their stories. Perhaps Ruari would read to him, he thought. He could imagine it well enough. Him curled up between the man's legs, watching the script flow by as Ruari narrated in his smooth, rich voice.

For want of something to do, he picked up another book and flipped through it, his eyes not really registering the words. It was hard to admit that he wanted that level of intimacy, especially when he knew Ruari would never have enough time to waste with him on something so pointless.

Corbet sighed, his mood spiraling downwards all the faster with the thought.

A door in the far corner caught his eye, too big to be a closet but innocuous enough that it hardly seemed to be another exit. Corbet set down the book in his hand and made for it, the sheet dragging along the floor with barely a whisper of sound.

He was snooping to avoid his loneliness. He didn't need to invite more by sulking over some unintelligible books.

It opened without issue and before he stepped inside, he let the sheet fall to the floor. He could tell now that it was a bathroom, so he didn't want to drag the clean blanket along the tiled ground. Wrapping his arms around himself instead, he walked in and took it all in, curious how anyone could live in such splendor regularly.

Compared to the bedroom, the bathroom was small. It was large enough to walk around, even with the large, ornate washtub situated in the center as it was. Corbet moved towards it and ran his hand along the cool porcelain. He'd never seen anything like this, even on his furthest travels.

The walls were laden heavily with more art, no frames to contain the wild bursts of natural and fauna teeming from the stone. He could tell that Ruari took great pains to make his personal spaces reflect the surface, and given the way he spoke about it, it was plain to see that the king longed for sanctuary from his endless responsibilities.

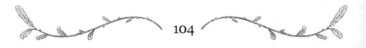

Corbet looked towards a low rack, reaching out his hand to touch the towels. They were fluffy, soft, and as warm as a lamb's fleece, all dyed a rather luxurious shade of crimson. He pulled one free and wrapped it around his shoulders, loving the feeling of it against his cheek.

Reaching out to the curved silver faucet, Corbet wondered how difficult it would be to run himself a bath. On the open road, traveling as he did, he never had the chance to indulge in this sort of luxury.

He certainly was making himself at home here. A little more intrusiveness probably wouldn't hurt.

The magic seeped into the place seemed to do most of the work for him. The large basin began to fill with just a gentle touch to the faucet. Steam wafted through the air and Corbet chanced a look at the door, wondering if he were really going to do this. If Ruari walked in, he knew all too well what would follow.

His cheeks flushed from something other than the rapidly warming room, and without a second thought, he shucked his sheer top and the undergarments. They fell to the cool tile in a silent heap. It wasn't as if they'd done much to hide him from Ruari's affections anyway.

Stepping carefully into the warm bath, he turned his attention away from the clothes and towards the myriad vials littering the nearby shelf. One had to have soap to bathe properly, so logic would assume that they held Ruari's collection. Why he needed some odd dozen was beyond Corbet, and he fussed with the assortment one by

one, looking for any rhyme or reason to the system.

Purple, green, crimson: every bottle was color coded and filled with some sloshing liquid. Corbet could tell quite easily which ones Ruari favored. Some were still filled to the brim, while others were noticeably emptied. He picked up a shiny blue bottle and popped the cork, curious to see why this one out of all of them held only a finger's worth in its cerulean base.

He didn't even need to hold it to his nose to smell the ripe, crisp scent of juniper exude from the open neck. Corbet's eyes went wide and for a moment, he had to keep himself from glancing around, his senses telling him he was in a forest though his body was firmly rooted somewhere far underground.

Was it magic? It had to be. Nothing man-made could ever succeed in bottling a forest. Bringing it closer, Corbet took a deep breath and let the scent fill him, the stress of his morning melting away like dew in the afternoon sun.

It smelled like Ruari and he knew he didn't care to check the other bottles for something else.

Gently, and before he could talk himself out of it, Corbet tipped the bottle to let a few drops fall into the water. The clear soap burst across the water's surface, erupting into suds. To his astonishment, flower petals rose up, speckling the bathwater as if Corbet himself had tossed them in.

"This is almost too much," he mumbled to himself, a bit embarrassed at the excess. It was just a bath, but it was obvious to him that for Ruari, it meant something far more than just a time to get clean.

He supposed it made sense, given how much the king worked. This might very well be the only time he allotted himself the luxury of relaxing. With care, Corbet corked the blue vial and sat it back alongside its brethren, biting his lip. He hadn't used much, but he hoped it wasn't an inconvenience all the same.

The mother-of-pearl overlay on the nearby scrubbing brush put the thought from his mind. An inconvenience? The wealth of the room itself was daunting, and it was idiotic of him to think that a few drops of fancy soap would be a hardship to replace when this was how the king bathed regularly.

And to think, if Ruari had personal rooms this nice, Corbet might have deigned to sleep with him earlier. A romantic entanglement might be worth it if he got to live as opulently as this. Even on the surface, bathing rooms like the one around him were reserved only for the richest of nobles.

Corbet huffed out a laugh void of any real joy and sank down deeper into the warm bathwater, blowing melancholic bubbles in the suds. Romantic entanglement might be downplaying it. He was nearly betrothed and they had shared a bed. There really wasn't much left to entangle.

It was a unique feeling, the calming water being so at odds with the tension tight in his shoulders. Deep in his stomach, he almost felt ill, as if afflicted with something beyond simple emotions. At least those authors had gotten it right, he thought. He certainly did feel heartsick.

Petals drifted by on the water's surface, scenting the air with their delicate perfume. He had hoped this would settle his mind, perhaps give him some introspection, but Corbet still felt as uncertain as he had the night before. His head lolled on the padded edge of the tub, his mood turning morose faster than the magically heated water could combat.

"Brrrrp" a small voice trilled, breaking Corbet from his thoughts.

His eyes widened and he looked over the edge of the basin to find the small hedgehog scratching at the tub's foot, his small snout snuffling erratically in the fragrant room.

"Tailan," Corbet laughed in greeting, reaching out a hand to stroke the prickly spines. "How on earth did you find me? For how much you seem to hate Ruari, I hardly expected to find you in his rooms." He bit his lip, realizing he hadn't come back that morning. "We're you worried about me?"

Tailan rolled his black button eyes and nudged at the proffered hand, his tiny feet scrambling at the fingers until Corbet placed his palm flat on the ground.

Corbet could hide his charmed smile, his head cocking. "Do you want to join me?" he asked, lifting the small animal up and onto the edge of the tub. "I didn't know hedgehogs liked water."

The moment his feet felt the cool wash basin, Tailan was kicking off to jump into the warm water. For a heart-stopping moment, Corbet feared he would sink, but a few nudges and a helpful prod had the hedgehog floating serenely on his back, spinning slowly in the gentle current of the bath.

The sight was so funny he barely smothered the laugh that rose up. Tailan's disgruntled snuffling only added to the sight. "You really are something," he teased, settling back into the bath with a smile on his face. "I'm glad you're here."

Tailan sniffled and bumped against his ribs, but with his spines relaxed, it only tickled. Corbet petted his soft underbelly with the tip of his finger, sighing into the silence. A wiggle and snort seemed to ask what was wrong and Corbet almost felt foolish for avoiding eye contact with a hedgehog.

"I have a lot on my mind right now," he finally said, turning back to meet the tiny black eyes and inquisitive nose. "Ruari is being, well. He's being Ruari and I'm not sure if that's a bad thing anymore."

Today was a day of firsts as Corbet had had no idea that hedgehogs were capable of snorting derisively. He grinned and tickled the soft stomach again, making

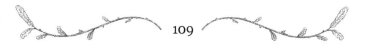

Tailan wriggle in the water. "You don't like him much, do you? That certainly bodes well, his own subject not being fond of him. Perhaps if there are more like you, I'd have enough of an army to stage a coup."

A lilac petal drifted close enough to stick to Tailan's prickly head and Corbet moved it so it sat like a little bonnet, pulling another laugh from him. He smiled sweetly at the small creature so content to bask in the water with him. It must have been scary, waiting for Corbet to return after leaving like that the night before, especially when Tailan held no love for Ruari. To think, he'd wandered all the way here, just to check up on him.

His smile turned melancholic. It was hard to imagine that only here of all places he had friends who cared enough to cheer him up. The feeling was a novel one, one that didn't help at all with his waning desire to leave.

When he watched Tailan smile at him from the water's surface, it was hard to imagine anything as kind waiting for him above.

"He's not all bad, you know. He beat me in a game and he still let me win, in his own way," Corbet continued, unsure of whether he felt the need to defend the king or his own reasons for why he was being so indecisive.

"And he's very handsome, so that makes it more bearable," he added with a grin, laughing as the hedgehog seemed to sputter and hiss in vehement disagreement.

"I can tell you don't like him, even though the other

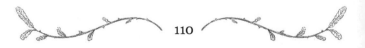

animals don't seem to care one way or another." It had confused him a bit, but Tailan was a bit cantankerous in general. "Maybe you're just too straightforward for these fae."

Tailan wiggled his nose, sniffing like he thought Corbet should feel the same too.

Corbet sighed, his lips quirked in a loose smile. "I just don't know what to do, Tai. He's an awful lot to take in at once, but he has his moments." He pinched a tiny little foot between his thumb and forefinger, using it to twirl the hedgehog around the bath.

They soaked together for a while longer, relaxing in each other's silent companionship. Corbet finally began to feel his mind quiet, the tight knot of uncertainty in his stomach loosening. He covered the hedgehog's stomach in flower petals and washed his hair, but before long, he had nothing left to do to occupy himself beyond his thoughts.

"What do you say we head back to my room?" he asked the small animal, flicking off the petals and cupping him gently to lift him out of the water. "Any longer in here and I might just melt away."

Tailan gave a sleepy little trill and waited patiently in a bundle of cloth for Corbet to rinse off. "Stay right there, alright?" he said. "I need to get changed." He wrapped himself in the towel and went back into the main bedroom to snatch up the clothing that he'd found in the room earlier.

The outfits just kept on getting more extravagant, this one embroidered linen as green as a forest in spring. It fell loosely like a tunic, belting in the middle as it hung off his shoulders. He pulled on the soft leggings, toed on the boots, and went back to gather up the hedgehog in his arms, letting Tailan burrow into his sleeves for warmth.

Corbet tried his best not to look at the messy bed as he passed by. Nothing had happened, but with the sheets mussed and the phantom image of Ruari reclining among the pillows laying heavy behind his eyes with every blink, his cheeks still flushed.

Tailan snuffled at his hands, his tiny teeth nipping at the ring he wore. Was still wearing. Why was he still wearing it? "I know," Corbet murmured, opening the door and moving quickly into the hallway. "I'm hurrying."

He made it almost completely down the first hall before running into the object of his distress.

The king stood lounging against the wall in a manner that almost came off as unplanned. Almost. Corbet sighed and raised a brow when Ruari looked surprised to see him, already prepared for the deluge of affection he knew was coming.

If he had the time to ambush him in the hallway, he had the time to write a note before leaving him in bed all alone, Corbet thought bitterly.

"Ah, Corbet," Ruari called out in greeting, walking

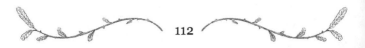

up to meet him far more sedately than expected. "I was wondering where you had wandered off to. I checked my room but you weren't there."

Oh. Corbet swallowed and shifted uneasily. So Ruari had come back for him. It still didn't explain the absence of a note, though. "I was in the bath," he said back, his tone a bit cool. It was a little odd that the fae had made no move to touch or kiss him, but given his current mood, he told himself that it didn't bother him one bit.

"I can see that. You smell like me now." Ruari smiled warmly at him and rested his hand on Corbet's cheek, his thumb tracing a cheekbone. "You look breathtaking," he remarked, and that sounded almost normal.

Clearing his throat, Corbet tried not to lean into the touch as much as his body wished to. "Did you need something? You said you had been looking for me." Hidden in his sleeves, he could feel Tailan lick his wrist in support.

"Oh, right," he gave, breaking contact to stand an almost respectable distance away. "I figured you might be hungry. I wanted to tell you that I had some food taken to your room."

Before Corbet could open his mouth to protest, Ruari was already charging on, his hands dancing in the air to calm him.

"Don't worry, it's not what you think," he explained. "Think of it as a continuation of yesterday's wager. I

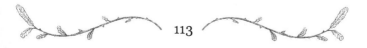

never said how many meals you would get. As long as it comes from me, you won't be bound here."

For some reason, the gesture made Corbet's throat go tight, constricting like a noose. "Thank you," he managed, his voice weak.

The look in Ruari's warm golden eyes was soft, and just a touch melancholic. "You don't need to thank me. Do you need help getting back, or have you grown familiar with the layout of the place? It'd be no trouble to walk you to your room," he offered, extending his hand.

Corbet knew where to go but he still shifted Tailan to one side, placing his hand in Ruari's. He had never noticed how small his was in comparison, how easily Ruari's long, clever fingers completely dwarfed his own.

"I didn't see you this morning," he found himself saying, looking up at the king.

Ruari sighed, the sound unexpectedly tired for all that Corbet had seen him sleep the night before. He squeezed Corbet's hand gently and brought it to his lips to kiss. "I'm sorry about that," he said, turning them down an arched corridor. "I've been busy."

Their footfalls echoed like muted heartbeats as they moved through the populated halls, the fae moving respectfully to the side to let them pass. Corbet tried to soften his steps, preferring the quiet over the sound of Ruari's thin excuse.

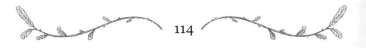

"Do you want to eat with me?" he tried, resituating Tailan against his hip as he squirmed a little in his sleeve. "Or maybe we can play another game. I'd like to learn some more of them. It'd be fun, taking some more of your wealth from you."

When Ruari smiled, it felt like the sun after a month of rain. "So eager to try again after what happened last time? You must enjoy sharing my bed with me," he laughed, gently pulling Corbet to the left and through an open courtyard. "There are so many things I want to show you."

The faux sky above them twinkled in the midst of a dusky sunset, bathing them both in a soft orange glow. It sent Ruari's fiery hair into a muted smolder, coloring him like the fall until Corbet half imagined he could hear the sound of crunching leaves underfoot. For a moment, he forgot he should be irritated with the man.

Tailan prickled against his wrist and it broke him from the reverie. Corbet glared, but before he could give a rebuttal, Ruari's jovial smile melted into a frown. They stepped through the courtyard's doorway and the colors left them just as quickly.

"What is it?" he asked, inching forward to follow the fae when he turned away.

"I fear I'm too busy right now to spend more time with you," Ruari said, his shoulders going stiff as if he were carrying a heavy weight. Gold eyes turned to meet Corbet's, the distance back like a physical force. "I'd like

nothing more to play with you again, but there's simply too much on my plate right now to allow for it."

It stung like a slap to the face and Corbet didn't even know if he had the right to feel so rejected. "It's fine," he managed to say, his voice a bit forced. "You're a king after all. You've got a kingdom to run."

Ruari let out a sigh that sounded how Corbet felt, but neither mentioned it. The room was just ahead, right at the end of the hall, and they spent the last jaunt of the walk in silence, the one moment of levity all the more missed for the weight of its absence now.

All too soon they came to his door. The ever-present guards dutifully ignored them, trying to give them the veneer of privacy though Corbet could tell they drank in every single detail. He gave the leafy-haired fae a small smile, and he was warmed to see her smile back, if only a little.

Corbet startled a bit when Ruari looked down at him and detached himself from his grip. "Here we are," he said, his hands only lingering a moment too long on his shoulders. "Have a good meal. Let me know if you need anything at all, okay? Corin and Gali here can reach me if you require me. There are plenty of books to keep you busy if you get bored as well, so don't go wandering."

Books? That he could actually read? Corbet bit his lip to hold back on the urge to tilt his head up for a kiss he could tell wasn't coming. "I will, Ruari. Thank you," he said again, unsure of what else he could say in light of the kindness.

Ruari smiled, his eyes flighty, and he said nothing more as he turned, the guards saluting him as he left.

Already Corbet felt colder. The bath had given him nothing compared to the heat retreating with Ruari's departure.

"Are you alright?" the tall, leafy fae asked, her voice soft. Corin or Gali, he didn't know, but she sounded like she cared, and that was something.

"You don't look well at all," the childlike one muttered, craning his neck to make sure Ruari wouldn't catch them breaking form.

Corbet sighed but threw on a smile, appreciating their concern if nothing else. "I'm fine, thanks," he answered, not caring whether they believed him.

He closed the door behind him and took in the concerned look from Tailan peeking out from his sleeve, the hedgehog the one thing he couldn't quite avoid. The spikes against his skin were impossible to truly ignore. "I know," he said, reading the look all too easily. "I shouldn't take it so personally."

It didn't stop the fact that he did, or that coming back to his unadorned, flavorless room after being in Ruari's only made him feel all the more miserable.

His desk was laden with the promised food, but

despite not having eaten in a day, he found his appetite smothered beneath the painful knot lodged in his stomach. On his bed rested the other animals, all waiting for him in a comfortable looking pile. That at least made him smile genuinely. They brought some life to the space, making it warmer in a way. More bearable.

Tailan bounced down onto the bed and joined his friends as Corbet kicked off his shoes, sliding in alongside them for the comfort he knew they would offer. The rabbit gave his knee a gentle headbutt and he scratched at his long ears, letting the birds sing and nip at his damp hair.

"I just don't know what to do," he groaned, hiding his face in the pillows.

Why had Ruari been so distant? He couldn't even tell why it stung so much. Tailan's cold nose bumped his cheek like a kiss and he pushed it from his mind as best he could. All of the animals seemed to settle in around him, coaxing him down into their dozing warmth.

Corbet curled into the warm bodies around him and closed his eyes, content to push off further introspection until later.

He had had more than his fair share of that today.

# CHAPTER 6

The coming days didn't aid in Corbet's growing discontent, especially when Ruari continued to hold him at arm's length. Every time he caught sight of the king, be it across the hall, down in the gardens, turning a corner, or even in the fae's own bedroom, he was routinely ignored.

Or well, perhaps ignored was a bit harsh. Ruari was nothing but polite to him. An utter gentleman, even.

Gone were the proprietary touches and dizzying kisses. When Corbet came to him at night, dressed in whatever he deigned to wear since Ruari no longer insisted on clothing him, he was given his half of the

massive bed, no petting or fondling or eye contact to be found.

Corbet couldn't stand it.

He kicked at the base of the bench, looking up at the faerie lights that danced around him, all vying for his attention. One swam closer, bumping gently against his hand to entice him to play. "At least you want my company," he sighed, letting the small creature chase his fingers.

The gardens were completely different during the day, or what passed as day in a world below the earth. Tall trees and expansive growth extended for as far as the eye could see, the colors bright and nearly magical beneath the faux sunlight streaming in from beyond the canopies. Corbet lay stretched out on the bench, losing himself in the songs of nature, begging it to ease his troubled thoughts for a moment.

If he was this bored, he should just leave. The playful light settled in his open hand, undulating and pulsing a low glow in time to his heartbeat. It wouldn't be that hard to escape, if Ruari really had gotten tired of him already.

A little exploring, perhaps a few well-worded questions: if he wanted to, he could do it. These fae weren't as tricky as they seemed when he first got here. He'd learned too much to let them deceive him now. The light seemed to settle in for a rest, it's colorful rainbow of petals curling like satin around his wrist. Corbet could leave this magical place behind.

Turning his face towards the ground, he frowned. Traveling was all he really knew, when it came down to it. He wasn't accustomed to residing in one place, wasting his time on frivolities and luxury. He was human too, a rarity here. An oddity. He may not fit in anywhere up above in the world beyond the fae, but he sure as hell didn't belong here either.

A small voice rose up in the din of his head, unwanted and unbidden. *You could have belonged*, it seemed to say, *if the king wanted you to.*

The faerie light sleeping in his hand woke with a start when he forced himself upright, his cheeks red and his eyes stinging. Flitting anxiously around his head, it brushed past his cheek, comforting him like a concerned friend. Corbet huffed out a rueful laugh and stood, giving it a soft pet before making for the door.

The worst thing was, he probably would. Ruari was infuriating, cocky, presumptuous, unrelenting, and overwhelming, all wrapped up neatly in a handsome, charming package. Corbet wasn't an idiot. He knew himself well enough to know when he was interested in someone, even if that someone couldn't seem to look at him, let alone court him properly.

If Ruari wanted him, he'd have a reason to stay. It was just a shame that Ruari didn't seem to want him anymore.

He exited into the hall and resolutely ignored the fae that turned to watch him as he walked by, leaving the

small trailing light behind at the threshold of the garden. Would it be worth it to try and hunt down the king? Corbet wouldn't boast to know the palace like the back of his hand, but days of solitude led to boredom, which inevitably led to him exploring the place thoroughly.

Abandonment had its perks, he thought cynically, turning down the hallway that led to his room.

It had its perks, but there was no denying how much it still stung. Corbet frowned at the tiled floor, his pace increasing ever so slightly. He didn't have to stomach it. If Ruari had truly grown bored of him, then it was well within his right to demand he just let him go.

"Have either of you seen the king?" he asked, calling out to the ever present fae guarding his door. "I've searched all over this damned palace and I can't find him anywhere."

The two shared an exasperated look, one that might have come off as fond were it meant for a small pet seeking attention. Gali, ever the more understanding of the two, sighed and gave him a pacifying smile, letting him get closer before she answered.

"He's busy, Corbet," she explained, and Corbet rolled his eyes, far too sick of hearing that phrase. "Tonight's the Solstice, so it's-"

"Why is that always the answer?" Corbet complained, doing his best not to let it come out as a whine but losing control of it rapidly. He was an adult, he told himself.

This was no time to be acting like a child, even if all he wanted to do was throw a tantrum.

Gali huffed out a sigh, telling him well enough that his attempts weren't good enough to make him sound his age. "Corbet, we've explained it to you before. The king is busy, that's just how it is given the time of year," she repeated. To her credit, she kept her temper in check far better than Corbet ever could, if their situations were reversed.

Corbet crossed his arms and sagged against the doorway, sliding down until he sat at the guards' feet. "Did he at least leave a message for me this time?" he asked bitterly, rubbing at his eyes.

Silence sounded above him like a forgone answer and it was enough to tell him that he'd been left to his own devices again. What was it now? The fifth day in a row? He couldn't even keep count at this point. He looked past his hand and up at Gali and Corin. With no one else to talk to beyond the animals, he had quickly grown familiar with the ever-present sentries lurking just outside his door.

"Was he like this to the others?" Corbet sighed, leaning his head against the door frame.

The two fae shared a look and shifted on their feet. "The others?" Corin asked, his voice purposefully flat.

Rolling his eyes, Corbet fixed him with a look. "I can't be the only mortal who's been whisked away by your

king, and I'm not prideful enough to think I am. Tell me," he pressed. "Did he treat the others like this too?"

Gali cleared her throat and hid behind her leafy hair. "It's been a long time since he last took a mortal. He really doesn't find himself with the time to devote to the ones he brings back," she said slowly, choosing her words with care. "He doesn't make a habit of it."

"The king is a rather romantic sort," Corin huffed. "He doesn't fall for just any mortal. Whatever he saw in you made him think you were worth the struggle of balancing you with his responsibilities."

Corbet narrowed his eyes. They could word it however they wanted, but it was as good as a yes.

"So what you're telling me is that Ruari avoids bringing home strays since he's a poor pet owner." It fell flat, more an accusatory statement of fact than a question needing answering.

Corin kicked his boot along the tiled floor. "When you say it like that, it sounds rather bad," he chuckled. Gali punched him on the arm and he quickly stopped.

"He really doesn't mean to neglect you," Gali tried, petting through his hair with her spindly fingers.

"Please don't call it neglect. You'll really make me feel like a pet if you do," Corbet groaned, burying his face in his crossed arms. At least the guards paid attention to him. So what if they were ordered to stand there all day?

They at least had the decency to speak to him.

"I don't really see why you're so maudlin," Corin let out, leaning on his bow. "Thought you weren't a fan of the king's courtship. The way I figure, you should be happy to be rid of him for a bit."

Corbet looked up, grimacing. "He's not all bad," he found himself saying, and he knew they latched onto that information with barely contained glee. Fae loved to gossip, no matter how friendly they were to the information source.

A light, jovial punch hit his shoulder and Corin smiled down at him, his face cherubic. "Sure," he said, his voice patronizing. "And if you wind up changing your mind, I'm sure the king will let you go once he realizes how needy a pet you are."

"Corin!" Gali admonished, pulling her hand away from his hair to properly hit her fellow guard. "Don't listen to him," she grated. "The king really is especially busy right now. You know he'd spend time with you if he were able."

Given how the last few days had gone, and the awkwardness surrounding the walk back from his room, he highly doubted that.

"Then why didn't he leave a note?" he pressed, feeling his resentment grow. "Or a message? Would it really have been so hard to do?" It was common decency, at the very least, to tell him why he kept waking up alone, why he was left to entertain himself in a strange palace that

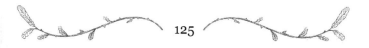

didn't always welcome him. Why he wouldn't even hold him while they slept.

The two guards shared another look and Corbet scoffed, shoving himself to his feet. "That's what I thought," he sighed, pushing past them both to start down the hall.

"Where are you going?" Gali called out, jogging a few steps as if to follow before she realized that would involve leaving her post.

"To see how much Ruari feels like neglecting his pet today," he called out over his shoulder, not sparing a look back to see their expressions.

Corbet had more than had his fill of it. He refused to take it any longer.

In his frustrated state, the trip to Ruari's room took no time at all. He paused for a moment outside it, clarity returning in a cold, liquid rush. What was he even doing? He had no idea if Ruari was even inside. If he were busy, conducting business and preparations, wouldn't he be in a study or a throne room?

He had no idea what he was doing. Corbet sagged, suddenly exhausted. His head fell to the cool door, his hands resting on the heavy oak. Neediness suited no one, and entitlement even less.

It was just so lonely, being left by himself like this. He didn't want it anymore. He'd rather just leave if this were

all he had now.

With more willpower than he knew he had, he raised his hand and knocked softly.

A reply sounded, something in that unintelligible language, and Corbet's eyes grew wide. He was in his room? This whole time? His stomach clenched and Corbet swallowed the bitterness coating his tongue. Reaching for the doorknob, he opened it without another wasted moment.

Ruari didn't even look up. He said something in the fae speech, his tone annoyed. Corbet figured it was probably some complaint about entering without being invited.

"Do I need someone to announce my presence to get an audience with you, or can I just come in?" Corbet said, and that got his attention.

He looked up from his reading to take in Corbet leaning in his doorway. "Did you need something, my lost one?" the king asked. He looked confused, like it didn't make sense for Corbet to have sought him out. "I don't think it's quite nighttime just yet."

Of course he would think that he'd come to sleep. As if that were the only reason for Corbet to come seeking him out. It was far from bedtime, not that Ruari cared to give him attention then either. Corbet frowned at the thought and came inside, crawling up onto the big bed to sit beside him.

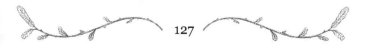

"Can I not spend some time with you?" he asked, hating how defensive he sounded. He would see for himself how much Ruari cared before he demanded his freedom. "I've finished all the books you gave me and I can only talk to the animals for so long until I begin to long for a reply." Did he even feel guilty about it?

"Ah, well, I'm a little busy with-"

Corbet didn't look to see what Ruari's expression was. He just went ahead and snatched the documents from his hands, tossing them aside to burrow his face into the man's chest. When he wasn't immediately wrapped up in an embrace, he moved Ruari's arms for him.

"You can take a break," Corbet mumbled into the shirt. "You work too much."

He had missed this, the feeling of Ruari holding him. They still slept together come nighttime, but the king had made a rift between them, leaving Corbet to curl into himself to stay warm. It was awful. The worst kind of feeling. He wanted that easy intimacy back, if it were even still within reach.

"Speaking of leaving you on your own, I noticed you went through my belongings," Ruari prompted, his tone curious but not reproachful. Corbet hummed and held himself closer, nuzzling his cheek into the fae's warm chest. "Was there a reason for that, or were you simply curious?"

Why wasn't he holding him tighter? Corbet was

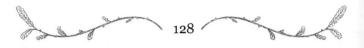

here, in his lap, as eager as could be, but still Ruari kept himself distant. "I wanted to know more about you," he said, looking up to meet golden eyes. "Is there something wrong with that?" Corbet winced internally, hating how vulnerable he sounded.

There was a beat of silence, one that stretched uncomfortably long between them. "Is...everything okay?" Ruari asked quietly, tightening his arms around him without further prompting. His fingers carded through his hair and Corbet melted into the touch, for the first time in days feeling content.

"Everything's fine," Corbet mumbled, inching higher to put himself within range to be kissed, staring at Ruari's lips as if he had to reacquaint himself with them after a long absence.

He was just about to dive in for a taste when Ruari sat up, holding Corbet away from him like he'd been shocked.

"Hold on," he breathed, his eyes wide. "What are you doing?"

Corbet struggled against the grip holding him in place and glared at the fae. "What does it look like?" he grunted, trying to slip out enough to pin the king to the mattress. They were so close. It couldn't just end there.

"It looks like you've planned something," Ruari shot back, a look of distrust in his golden eyes. "You're never this forward." He held tighter and rolled them, holding

Corbet down against the sheets with the length of his body.

Narrowing his eyes, Corbet scoffed derisively. "So you're the only one allowed to make a move? If that's the case, maybe you shouldn't give me the cold shoulder for days on end." His voice was biting and he struggled against Ruari's weight, trying to get enough leverage to reclaim the upper hand. "Just some advice, your royal highness."

"Cold shoulder?" Ruari asked, using his legs to pin Corbet's effortlessly. "What on earth are you talking about?"

He held him down but Corbet simply struggled harder, his anger coming to a crescendo now that he had the king before him. "You kidnap me and then play with me for a few days before growing tired of me," he hissed, trying to throw off the hands keeping him in place. "Is that how fickle you fae are? I don't deserve much, but even I deserve better than this."

Ruari looked like he had been slapped.

"Tired of you? Corbet, what are you talking about?" he grunted, pinning Corbet's wrists above his head. "You're the one who needed to figure out how you felt. I was trying to give you space. Isn't that what you wanted?"

Corbet's eyes went wide and he froze in place, suddenly far too aware of how closely Ruari was watching him. He bit his lip and avoided eye contact.

That had never occurred to him. Not even once.

Ruari seemed to realize that, deflating a bit with a humored sigh. "You're going to be the death of me," he murmured, ducking down to kiss him deep enough to make up for the days of no contact.

There was no way Corbet was going to be shy when this was all he had been craving and more. He surged up into it, meeting Ruari for every move he made. Warm hands loosened their hold on his wrists to cradle his face, letting him touch Ruari himself. He immediately sneaked beneath the hem of the fae's shirt to touch the smooth skin, the firm muscle.

The relief he felt at learning he hadn't been cast aside was debilitating, much like Ruari's kiss.

All too soon, he was forced to break away to breathe, taking in ragged gasps of air as Ruari moved the assault to his throat. "I can't believe you thought I was trying to trick you," he groused, tangling a hand in the wild red hair. "Why is everything with you fae all double crossing and subterfuge?"

It was an interesting feeling, the sensation of a laugh playing out against his neck. "It seemed too good to be true, my lost one," Ruari teased, sucking a mark against the skin. "Let me make it better."

Corbet closed his eyes and went boneless, his entire body tuned like a harp to what Ruari wished to do. He parted his lips and his thighs, dragging the man down to

him in a hungry move to taste more of his skin.

This was harmless, he told himself, savoring the building heat. There was no rule that he knew of saying he couldn't have Ruari and still leave. A muscled thigh fell between his legs and he rubbed against it, moaning. And if it turned out there were, then he could think of considerably worse ways to lose his freedom than from under the touch of a handsome fae.

It was some sort of cosmic joke that a knock chose to sound on the door at that moment, dousing Corbet like a cold burst of water. Ruari ignored it, tugging at the laces that held shut the soft front of the shirt, but it was too present to let him just relax back into it. The rapping grew louder and Corbet pushed Ruari away, a pointed look thrown at the door.

"You should probably see what that's about," he gasped, licking thoughtlessly at his swollen lips. "It could be important."

Ruari made a childish groan as if he were dying, burying his face in Corbet's collarbones. "I suppose I could use the excitement. I don't want to always put work above the time we spend together," he grinned, throwing his hand out to fling the door open from there.

"What are you—" and then Corbet's confusion crumpled into horror, his entire face flushing as the caller walked inside, scroll in hand, to talk to Ruari from the foot of his bed. He struggled under Ruari's figure, trying to cover his chest from sight, but he was held firmly in

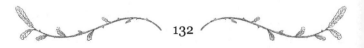

place by the fae's bulk.

"What is it?" Ruari asked, speaking as if he normally conducted business of the state while obviously in a compromised position. Errantly, he twirled a lock of Corbet's hair between his fingers, his hips still rolling deliciously slow against the trapped human.

The reply came in the fae language and Ruari shifted to that seamlessly, the melodic words falling like muffled music around him. Corbet could hardly force himself to make eye contact with the page but he did anyway, biting his lip and struggling to cover himself a bit more. He could only imagine what this must look like.

The rumors of their engagement consummated, no matter how false, would no doubt be common knowledge by evening.

Ruari chose that moment to let out a loud sigh, his tone growing annoyed and his grinding near unbearable. The page jumped a little, her green cheeks flushing dark, but she stayed firm and held out the scroll, gesturing emphatically at some line. Corbet almost felt sorry for her as he failed to hold back a choked moan. She must not enjoy handling Ruari's capricious moods either.

When the tension only seemed to mount, Corbet slowly let his hands fall to Ruari's thighs, massaging the muscle lightly in hopes of getting him to ease up, on him and the page both. Golden eyes flicked down to look at him curiously for a moment, a sharp smile following as soon as he realized what Corbet was up to. Corbet

blushed messily again and pointedly turned his head towards the wall, determined to count the vines creeping up the fresco before he hazarded another look at the pleased king.

The conversation carried on for another few minutes, much less strained than it had been before. Ruari kept up his shameless touching, even going so far as to cup Corbet through his leggings. Corbet let out a mortified gasp, digging his nails into the muscled thighs viciously in return. He was so embarrassed he feared he might faint, his panic spared only by the page rolling up her scroll and leaving just as easily as she had come, her face pointedly turned away from the bed.

Ruari watched the page go, collapsing next to Corbet with a childish noise of displeasure. "I had almost forgotten we had to celebrate the Solstice tonight," he explained, running his fingers through his own hair. "The ball is going to happen soon. They need me to oversee some things. Apparently there is going to be a storm tonight and they don't feel as if they can handle it themselves."

Corbet sat up and held his shirt closed now that he finally could, his embarrassment quickly morphing to anger now that they were alone again. He opened his mouth to complain, both about the exhibitionism and the sudden stop, but the first syllable muffled into a startled yelp as Ruari rose up to kiss him, a smoldering ember instead of the raging fire it had been only moments before. With gentle hands, he guided Corbet to lay back down.

"Heavy is the head that wears the crown," the king said against a conflicted mouth. "I have to go, but I'll see you later tonight. We might even have a moment to ourselves once this is over."

"Do you promise?" Corbet asked, latching onto Ruari's lapels to keep him from pulling away. "I know you're busy, but I want to see you. You can't kidnap me and then leave me to entertain myself. It's bad form."

To his credit, Ruari looked apologetic. "Get kidnapped often, do you?" he teased, leaning into Corbet's arms for a warm embrace. "What would you like to do? Name it, and I will move mountains to make it happen."

Corbet worried his lip with his teeth, glad that Ruari couldn't see his face while holding him like this. He looked over the broad shoulder at the bookshelf, filled to bursting with the books he couldn't read. "Will you read to me?" he asked, teasing the king's pierced ear with his lips. "I want to sit with you and hear you read, since I can't understand your fancy language on my own."

Ruari laughed, low and heady. "If you wish it, I'll make it so," he swore, bringing them in for another devastating kiss.

Slowly, the fae guided Corbet down, laying him out on the sheets to kiss him until there was no breath to spare between them. A clever tongue teased his lips and he parted them, giving Ruari entrance to deepen his

touch. He wanted him. Corbet wanted him so much, and he could hardly think of a reason why it would ever be wrong to have him.

All too soon though, Ruari pulled away with a look of longing on his face.

"I'll read you a library, Corbet," he whispered, bringing up one of Corbet's hands to kiss. "Just be patient with me until this all ends."

Speechless and breathless against the pillows, Corbet watched him get up and fix his appearance with merely a snap of his fingers. With his hair slicked back from his forehead and his clothing shifted into that of a monarch, he truly looked like he hadn't just been about to debauch Corbet senseless.

He wondered what he looked like, and if he seemed as if he'd been about to let him.

He blamed the lack of oxygen as the reason why he leaned into the proffered kiss goodbye, his body still thrumming in hopes of more. "Do you promise?" he asked, biting his lip. There was no way he could handle another bout of loneliness. Not now. "Will you really do that?"

Ruari stared down at him, drinking in the sight. "I promise," the fae swore, sealing the vow with a press of his lips to Corbet's hand.

Corbet watched him leave, his heart racing.

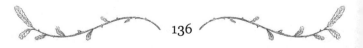

If eternity felt like this, perhaps staying wouldn't be as unbearable as he had thought.

# CHAPTER 7

"Thank you for this," Corbet said after a terse moment of silence, the shifting of fabric the loudest thing in the hallway. "I don't know how I would've figured this thing out on my own."

The two guards gave matching grunts and continued to fuss at his fancy snaps, each fiddling with the persnickety clasps that had given Corbet so much trouble before. He felt foolish standing in the middle of the corridor, the two fae intently helping him dress. Apparently it was a serious thing, leaving one's post. Far too serious to take this inside the room at any rate, or so they told him.

To be perfectly honest, Corbet thought they just enjoyed showing off to those passing by that they were allowed to touch the king's mortal.

"He has such a fondness for the frivolous," Gali huffed, blowing a lock of her leafy hair from her eyes.

Corin nodded, his tongue poking out of his mouth in his concentration. "That he does," he replied, finally getting the silver piece to snap into place. "Lean down here a bit, you settled your brat wrong. It should lay behind your shoulders, not in front of them."

He did as he said, letting him fix the oddly named cloak until it hung properly. Corbet flushed a little as both fae primped and prodded at his outfit until he met their standards of neatness. Gali stretched up to fix the knotted mess that was his hair. He winced when she tugged out a particularly bad one, hissing in pain.

"Oh hush," she chastised, pulling him back down so she could smooth the back into some semblance of order. "If you didn't spend so much time with the king you wouldn't have faerie locks in the first place. Your hair is so shaggy, too. If you cut it, you might not have such a problem with this."

"Excuse me?" he said, straightening the bottom of his léine. Every move had him feeling the gentle swish of the uneven hem, the tunic-type garment long enough to graze his calves. They'd told him that the longer the léine, the more wealth being displayed, so he could only imagine how expensive his ensemble must be to warrant

such length. "What does Ruari have to do with my hair being a mess?" He hoped this wasn't more innuendo. He'd gotten enough of that walking back to his room after their first night of sharing a bed.

The two guards exchanged a fond look and sighed, Corin leaning down to make sure his boots were properly fastened. "Those are faerie locks. They're from sleeping near a fae, one who likes to tie knots in your hair while you dream."

Corbet was glad both were occupied with his outfit so that they missed the look of flustered surprise no doubt at home on his face. "You're telling me that Ruari's the reason why I've been having to wrestle with my hair every morning since I got here?" he shot, masking his embarrassment with annoyance.

"Are you telling us you hadn't worked that out on your own?" Gali shot back, much more confident in smarting off to him after having seen him walk out of his room with his shirt hanging unevenly, asking for help like a lost child.

Huffing, Corbet glared at the both of them and their entertained grins. "Sorry for not knowing everything about you fae," he groused, slouching under the weight of the finery. The trousers hadn't been so bad, since they were similar to the leggings he wore daily. It was the upper layers that had him feeling stiff and restricted. The heavy violet cloak weighed him down like an anchor.

Corin patted his knee and stood up, having deemed

his boots acceptable after only minor fussing. "Give it time, you'll pick it up quickly enough. Have you got your gloves?" he asked while he hefted his discarded weapon, shouldering the bow.

Corbet pulled them from his pocket and tugged them on, letting Gali take one last look at him to make sure he had everything in order. He really was grateful, as much as he complained. There was no way he would have gotten dressed on his own if they hadn't saved him when he'd asked.

Like proud parents, they tugged at his already straight cloak, fretting a little about his low collar. Corin snatched up the end of the brat and helped guide it around his shoulders, letting his taller friend cinch it into place with a fancy, and no doubt expensive, brooch shaped like an oak leaf.

The soft fur trimming on the collar tickled his throat, an obviously Gaelic touch. The whole outfit was foreign to him. He let himself believe it was the unfamiliar sensation of it that caused his voice to waver a little as he thanked them once more for their help.

"Really," he said emphatically. "I appreciate this."

"Hurry up or you'll be late," Gali chided, hiding her smile behind her autumn rust hair. "Perhaps we'll see you there once our shift ends."

They waved him goodbye as he started off down the hall, the long hem of his cloak whispering across the floor

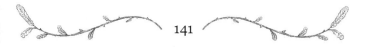

as he went.

A flutter of nerves settled in his stomach as he grew closer and closer to the main hall. Would it be like the first night he had come, he wondered, already picking up on the sounds of the ball echoing through the palace.

Maybe he'd actually be able to sample the food this time, so long as it came from Ruari's hand first. He could only imagine the kind of delicacies served at a faerie ball. Meats, sweets, vegetables that had no right to be as attractive as they were while picked out of season; the possibilities were endless, but knowing the fae and their magic, he knew that it all would be delicious.

Thoughts of food left his mind the moment he entered the hall, the ball in full swing.

A Court of fae paraded past the entrance, all of them decked out in their finest outfits. Some were hanging off the arms of their friends and paramours, others consumed in conversation. From the ceilings hung lights and ribbons of fabric, adding to the dizzying height of the room. It all culminated into a singular focal point at the very apex of the vaulted ceiling, a brilliant glow emanating from a bright orb.

Its shape was in constant flux, a stochastic rhythm that had it in a perfect sphere one moment, and then a jagged shard in the next blink of his eyes. Corbet took in a deep breath and forced himself to look away from it, the sharp outline of its latest shape still seared atop his vision. He blinked rapidly to help it dissipate, turning his attention instead to the focal point of the floor itself.

He watched in awe as one fae, tall and slender like a willow tree, gracefully danced through the mingling crowd as their snow white gown followed, lifted from the floor and milling feet by an entourage of small field mice. Their head was held high, their night black hair held up by a glittering crown. Where they moved, others jumped back, clearing the way for the regal figure as they made their way around the hall.

Whispers followed them and Corbet inched closer to the nearest fae, hearing them gossip of the Unseelie Court's Monarch arriving as decadently as ever.

Unseelie? Ruari was king of the Seelie, so did that mean this fae was some sort of counterpart? Corbet bit his lip and worried it between his teeth, hoping that the two weren't married, or whatever the fae equivalent was. It probably would be akin to suicide to be the king's mortal lingering so close to what could potentially be his spouse.

To be safe, he held back from exploring the center of the festivities and instead made his way around the outer edges, trying not to attract too much attention himself. A platter filled with candies passed by him and he snatched up a couple, discreetly putting them into his pocket for later. Once the king came, he could have Ruari give them to him to eat, and also an explanation on what exactly his role was at his side.

He peered around the party, searching for red hair

and that low, musical laugh. There was no sign of Ruari though, and he shifted awkwardly, overly aware of how long and heavy his outfit was in light of the airy, loose garments worn by most present. He longed for the day clothes he normally wore. At least then he wouldn't feel so conspicuous in them, like an overly plumed peacock in a field of Seelies.

"We hadn't thought we'd be graced with a mortal in our presence this Solstice-night," came a melodic voice from above, and Corbet broke from his thoughts to find that he hadn't been as inconspicuous as he had hoped.

He looked up to meet the voice and found himself craning his neck. The fae before him, the one whispered to be the Unseelie ruler, stood before him with a look of regal indifference upon their sharp face. Corbet swallowed and put on his best smile, unsure of what to expect.

The books given to him by Ruari made mention of the Winter Court, which he assumed must be the Unseelie. They made them sound far more malicious than that of the Seelie, but when dealing with fae, that didn't amount to much. They all seemed to have their nasty sides.

"I hadn't thought I'd ever be here myself," he replied, inclining his head politely, taking it as a positive sign that he hadn't already been struck down. "It's lovely though. Ruari certainly knows how to throw a party."

Was he meant to bow? No one seemed to pay them any mind but he hoped someone might intervene if he were

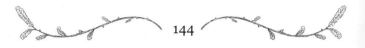

about to get himself killed.

The Monarch raised a razor-edged brow, their expression entirely unreadable. On their head glimmered a delicate crown, woven like coiled vines around a golden frame.

"Yes," they said after a moment's pause. "Ruari is rather fond of his frivolities." The barest inflection to Ruari's name, even in such a passionless voice, rang with distaste.

Corbet blinked and put on a smile, though he knew they included him in that list. "In any case, I hope you're enjoying the night. I'm not too sure what we're celebrating, but it's certainly fun," he returned, deciding to be as diplomatic as he could.

Burnt orange eyes stared him down and it was only when the Monarch's lips quirked that Corbet released the breath he hadn't realized he had been holding.

"Did Ruari not tell you of the Solstice?" they asked, a rueful smile breaking their cold composure into something almost human. "How rude of him, not even taking measures to include you in his royal duties. One would think to treat the object of their affection better, lest they lose them to someone kinder."

The tone rankled and he didn't think he was imagining the note of prospect layering their words. It told him that at the very least, this wasn't a jealous spouse. "He mentioned something about a Solstice

celebration, but his considerable duties tore him away before he could tell me more," Corbet said, clasping his hands behind his back to hide how they clenched.

Not a jealous spouse, but a bitter rival all the same.

"Of course," the Monarch said patronizingly. "We know well of how Ruari conducts his duties."

Biting the inside of his cheek, Corbet kept his smile light. It wasn't as if he could just tell this person how hard Ruari worked, or how often he had been forced to leave Corbet to his own devices as he personally handled every problem that seemed to arise.

Whatever this Solstice was, Corbet knew Ruari did his utmost to make it perfect.

It really should have startled him more to feel strong arms wrap around him from behind, a sharp chin resting on his shoulder as a kiss was pressed to his cheek. The warm, wild scent of the forest pervaded his senses and just like that, Corbet's frustration melted away.

He relaxed, leaning back against the man's chest. "Hello, Ruari," he murmured, tilting his head to the side to kiss him. "I think you're late to your own party."

"Oh, come now, it's not my party. It's the Solstice," he crooned back, spinning him slowly to take in his appearance fully, paying no mind to the Monarch watching with palpable distaste.

Golden eyes traced up and down his form, Ruari's

hands smoothing down the already impeccable front of his léine and the leather belt cinching it around his waist. He snatched up both of Corbet's hands, bringing them to his lips to kiss the black leather of his gloves. "You look so lovely, my lost one. You shame everyone here."

Corbet shifted and looked at Ruari's ensemble, taking in the brilliant carmine of his own brat, the front of the cloak parted perfectly over his shoulders to display the saffron of his shirt. Corbet took some comfort that Ruari's léine was as long as his own, giving him some company in the room filled with shorter cuts.

As unused to the fashion as he was, he still couldn't help but admire how well it suited Ruari. He caught himself staring at the man's collar bones, the dip of skin showed off by his low neckline. Like this, he looked every ounce of the wild king he was. His crown twinkled merrily in the bright fae light, oak leaves tucked in alongside the band to match the one on his brooch.

"You look nice," he managed, flustered and aware of the eyes already beginning to draw towards them.

Ruari laughed, unfastening the brooch holding clasped Corbet's cloak. "Only nice? And here I was, thinking I'd charm you with my handsomeness. Alas, there is no winning with you," he bemoaned with a faux grimace, tossing the no doubt expensive garment to the nearest attendant. With consummate care, he fastened the brooch to the front of his léine, letting his hands linger longer than necessary on his chest.

147

"We see you've acquired a new distraction," the Unseelie Monarch stated, bringing the conversation back to them. "We pray you haven't ignored your responsibilities playing with it."

It was astonishing, watching the joviality fade from Ruari's eyes just like that. He turned towards the tall fae and Corbet bit his lip, noticing how Ruari's face had become a perfect mask. Ruari dipped into a graceful bow and rose up, kissing the elegant, proffered hand.

"Always charming to see you well, Avenir," he gave, his smile cheeky and gaze pointed. "If you pray for my successful courtships, I'll have to wonder about your priorities."

Corbet barely held back the snort of laughter that longed to break free. Instead, he pressed his cheek to Ruari's shoulder. For his efforts, an arm was wrapped around his waist. The Monarch stared, nonplussed, and fixed them both with a heavy look.

"Take care you remember yours," they intoned, though Ruari had turned towards Corbet to fuss with his outfit and kiss his hands again.

If Ruari cared, he didn't show it. Corbet rolled his eyes at the attention and couldn't quite hide his smile from the disapproving Monarch.

"You, my lovely lost one, look like you could use some refreshment," Ruari crooned, taking Corbet's cheek in hand. "There are so many delicacies I've had prepared for

you to try."

He spared a glance to Avenir and quirked his lips into a grin that somehow managed to look equal parts bragging and sincere. "Please, excuse us. I pray you enjoy your evening," he jabbed, pulling them away before the Monarch could retort.

"Well, that wasn't very pleasant," Corbet said the moment they were out of earshot of the fae still watching them walk off. "I don't think you're very popular."

Ruari sighed and guided them through the crowd, his hand burning against Corbet's lower back. "They've never much liked me, though that's always how it is between the two Courts," he explained, nodding at the fae who stopped their dancing and revelry to bow to him as they walked a ring around the expansive hall. "We live long enough that we amass plenty of time to make enemies of most."

Curiosity piqued, Corbet probed deeper. "You'll have to tell me all about it. How long have you been king? Do the two Courts come together like this often? Is there something wrong with you courting me like this?" he asked, more questions coming to mind before he had even verbalized the first. "You need to tell me how to address other royalty so I don't get myself killed."

"You're so eager," Ruari teased. "Finally curious about the workings of your new kingdom?"

Just then a loud, muted rumble seemed to exude

from the walls, shuddering through the floor and cutting off any reply Corbet might have had at the ready. The shifting orb above dimmed slightly before flaring bright once again.

The guests didn't seem to pay it much thought, their conversation only dipping in volume for the barest of moments. Corbet looked up at the fae, the question furrowing his brow.

"Pay that no mind," Ruari sighed, pulling him from their secluded corner and out into the open space reserved for dancing and talking. "It's an odd sensation, isn't it? Feeling the thunder from below the ground."

"That was thunder?" Corbet asked, dumbstruck. "How bad of a storm must it be to feel it this far down?" He let himself be led through the crowds, his arm hooked through Ruari's. They must look like such a pair, arm in arm like a normal couple.

Ruari shrugged, a tired look passing over his youthful face. "The worst I've seen in a long while. The wards will handle it, but it's a drain nonetheless. Put it from your mind though," he said, snagging a crystal flute of some sort of alcohol from a passing tray. He took a single sip before pressing it to Corbet's lips. "Tonight is a night for revelry and rejuvenation."

His eyes flicking down to the glass, Corbet trusted Ruari that it wasn't a trick and took a sip. The taste was crisp and full, like ripe apples and champagne bubbles. It tickled his nose and he giggled a bit, resting his fingers

on Ruari's wrist to get him to tilt the glass so he could have more.

"Do you like it?" he asked, smiling down at him with a smile not completely innocent. "Try to take it slow. It has a rather strong effect on mortals."

Corbet raised a brow and took another pointed swallow, as if in challenge. "I bet I could drink you under the table," he issued, though already his mind had taken on a rather pleasant hum. He leaned into Ruari's chest, forcing him to support his weight as he grinned.

To Ruari's credit, he didn't jump on the opportunity to test it. Ruari sat the empty glass back on another passing tray, wrapping his arms around him to pull him up for a boozy kiss. "Maybe we can test that some other time, when I'm not surrounded by political enemies and ambassadors alike."

Instead of replying, he went in for another kiss, losing himself in the warm embrace of the king. "And here I was, thinking you were the adventurous sort," Corbet lamented breathlessly, looking up at him through his dark lashes. "I want to give them something to disapprove of."

"I think you might be a terrible influence," Ruari breathed, his eyes hot and hungry.

The music seemed to shift into something new, something more suited for the dancers beginning to get tipsy on the freely flowing wine. Corbet turned to look at

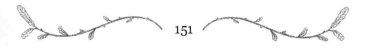

the fae all pairing up, some even in small groups to dance along in their strange, unique ways.

Ruari held him as he began to sway to the song, and slowly he guided him towards the dance floor.

"Would you honor me with a dance?" he asked, batting his eyes winsomely like a fair maiden, innocent and pure, though his smile proved him to be anything but.

"What would you do if I said no?" Corbet teased, already letting Ruari position him properly for the strange, foreign dance.

"Oh, I'd no doubt cry. You wouldn't want that now, would you?" he pouted, kissing Corbet's hand before he held their joined hands fall. "Try to keep up, dearest, this dance is a quick one."

It was then that he noticed the fae had begun to line up with their partners in tow, Ruari and he prominently positioned at the head of the line. He looked up at the king, vague panic mounting. He didn't know how to dance his own country's dances, let alone theirs.

"I don't know, you might deserve it," he muttered in a rush, watching Ruari's feet carefully as they skipped forward a step and then back a step, their legs moving in tandem, almost as if they were in tuned to each other's rhythms. "You've been mean to me too. Maybe you should get a taste of your own medicine for once."

There was the deep thrum of the thunder again, this

time louder, but with Ruari's hand so warm around his own, he couldn't find it in himself to think about what could be occurring above their heads.

The music stepped up its rhythm and Corbet found himself tugged forward, the row shifting in time to the drum's beat. Skipping forward and back, forward and back: he chanced a look at the king and saw how he watched him flounder, a grin blooming on his handsome face. It was the only warning he received before he let go of his hand and broke form to walk around the outer line of dancers, signalling with just that damnable smile that he should do the same.

Corbet turned to the left and tried to match Ruari's pace on the right, catching him in glimpses through the dancers still skipping and waiting their turn to break rank and follow them to the back of the line. The king was smiling brightly, looking carefree and weightless in a way that he hadn't seen before. Perhaps it was freeing, knowing that his hard work and tireless preparations had paid off. It was a good look on him, he thought, approaching the end of the line.

They reconvened at the very back of the dancers' train, grasping hands once again as if drawn together by something stronger than a pervasive rhythm and the traditional movements of the dance. Before Corbet could gather the breath to complain about the unexpected separation, Ruari proceeded to be Ruari.

"I'd rather just taste you," the fae gave in the moment

they had before they were forced forward again, his smile sharp as he tugged Corbet closer. They stared into each other's eyes, the air between them crisp and heady like the taste of alcohol. The dance continued while their world slowed, and they dipped below the other dancers' uplifted and arched arms, like children playing a game.

Corbet's mouth watered for more and he raced to keep up. He didn't want an inch of space between them. "Perhaps I'd let you," he whispered breathlessly, mischievous as any fae, "if you made a good argument for it." Ruari lifted their joined hands, a pair of dancing fae dipping beneath. Their long léines billowed as they danced back to the front of the line, the repetition echoing the thrumming music.

The grin that bought him was truly breathtaking. Ruari guided him through the arches of raised arms, surprising Corbet by breaking the chain of dancers to spin them both away from the group entirely. Corbet laughed against his chest when the world twirled along with them in a dizzying stream of light and color.

"Are we done with that then?" he asked, leaning up on his toes to kiss the fae's cheek. They swayed slowly, savoring each other's heat and touch and sharing the air between them like the most intimate of secrets.

"I figured we should stop before one of us gets embarrassed," the king teased, holding him close, the mood heady.

Corbet smiled, staring up into warm, golden eyes.

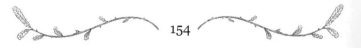

"You're talking about yourself, right?" he teased right back, suddenly so aware of the soft, inviting mouth drawing him in. "I think we all know which of us is the weaker partner."

He could sense the kiss coming and he welcomed it, closing his eyes. Had he ever felt this content before?

A loud cry cut through the music and chatter, snapping them apart mere inches from each other's lips. Corbet was the one to pull away. Ruari kept moving, pressing his kisses to his cheek and down his neck.

He turned towards the sound, catching sight of a frantically flapping bird just as it swooped down, aiming its path straight towards them. Corbet recognized the bright yellow canary as one of the usual creatures that spent time with him. The songbird landed heavily on Corbet's raised arm and immediately began to chirp and squawk, her feathers fluffed into an agitated mess.

Confused, Corbet looked between the bird and Ruari. "What's wrong?" he asked, his concern burning through the buzz like a flame through paper. "What's she saying?"

Ruari's face fell the longer he listened to the erratic sounds. "Not all of the animals made it back in before the storm hit," he finally answered, his voice tight. "Shal's saying she can't find your hedgehog friend. Phren, your rabbit, hasn't seen him since they were last above."

The words didn't fully sink in.

"Tailan? But, he can't be outside in this. He has to be here somewhere." Corbet glanced around the room, looking in between the dancers' feet like he might spot the small creature among the festivities. Another loud thrum marked the thunder in crescendo, sending the canary into a renewed fit.

"She's certain that Tailan didn't make it inside," Ruari replied, even going so far as to take the bird from him in hopes of calming her.

Corbet looked at the small bird cradled in Ruari's hands, taking in her frightened eyes. The thunder sounded again, this time stronger.

Fear gripped his heart like a vice and he grabbed Ruari's shirt, tugging him down to look him in the eye.

"You have to help him," he whispered, his voice nearly strangled in his throat. "Ruari, Ruari, he's out there all alone—"

Ruari took him by the shoulders and tried in vain to calm him. "He'll be okay, Corbet. He knows the forest too well to let something happen to him." Even as he spoke though, another rumble rattled the hall, the plates and glasses and dancers trembling in its wake.

Corbet bit his lip hard enough to bleed and couldn't erase the vision of Tailan out in the tempest, alone and so small as the forest crashed around him. If Tai wasn't in a safe place, there was no telling what could happen to him.

"Please," he begged, looking into Ruari's golden eyes. "Please help him."

Ruari's eyes narrowed, bringing them closer to avoid drawing attention while he led them away from the middle of the dance floor. "It's not that simple, Corbet. It's the Solstice and he's above ground. It's not exactly easy for me to bridge the gap tonight," he tried to explain. "Or smart for that matter."

"Then I'll go on my own," Corbet shot. "Where is the opening? Show me and I'll find him myself."

"I'm not going to let you go out there either, Corbet," Ruari sighed, his temper flaring a bit. "You'd get yourself killed or injured, and then I'd have to come to your rescue as well."

Corbet ground his teeth. He wasn't about to let one of the only creatures that cared about him to die in some terrible storm. "He's my friend," he insisted, taking Ruari's jacket in his hands.

To his credit, Ruari looked thoroughly miserable. "I can't," he said. "I'm sorry, but there are things at work here beyond our own desires. This isn't a night to be breaking rules."

Corbet didn't care about idiotic fae rules. He clenched his fists and raised himself up to put his mouth at Ruari's pierced ear. Belatedly, he realized they were different from his usual ones. Shaped like fleur de lis interwoven with leaves, they were a perfect representation of their

cultures combined.

"Do it, please," he whispered, imploring while his voice shook. "Do it and I'm yours. No more running. I'll eat the food. I'll sleep with you. I'll be yours forever. Just do this one thing."

He almost thought Ruari was going to refuse again, the silence between them stretching for a dozen painful heartbeats.

"Alright," Ruari finally agreed, taking Corbet by the hands to sit him back down outside of the ring of dancers still making merry, oblivious to their conversation. "I'll go find him. Stay here though," he ordered, kneeling down to make sure their eyes connected. "I don't need to get sidetracked looking for you if you decide to try and find him yourself."

The accusation smarted but Corbet only nodded, pushing at Ruari until he finally stood and disappeared somewhere behind that same tapestry from before, the one that showed the figures around the throne, the red king at the very center of its colorful expanse. The partygoers around him didn't even notice, none picking up that their king had vanished or that their mortal guest was off in the corner, waiting in a state of panic.

It was nearly impossible to stop thinking about it, but the music at least provided a lovely backdrop to his worry. Flutes, harps, and bagpipes chased each other in quick melodies, trilling and looping like the most convoluted of games. Pipers raced and the tempo charged, following the cadence of the storm. Like this, it was easy to forget it was happening if you weren't listening for it.

Corbet was definitely listening for it. He couldn't not. In front of him danced hundreds of fae, celebrating their Solstice in complete joy as the walls vibrated with the force of the thunder above. The light from above dimmed and flickered, fluttering in time to the storm raging on the surface. How much longer would it be?

He wondered where the other animals were, if they weren't here. They must be inside, maybe even snuggled up in his room, worried about their missing friend.

A new wave of worry washed through him and Corbet forced himself into place, knowing that following Ruari through the tapestry would only cause more problems. No wonder he had found his pack there, that first day he had awoken. The tapestry must hide the gateway through which the fae crossed.

He bit his thumb, worrying the flesh between his teeth until he tasted blood. If only he had known, Corbet doubted he'd still be here. To think he had sat so close that first day, not even realizing how close he was to escaping. Would he have had the foresight to take Tailan with him? He hoped so, though they hadn't bonded truly until later.

Corbet clenched the wood of the seat in his hands. It was such a large forest. He couldn't help but think back to how easily he had gotten lost himself, a week ago, maybe

more. The days all ran together and the panic wasn't letting him think clearly enough to count. There were so many places to look, so many ways for a small hedgehog to be hurt out there.

The ball carried on and Corbet contemplated grabbing another glass of whatever that drink had been. His nerves were frayed and on edge, but he had enough self-preservation to remember the restriction.

A few curious and drunk fae stumbled up to him, one after the other, to ask him for a dance. He gave them a tight smile and a terse no. All the while, he kept his eyes focused on the tapestry, waiting for Ruari to return.

What must have been an hour passed like that, with no sign of Ruari or Tailan. He could hear the guests beginning to notice that something was wrong, some whispering that their king was missing, others that something just didn't feel right with the air.

The Monarch from the other Court whispered demurely behind their fan, no doubt gossiping. Corbet folded his arms around his stomach and tried to hold back the nerves. Burnt orange eyes weighed down on him like an anvil and he pointedly ignored them. They turned instead towards the ceiling, their impassive face turning hard like stone.

And then he saw the tapestry move, the fabric rippling like the surface of a lake in the wind. Corbet was on his feet and rushing towards it before he fully processed what it meant or what he might find on the other side.

Ruari was just poking his head out and pulling back the heavy piece when Corbet came upon him, dragging him out by the arm. The fae was completely soaked through, as if he had been dunked clothes and all in the ocean. Water dripped from his hair and face and he seemed to tremble from the cold, his arms wrapped around his middle.

Corbet smoothed back his wet hair from his face and looked for any sign of Tailan.

He saw nothing.

"What...what happened?" he asked, his voice a weak whisper. "Where is Tai?" He could feel the guests looking at them strangely but he couldn't bring himself to care. Ruari looked weak, like he had run halfway across the world and given no rest for his effort.

The king sighed and straightened up, wincing as he unbuckled his belt and dipped his hand inside the shirt beneath. "Hold on," he grunted, his expression pained.

Corbet flushed and the curious onlookers grew even more curious now that their king seemed to be soaked and stripping in front of them. He tried to cover Ruari from view to the best of his abilities, the fear clamping his throat closed in a tight fisted hold.

Ruari smiled and reached into his léine, gently pulling out the handful of spines and hisses that made up the prickly hedgehog. "He didn't appreciate me coming to his rescue, but once I said you were worried, he at

least let me pick him up," Ruari complained, plopping the hedgehog into Corbet's hands as he rubbed at the scratches no doubt littering his abdomen.

Tailan uncurled from his defensive ball and snuffled at Corbet, his tiny black eyes frightened yet affectionate. Bringing him to his cheek, Corbet let the cold, damp nose kiss him. "Thank you, Ruari," he managed, his voice a ragged mess of relief. "Thank you so much."

Still a dripping mess, Ruari smiled warmly back at him. Though his eyes were kind, his posture looked drained, and he fastened his belt sloppily, more to have it on than to put his outfit back in order. "Make sure he gets dried off," he said.

That was a good idea. He grabbed the long hem of his tunic and wrapped the hedgehog in the expensive fabric, cradling him to his chest like a mother with a swaddled baby. Corbet leaned into the hand that fell to his waist and he moved when Ruari did, letting him guide them towards the hall where the rooms lay. With a wave and a commanding glare, the king sent the onlookers back to their activities.

"What about you?" Corbet asked, rubbing gently at the shivering hedgehog to warm him.

Ruari sighed. "I'm going to do the same. I think the party can function without me for the rest of the evening, or at least until someone comes hammering at my door with another problem." His eyes glanced up at the still

flickering orb, and a shadow passed over him.

"Let me escort you," he said, tearing his eyes away.

Corbet pressed close to him. "I can make it back on my own," he gave. "You should take care of yourself first."

"I think I'd rather see you safely back."

Tired though he sounded, he still seemed determined to walk Corbet to his room before heading to his own. Corbet couldn't find it in himself to argue about it, and they left the crowds behind and with them, the gossip and stares.

"Where did you find him?" Corbet pressed, holding Tailan close to check that he wasn't any worse for the soaking he got. "What happened to you? You look terrible."

Water dripped from his clothes, leaving a trail of puddles that marked their way. "He was huddled under a fallen tree near the entrance. It seemed that once he realized the door had been sealed, he was intent on digging himself back home." Ruari looked at Tailan with some measure of annoyance. "It took longer to convince him to come with me than it did to find him."

Corbet lifted Tailan to eye level and frowned. "Did you make him stand out there in the rain just to give him a hard time?" he asked, disappointment coloring his voice.

Tailan looked away, only somewhat guiltily, and Corbet sighed. "You're lucky he came for you," Corbet told

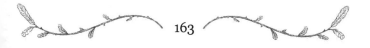

him. "You could've drowned, Tai."

Ruari managed a worn laugh. "Don't give him too much grief, though he should know better than to be out on a night like this," he said. "We all should, for that matter. Maybe we'll think clearer after some rest."

Before Corbet had even noticed, they were outside his room, Gali and Corin both conspicuously absent. He paused and looked at Ruari, unsure of what came next. "Do you want to come inside?" he asked, en lieu of any idea of what else to say.

For his efforts, he was kissed gently. "I think I'll just retire to my own, though I thank you for the offer." Ruari looked down at Tailan, who for once didn't hiss when he reached out his hand to touch his small head. "I'm feeling rather worn, all things considered."

"Do you want me to come with you?" Corbet asked, brushing a wet lock of hair from Ruari's eyes.

The fae smiled tiredly and opened his door for him, the hand on his lower back nudging him inside. "Take care of Tailan," he answered. "Make sure he's fine and feels safe. No matter what he says, he was scared up there."

Corbet bit his lip as he watched him head off, confliction heavy in his chest. He hadn't forgotten his promise and it didn't feel right to leave Ruari to himself after all he had just done.

Entering the room quickly, Corbet found the other animals burrowed in his bed, exactly where he had thought they'd be. Tailan was quick to let his desire to join them be known. The canary, Shal, and the hare, Phren, dove to smother him in their combined feathers and fur.

With a soft blanket, Corbet carefully bundled up the damp animal, rubbing gently at his spikes until his shivers morphed into tired snuffles. He thought of Ruari in his room, drying himself off in the quiet dark. Black eyes looked up at him and Tailan sneezed to tell him to let him be so he could sleep.

"You don't mind?" he asked quietly, settling the small creature back into the pile of warm bodies waiting for him. "I don't want to leave you alone if you're scared."

Tailan rolled his eyes in a way only he could, turning his face to bury it into slick fur. It was as much permission as he was likely to get and Corbet bent down to kiss all of the animals in turn, thanking them silently for understanding him so well, far better than he understood himself.

# CHAPTER 8

When Corbet finally found himself staring at the wood of Ruari's bedroom door, he didn't waste time in thinking, let alone knocking. He turned the handle and walked in confidently, determined to settle whatever it was between them.

He made it all of three steps before he realized that Ruari was still soaking wet and in the midst of getting undressed.

"So I heard you're the one who's been tying my hair into knots," Corbet blurted out, his mind searching for something to say beyond what was already heavy in the air.

Ruari's eyes grew wide, obviously thrown by both the entrance and the non-sequitur. His pale cheeks flushed a little, nearly indiscernible in the low light of his room. "Now who told you that, I wonder," he muttered, fumbling with the buttons at his wrists to no avail. Strewn across the floor lay his boots, the heels caked with mud and leaves.

Corbet took pity on him after another moment of watching, crossing the room to take Ruari's hand in his. It was no wonder why he was having trouble. Where they touched his skin, he could tell that Ruari's fingers were numb, the cold and wet clothing only sapping him of what little warmth he had left.

"Just a helpful little faerie is all," he replied with a small smile, unfastening the pearl loop and then the next. "Is there a reason why, or do you just like lengthening my morning routine?"

The next thing to go was the waterlogged brat, the léine following soon after. Ruari stood patiently and let Corbet help him navigate the miles of fabric, bowing his head to help him slip it off. He shivered when the cold fingers slipped beneath the flowing cuffs on his sleeves, warming themselves on his bare skin.

"It wasn't like I meant to," Ruari defended quietly, rubbing his fingertips along Corbet's wristbones. "It just happens when I'm not thinking. I won't do it again."

Corbet frowned, slipping the see-through shirt off broad shoulders to add it to the pile growing on the floor.

"I didn't say I minded. You can help me untangle them come morning next time." He eased up on his toes for a kiss. "I like your hands in my hair."

Ruari warmed up quickly under his hands, his bare chest near flush with his own. A cool cheek met his lips instead of a warm mouth, the fae turning away at the last moment.

Corbet's brow furrowed and he tried again, only to get the same result. "What's wrong?" he asked when Ruari's hands came up to pull his from his skin. "You can have me, Ruari. I'm yours."

"I don't want you like this," Ruari stated, his eyes uncharacteristically serious. "Not because you felt backed into a corner. It wouldn't be you, and you've made me want you."

He almost balked, the tone seemingly out of nowhere. "But I said I was yours," Corbet repeated, his voice almost a whisper in comparison to Ruari's commanding tone. "I'm not doing this because I feel honor bound. If I didn't want you then I'd find a way out of it, like I always do. This is all me."

It probably said something about their relationship that that was meant to be comforting. As it stood, Ruari merely shifted, his eyes focused somewhere on the floor.

"You don't believe me do you?" Corbet glared, stepping back to take in the suddenly scrupulous fae. "You don't think I'm serious."

Ruari continued to stare at anything but him and Corbet clenched his jaw. With a roll of his eyes, he brought his glove to his mouth and bit down on the fingertip, slipping it off his hand. When he realized he had Ruari's attention, his eyes sharp and hot, he did the same with the other, only slower.

"Let me show you how serious I am," Corbet proposed, digging into his pocket for the treats he had stashed there earlier. Upon closer inspection, he found them to be small candied figs, petite and sugary and enough to make the king look up from where he had been staring at Corbet's lips, his expression one of surprise.

"I didn't give that to you," Ruari said slowly, the puzzle pieces slowly lining up behind his eyes. "What do you think you're doing?"

Corbet rolled his eyes and moved to pop the candy into his mouth, the fruit just barely touching his lips before Ruari seized his hand and waist, pulling him against his chest. Golden eyes bored into him, disbelief warring out with desire.

"I was going to bind myself here. To you specifically. Because I'm yours," Corbet spelled out, as if he were explaining himself to a small child. He tugged at his wrist in hopes of freeing it, but Ruari merely leaned forward, taking the candy from his hand with his lips to eat it himself.

Corbet frowned. "Now how am I supposed to show you I want you?"

He was abruptly answered with a ravenous, sweet kiss, desperate enough to melt away his frustration and hot enough to make him moan. Ruari's hair was cold in his hands, still damp and loose and he tangled his fingers in it as he was lifted into strong arms.

The world went hazy and before he knew it, his back met the mattress with a soft thump. Ruari folded himself along Corbet's body, tugging messily at all of the hard work Corin and Gali had done to make him presentable for the evening.

"Are you excited?" Ruari asked, his smile so wide it blinded. "I can hear your heartbeat from here, as quick as a hummingbird's."

The brooch went flying and Corbet quickly reached for Ruari's hands to slow him down, lest he ruin the outfit completely or send his heart pounding even harder.

"Hey, be careful. This looks expensive," he panted, his head falling to the side when Ruari let him ride his thigh.

"I paid for it so I can ruin it if I want to," Ruari shot back, offended by the very notion of taking it slow. His hands yanked and tugged, to impatient to bother with undressing him properly. Corbet winced at the sound of tearing fabric.

With a strong push and a kiss for distraction, Corbet managed to roll them. Ruari's surprised eyes stared up at him with a curious heat. "Maybe I don't want you to ruin it," Corbet whispered against his lips. He took Ruari by the wrists and placed them above his head. "Stay still and watch, since I don't trust you not to be destructive."

To Corbet's utter delight, he listened. Ruari moaned as if in pain when he made for the snaps on his upper sleeves, unfastening each one with consummate care. Golden eyes raked down his form, his hands clenching in the pillow hard enough to tear the delicate stitches. He bit down on his lip and breathed through his nose, watching Corbet's slender fingers open each button until his léine opened up like a flower blooming.

"You're going to kill me at this rate," he complained, whining when Corbet slid off the long garment and folded it neatly before setting it on the floor. His undershirt still remained, his trousers hiding the rest of him yet from the hungry eyes.

Corbet smiled and slowly unlaced his boots, grinding himself into Ruari's obvious erection a little to make him really sweat. "You doubted my sincerity, my king," he chimed, throwing in the title to see what it bought him. "You didn't want me, so now you have to work to make me think you do."

The boots fell to the floor and Ruari bucked weakly, his face flushed and wanting. His muscles bulged and tensed when he clutched the pillow above his head with all his strength. "Would it help if I say how sorry I am?" he asked, voice strained.

Letting his head loll on his shoulder, Corbet smiled sweetly down at the fae as he unbuttoned the shirt as

slowly as he knew how. "We're a little past that point, don't you think?" He leaned forward enough to let their chests barely touch, Ruari arching up as much as he could to chase the contact. "Let's see if I can't make your heart race too."

He pressed a feather light kiss to Ruari's tortured expression before sitting back up, shrugging off his loose layer and letting it flutter to the floor. His hands fell to the belt at his waist next, coaxing the leather through the straps slowly, making a show of the thick strip sliding through his hands.

Every few moments he rewarded Ruari with another slow roll of his hips, just enough to make him keen. It really was astonishing that the fae had held still long enough for him to get this far.

That uncharacteristic patience ended the moment he tugged his trousers down, revealing the soft undergarments from that first night together. Corbet averted his eyes as he stripped, having forgotten he had even been wearing them.

Ruari took one look before his hands flew to Corbet's hips, rolling them back over before Corbet could even process what had happened.

"You kept them," Ruari growled, his mouth already falling to the miles of pale skin begging to be marked. His eyes darted up to meet Corbet's, just enough to send him blushing and paint Ruari's grin predatory. "You actually kept them."

Corbet turned to face the wall, his hands buried uselessly in damp hair. "I wasn't going to just throw them out," he muttered, gasping a little as Ruari mouthed at him through the thin satin.

"I don't think that's the only reason why," Ruari sang, making wide, rough passes with his tongue to keep Corbet fidgeting, his hands pinning his restless hips to the bed.

His eyes taunted him to tell the truth and Corbet held out for all of a minute before the teasing licks became torturous, a barely there fondling. Breathing ragged, he clenched his eyes shut and tried to bite down on the moan.

It only took a targeted snap of the waistband to make him jolt and cry out, the dam broken just like that.

"I liked them, okay?" Corbet rushed, writhing against the sheets for more contact, any contact. "Ruari, please, touch me. I want you to touch me," he moaned, tossing his head as he tried to force Ruari's down for more.

"I like them too," and Ruari gave him what he wanted, slipping the satin off his hips. "You're so slender for such a dangerous mortal. You fit so well in my hands," he chuckled before taking him into his mouth.

He had planned that observation perfectly, because with the wet heat around his cock, he had no time to get angry. Corbet's lips parted in a soundless moan and he writhed against the sheets, yanking at Ruari's hair. It was

too much, not nearly enough, more than he could ever take and he nearly sobbed when the fae pulled off to look at him, leaving his cock flushed red and painful against his thigh. A whine sounded when a clever tongue flicked out to tease him, soft lips following to kiss at the head.

Thighs trembling, Corbet couldn't keep watching the obvious show the king was putting on for him. His head fell back into the pillows and he threw an arm over his eyes. It was laughable, the idea that it would be enough to hide behind.

Gentle but strong hands took him by the thighs to open his legs, the fingers of one trailing down to prod at his entrance. The air tingled with the taste of magic and when the fingers touched him again, they felt wet and slick with some sort of liquid. Corbet stuttered on a breath, jolting a little as the first slipped inside him and began to stretch him, every slow press matched with a lick or a suck from Ruari's talented mouth.

Peeking past his arm, he watched Ruari work him open expertly, the second finger moving in alongside the first with barely a twinge. A warm, heady pressure began to build inside him and he keened, pushing his hips back to meet every thrust. Ruari kept him from bucking deeper into his mouth, but he rewarded him with a third finger, this one enough to punch the breath from his lungs.

"You're awfully slow," Corbet managed to say, shifting constantly to try and get more friction. Ruari had taken to licking up and down his shaft, skimming his soft lips against him to keep him on edge. "Come on, my king. Show me how much you want me."

"If that's what you want, my lost one," Ruari grinned, giving one last lick before he pulled away entirely, his fingers retracting to curl around his hip.

Corbet flushed when he was maneuvered up, a pillow slipped under him to lift his hips higher. The hot, wet brush of Ruari's cock against his entrance came like a promise of something much more, of all that the fae was willing to give. He looked into the fae's eyes and arched beneath his hands.

"I want you," he pleaded. "I want all of you."

There really was no stopping the outpouring of desire emanating from the man above him. Ruari grinned against his lips as he thrust inside, all teasing lost as they came together. His moan swallowed in the kiss, Corbet dug his nails into the fae's strong shoulders, dragging them down his back when he began to move.

"Ruari," he choked, his lips barely forming the words. "Oh my god, Ruari."

"You're so beautiful, my lost one," Ruari mouthed against his neck, rolling his hips in sync with their fevered breathing. "I've wanted you for so long."

Corbet keened and closed his eyes, the note of pure adoration too much to bear alongside the building

pleasure. He gasped for breath and took in the king with half-lidded eyes, his vision dominated by the sight of the handsome man, his strong chest and wild hair falling into his eyes as he took him apart. With desperation, he touched as much of him as he could, digging his nails in hard enough to leave marks whenever Ruari struck the spot inside him that sent him shaking.

Biting his lip, he tried to hold back the cries and words that threatened to spill, but it wasn't enough. He pulled Ruari down for another kiss but it failed to sate. He needed more, he needed to feel him in every way, in as many ways as he could.

"Please," he felt himself say, yanking at the thick red hair until golden eyes met his own. "Ruari, I can't, I can't take it—"

The words dried up the moment Ruari looked at him, slowing the rhythm to an almost mind numbing roll.

"What do you need, my love?" he breathed, mouthing along his neck like a reverent worshipper at the foot of his deity. "I'll give you anything. You make my still-heart sing."

Moisture pricked his eyes and Corbet felt so hot, the oxygen in the room not enough to keep him coherent. He lunged for a kiss, stealing the breath from the king's lungs, treating it like it was freely given. He kissed like it could be the answer Ruari was waiting to hear.

He felt Ruari hitching his thigh up higher, nearly

bending him in two. At first, all he registered was the hot, fiery hand burning a trail along his leg, but then something shifted, some minute change in the angle that sent him crying out.

White flooded his vision and the world sharpened to a razor-fine point, Ruari and his heat the only things in sight.

Ruari nipped sharply at his pierced ear, chuckling breathlessly as Corbet scratched wildly down his back. "Are you about to cum? Is this what you were wanting?" he asked, speeding up the rhythm of his thrusts. The hands tilted up his downturned chin, forcing Corbet's eyes to meet his own.

There was no way Corbet could answer or even consider admitting it, even as his body trembled, his muscles tightening like a coiled spring. He flushed and bit his lip, turning his face into the hand cupping his cheek. Ruari was so warm, so beautifully warm against his skin.

A soft thumb trailed over his lips, Ruari's following to taste the tongue that flicked out to meet it.

The kiss combined with another thrust sent Corbet over the edge, crashing like a waterfall. Corbet shuddered, the pleasure licking along his limbs, an all-consuming fire that was so entirely Ruari that he buried his cry of the king's name in the drowning kiss.

Ruari held him as he shook apart below. The king

faltered in his thrusts, his own release following quickly. He fucked his way through it, sending shivers of aftershocks through Corbet's over-sensitive nerves until he cried out, struggling weakly beneath the fae's bulk.

His belly was slick with the mess of their coupling and he flushed when Ruari finally saw fit to cease the torture, pulling away to kiss down his heaving chest, licking and marking his stomach. In wet, slow passes, he cleaned the cum from his skin, grinning when Corbet groaned. The sight was too much too soon.

"Ruari, don't do that," he whined, still trying to recover his breath. Ruari's hair had dried at that point, probably from the heat and movement, and he pushed the wavy locks from his eyes to better see his smug face.

The tongue made another pointed lick, this time along his cock and Corbet let out a strangled yelp. "But I want to," he chuckled, his voice carrying a heady rasp to it. "You're mine now, aren't you? Let me have my fun and pamper you a bit."

To Corbet's horror, Ruari's idea of pampering involved shifting him onto his stomach to better lick at the release dripping from his entrance.

"Ruari!" he cried, his hands clenching in the sheets as his hips were seized and held in place for the roving mouth. Embarrassment swelled and Corbet struggled and he couldn't help but spread his thighs wider. "Oh my god, Ruari, that's—" He cut himself off with a broken

178

moan, his body heating up again with the help of the warm hand palming his cock.

The fae paid his pleas no mind and took his time, licking into him until Corbet thought he was going to black out, unable to breathe for the sensations tearing through him. His arms gave out and he bit at the sheets, his eyes watering.

Ruari trailed sharp kisses along his inner thighs, laughing quietly against the trembling skin before he pulled away to take in his hard work. "You're amazing," he sighed fondly, easing up to join Corbet at the head of the bed. "Simply breathtaking. I want to touch you all night, for as long as I live."

Corbet barely gave him a frustrated glare before turning away, his body a mess of half-realized excitement and aching muscles. "You're incorrigible," he snapped back, yanking at the blankets until he could cover himself and hide his face properly.

"Don't tell me you didn't have a good time," Ruari crooned, wrapping his arms around him to pull his cocooned mass into his chest. "I never expected you of all people to be so bashful after the fact."

A kiss was pressed to his head and Corbet resolutely ignored him.

Whining like a child, Ruari buried his face in Corbet's neck. "You're going to hurt my feelings, Corbet," he pleaded, raining little kisses to his skin like a begging

179

apology. "At least let me look at you."

His resolve crumpled like paper and he let himself be turned, leaning into the proffered doting like it was his due. Kisses fell to his cheeks and hair, almost making up for before. The silence between them was comfortable, only broken by Ruari's quiet praises and the dripping clothes off to the side.

"You don't look cold anymore," Corbet observed as he let Ruari explore him with gentle hands. A healthy flush colored the fae's cheeks, no longer showcasing the pale chill it had held before.

"That's because you did such a good job warming me up."

Corbet swallowed hard, knowing it was his fault that Ruari had even been so wrung out. "Thank you," he said slowly, his voice muffled in the blanket. "Again. Ruari, thank you. You didn't have to do it."

Ruari uncovered his face and cradled his cheek, refusing to let him hide in his sheets. "There's not much I wouldn't do for you, if you but ask. The fact that you were willing to throw away everything just for Tailan was enough to tell me how important it was to you." He drew his eyes down along Corbet's hidden body, his tone turning cocky though something in his eyes stayed reserved. "Who am I to spit in the face of such devotion? Especially if I can expect such a grateful response from you. You drive me completely mad."

"Do you even listen to the things that stream from your mouth, or does it have a mind of its own?" Corbet asked. "You're so forward. It's overwhelming." His tone was annoyed but inside he was pleased.

"I think you really enjoy my mouth, when it's directing its skill at you." Ruari punctuated the line with a lascivious grin and got a shove to his chest as a reward.

"You're an ass," he mumbled, hiding his face in Ruari's neck. "I'm trying to be appreciative and you just won't take it with grace." The blankets were eased away and Ruari quickly replaced them. He was so much warmer than the sheets, so Corbet put up with it.

Ruari nuzzled into him, smiling gently against his hair. "But I'm your ass, so bear with it for a while, okay?" he whispered, his tone soft, almost apologetic.

Corbet glanced up at him, still struck by how handsome the fae was. How sharp his face, how gold his eyes. He brought his hand up to cup his cheek, pressing a chaste kiss to Ruari's sincere smile.

Aggravating as he was, he could always trust that smile and the feelings it held.

"Just for an eternity, right?"

Ruari tugged him close and tangled his hand through his hair, his sigh a laugh.

"And what a pleasant one it will be."

# CHAPTER 9

Corbet opened his eyes to a sight so beautiful that for a moment, he thought he might still be dreaming.

Ruari lay at his side, dead to the world, but so handsome that Corbet forgot he was his to touch. He took a breath and held it, drinking in the sight. Warm skin greeted his careful fingertips.

Whatever magical light there was in the faux morning of the room, it played across the planes of his sleeping face as beautifully as natural sunlight. Soft gold kissed the dark rings below his eyes, accentuating the vibrant hue of his crimson hair. Corbet inched closer to kiss the tired eyes himself, seeking the warm contact. Ruari didn't stir.

For all that they both had rested, Ruari still looked as if the draining exhaustion from the night before hadn't eased in the slightest. A cold sweat dotted his forehead, and his eyes flitted uneasily behind his eyelids, caught up in a dream less kind than what wakefulness promised. Corbet was tempted to rouse him, but the image of him wet and shaking from the night before rose up in his mind.

He had looked terrible. Weak. Corbet frowned and stroked his hair gently. Ruari needed the rest.

A flicker of guilt teased his stomach, but Corbet swallowed it down. Instead, he focused his attention on the way his lover's skin glowed in the morning light despite the discomfort on his brow. It looked inhuman. Gilding and gentle, it painted him completely ethereal.

Corbet had no idea how he had ever doubted Ruari's claims when they had first met. His fingertips brushed the fae's petal-soft lips and he chased the touch with his own, tasting the sweetness of the night before still lingering on his mouth, his cheek. There wasn't an ounce of mundanity beneath his fingers to suggest that Ruari could ever be mortal. The exhaustion was the only flaw on him, and even that did little to daunt his beauty.

Nectar sang on his palate and he couldn't help but kiss deeper, coaxing the somnolent mouth into a lazy press of tongue and heat. A hand came up to cradle Corbet's head, so Corbet tangled his fingers in thick, red hair in return.

He smiled despite himself when Ruari finally woke enough to realize his surroundings. He stumbled his way to wakefulness just in time for Corbet to roll atop his strong chest, making Corbet's face the first thing he saw as he opened his eyes.

"Good morning, love," Ruari greeted, his voice weary but as full of adoration as it always was.

"Good morning, love," Corbet parroted back, running his fingers through the messy hair to angle him up for another kiss. "I'm sorry for waking you," he whispered against his lips.

The moment Corbet left his lips to mouth at his neck, Ruari was laughing quietly, his hands resting on Corbet's waist to explore his bare skin. "Can I expect this sort of greeting every time I wake up? I never knew my mornings could be so pleasant," he murmured.

"It'd be more pleasant if you'd stop talking so much," Corbet purred, rubbing himself against Ruari's slowly growing excitement. "I'm trying to take advantage of you," he said, arching his back. "You look like you could use some pampering, so hush."

Ruari's grin was a lazy, pleased thing, and he rested his hands above his head, surrendering to Corbet's advances. His golden gaze was warm where it fell on Corbet's back, tracing down his spine as he folded himself between muscled thighs. He gave a little huff, barely more than a sigh, when Corbet kissed the head of his cock.

The attention made him flush, but Corbet kept his focus on the task at hand. He laved his tongue along the hard length, kissing teasingly along the vein. He let out a small hum as he worked, taking just the tip into his mouth to suck. Ruari's thighs twitched beneath his hands, his muted groan sending a shiver of pleasure down Corbet's spine.

"You're very good at this," Ruari let out, rolling his hips to chase the warm heat of Corbet's mouth.

Corbet raised a brow, pulling off and working the shaft with his hand while he caught his breath. "You sound surprised by that," he said, leaning down to give a small lick to the head before running his thumb over the slit. "Do I not seem the type?"

"You seem the type to be full of surprises," he sighed, squirming breathlessly when Corbet took him in again, adding just the barest hint of teeth to every bob of his head. It made his voice come out higher, broken.

He worked the fae until he was an inch from completion and only then did he pull off to breathe, making Ruari whine like a denied child. "Anyways, didn't I tell you to hush?" he chuckled, a little hoarse. Corbet pressed his lips to the slick head before he crawled up for another kiss.

"You make it so hard to behave," Ruari murmured breathlessly, the color sitting high on his cheeks. "You're a terrible influence. Please don't stop."

"Well, when you say it like that..." Corbet said, using his hand to rub them together. The saliva kept them slick and he made sure to direct his every sound to Ruari's pierced ear. "You really do like to beg."

Ruari shook and rolled his hips into every stroke, matching Corbet move for move. "Only you," he laughed, so breathless it was nearly lost in the space between them. "Only you can make me beg."

A thrill of power trickled through his veins and Corbet sped up the pace until they were both too out of breath to speak. The king gasped in his ear and tore at the sheets above his head, somehow, despite all of the teasing, still managing to keep his hands in check.

That, if nothing else, proved his devotion, and Corbet lasted hardly a minute more, burying his cry in Ruari's pleading kiss.

"Come on," he whispered. "Cum for me, Ruari."

And the fae did, growling as the sheets ripped in his hands. His golden eyes were molten, his wild hair a firestorm against the pillows. Corbet felt he could drown in the beauty. Adoration colored his every move, like fallen leaves along a forest floor.

Corbet still could hardly believe that any of this was for him. To think, it only took being kidnapped and thrown into some mystical wonderland for him to find a place that felt like belonging. Sticky and messy as they were, he plastered himself to Ruari's body, unwilling to

relinquish an ounce of it.

"You really never stop surprising me," Ruari gave, still trying to get his breath back. He wrapped his arms around Corbet and covered his face with kisses. "Oh, how I want you to be mine."

"Aren't I already?" Corbet asked, letting himself be rolled onto his back. The handsome fae hovered over him, his tired eyes perusing his skin hungrily. "I did try to eat the food. It's your own fault if you stopped me."

Ruari rolled his eyes and looked a bit embarrassed with himself. Corbet figured it had to be a bit humiliating, doubting his sincerity like that. He knew he wouldn't have hesitated for a moment if their positions were reversed. If he wanted Ruari, he would have taken him in any way he could get him, honorable or otherwise.

"Would you care to try again?" Ruari asked, marking a trail down Corbet's neck with his lips and teeth and tongue. Corbet found his hand taken gently, the fae placing a chaste kiss to his every finger. "I could have some food brought. We could make it a party, just for the two of us." His eyes were hot, but filled with such excitement. "Just one bite and you'd be mine forever."

Corbet pretended to think about it.

"I don't know," he teased, his tone serious while his eyes danced. "It might be more fun to drag this out. You do love begging, so maybe after enough of that." His head fell to the side and he took a shaky breath as Ruari's

mouth kissed along his pulse point, down his neck, along his shoulder, ending with his lips so soft on the thin skin of his inner wrist. "If I just give in, you won't have learned anything."

"How cruel you are to me."

"Yet you still love me."

Ruari didn't even try to deny it. He just smiled warmly, staring down at him like he was the most beautiful thing he'd ever seen.

Corbet bit his lip and looked up at the king. "You do love me, don't you..." he asked slowly, more confirming his assumptions than doubting them. "Why would you love me? I'm nothing but trouble for you."

Sighing, Ruari kissed his cheek and tipped himself onto his side, situating them so they lay face to face. His warm hand traced over Corbet's bare arm and down his hip. "I've lived a very long time, Corbet," he began, his thumb stroking along his hipbone. "And I've lived a very large portion of that alone."

He stopped him there, pressing his forehead against the solid chest. "I forgot how embarrassing you are when you open your mouth," Corbet mumbled, only showing his face when Ruari tugged gently at a lock of his hair. "Forget I asked, let's go back to kissing," he frowned, his cheeks burning when he looked up.

"I've barely said anything yet," Ruari laughed quietly,

holding him close. "At least let me finish. You did ask."

"Fine," he said, making it sound put upon. "Be embarrassing." A kiss was pressed to his temple and it was hard not to smile.

Ruari ran his fingers through his hair and smiled back. "I've been alone a long while, Corbet, with only responsibility as company. I'm long due for a little trouble to come my way." The exhaustion in his eyes was less pronounced when he looked at him, the intensity of his adoration outshining the dark circles. "I've been trapped below in this earthen prison, and for once I feel as if I can taste the sunlight on my brow, so long as I'm with you."

The words were almost too much, and Ruari kept going, quicker like he was eager to say the words aloud and make them known.

"You're beautiful and clever and unpredictable," he breathed, stroking Corbet's flushed cheek. "And my rival disapproves, so you must be absolutely perfect."

Looking up, Corbet held the hand to his cheek and leaned into it. "Does Avenir disapprove of all of your distractions?" he teased, curious about how deep the distaste ran between the two royals. "Or am I just that terrible for you?"

The fae rolled his eyes as he grinned. "They don't care for much if they can't control it. They've been that way since I first met them," he explained, entertaining himself by tracing shapes along Corbet's bare skin. "You

should have seen it the first time we were forced into a room together. They slapped me across the face and called me a usurper."

Corbet perked up at the information. "Usurper?" he asked, raising a brow. "Now why would they call you that?"

"Probably because I usurped the former ruler," Ruari chuckled, as blasé as if they had been discussing the weather. He caught the look on Corbet's face and grinned, resting his head on his hand. "Does that bother you?" he asked, raising a brow. "Is the heroic image of me in your mind forever tarnished by this startling revelation?"

"Heroic? I wouldn't flatter yourself with such a lofty idea," he smiled, inching closer to curl into his warmth. "Why did you usurp them? I had figured you were born into your role. That's usually how it is above. It's all settled by blood and family."

"I'm more flattered by the idea that you thought I was groomed for my crown," Ruari laughed. "We usurped her because we were unhappy. It's as simple as that."

Corbet raised a brow and pushed at his chest a bit, not appreciating his withholding tease. "You can't just say that and not tell me," he complained, leaning in to kiss him. Pulling away, he smiled up at his lover winsomely. "Tell me why you did it. Tell me a story. I want to know."

Ruari was the worst at denying him anything, and he

190

seemed to know it. Smiling, he leaned in for another kiss before finally giving in.

"We didn't always dwell beneath the earth, you know," he explained, entertaining himself as he spoke by tugging playfully at the sheet clinging to Corbet's hip. "The old Seelie queen took us below after the Milesians came. They came in ships from across the sea, and when they made landfall, they fought us and won."

Corbet smacked the hand before it could completely bare him. This was no time to get distracted. He wanted to hear every detail.

"Milesians? I've never heard of that before," he said. "Were they really so strong that you couldn't stay on the surface?" It was hard to believe that there was anything in this world stronger than the displays of magic he'd witnessed.

Ruari scoffed. "They came in droves and the war was long. They thought of us as pagan gods, creatures to be slaughtered so their new religion could take root. We fought hard, but it's difficult to hold out against blind fervor. By the time they won, we were too tired to prolong the fight. The queen brokered a deal and said we'd share the land."

His expression was bitter, and he laced his fingers with Corbet's. "Their idea of that meant we'd be below it."

"Why haven't you gone back up? Haven't they died out if I've never heard of them?"

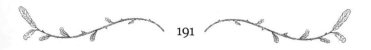

Golden eyes closed as Ruari sighed. "In your tongue, the Milesians are the Celts. Mortals forced us below, and there are too many above now to hope for victory. We realized that quickly enough after we deposed the queen."

He stayed silent, waiting for the rest of the tale to be told. Ruari squeezed his hand gently and went on.

"It took a lot of energy to bring the Courts below. She built the barrier with the help of Avenir, who was still the Unseelie Monarch, even back then. They were both drained once it was done." He found Corbet's eyes and smiled. "Those of us who weren't happy being ripped from the surface took the opportunity while we had it to get rid of the one we viewed as responsible for our displacement."

Corbet cocked his head, engrossed. "Did you lead the charge?" he murmured, seeing the tapestry from the main hall behind his eyes: the red king, the rioting fae... the broken, prone woman, crawling away with her face hidden.

Ruari smiled to himself and nodded. "I did. We threw her from her throne and I took her crown. I had such lofty goals back then. I wanted to reclaim the surface. Bring both kingdoms back to their former glory," he sighed. "I realized quickly enough that time hadn't waited for us. The mortals had spread along with the stories, and we found ourselves trapped below in an earthen kingdom with no chance for victory."

He swallowed and looked at the king. "I'm sorry," Corbet gave, though he wasn't sure what else could be said when he was another mortal in a sea of those preventing them from going above. No wonder some of them looked at him with such disdain.

He got a kiss for his worries.

"Don't apologize, my lost one. This happened so long ago that it's but a memory to most. Only the oldest of fae even remember the old surface kingdoms." Ruari brushed Corbet's dark hair behind his ear, kissing his forehead. "This is our home now, and we've come to accept it."

He smiled and shifted, tangling their legs together beneath the sheets. It certainly did feel like home, even to him, an outsider. "What happened to the old queen? Did you kill her?" Corbet asked, eager for more of the history he was only beginning to learn. "I remember the tapestry. Was she the blonde in the corner?"

"So you noticed that, did you?" Ruari huffed. "I'm not entirely sure what became of her. I didn't kill her, since I had no idea what would become of the barrier should she die. I sent her away from the Court, and I heard nothing more of her after that."

"You have to have some idea," Corbet frowned. "She couldn't have just disappeared."

Pensively, Ruari looked over his shoulder. "If I recall correctly, she was quite close with Avenir. Perhaps

she took up asylum in the Winter Court," he posed, shrugging a shoulder lazily. "Fae are fairly free with their lovers, and it wouldn't surprise me if those two were together. It wouldn't be the wildest of speculations, given how intertwined the Courts and royals can be."

The words hit him hard and Corbet couldn't shake the idea they put in his mind. There was no way, right?

"Did you and Avenir ever..." he led, and Ruari's eyes went wide before he broke into wild laughter. Corbet wrinkled his nose and frowned. "Don't laugh at me. It's a simple question."

Jealousy wasn't something he was used to feeling, and he didn't appreciate being made fun of for wanting his concerns proven baseless.

"Oh, no, never," Ruari assured him, wiping a bit at the tears in his golden eyes. "The two Courts are about balance, and I've never cared enough for them to risk something so important for the sake of some hate-filled tryst."

Corbet raised a brow. "So it was only duty that kept you from pursuing it?" he asked, tugging on a lock of red hair punishingly. "How comforting."

A warm hand wrapped around his own, soft, smiling lips kissing his fingers. "They're a bit too cold for me," Ruari said. "We share a mutual distaste, and that's all we've shared for nigh on a millennia."

That was the second time Ruari had made mention of his age. Corbet swallowed and watched the king kiss his pulsepoint. "How old are you?" he murmured, taking the fae by the chin to bring his attention back to him. "You keep saying millennia, and speaking of things from antiquity. Are you really that old?"

Ruari had the appearance of a strapping young man, looking no older than perhaps thirty. But if he'd learned nothing else during his time here, it was that the fae appeared how they wished to be, not as they truly were.

"Come now, isn't it a bit rude to ask my age?" he teased, letting Corbet turn his face this way and that. "I'm very sensitive, you know."

Corbet scoffed and flicked him in the nose. "So you're a middle aged housewife? I had no idea," he joked, delighting in the over-exaggerated grimace that passed over his lover's face. "Come on," he pleaded. "Tell me how old you are."

Humming deep in his chest, Ruari rolled them so Corbet rested atop him. "Old enough not to remember," he sighed. His fingers settled over Corbet's lips before he could complain. "I'm older than the language you speak. Older than any city you've ever seen. I don't count the years anymore, but I remember them all."

He felt a bit cowed by the admittance. Gold eyes looked tired now, and infinitely old. Be it from the memories the questions arose or the purposeful slipping of his glamor, Ruari suddenly looked the aged fae he was.

Corbet cupped his cheek and kissed the king's brow. "There's still so much about you that I don't know," he breathed. "I can't imagine all you've seen and done."

Ruari leaned in and sealed their lips together into a kiss. "That's fine though," he breathed, tangling his fingers in his hair. "Because we've an eternity to share it all. I want to know you as well. Every moment you've ever lived, I want to know it like I know myself."

He hardly thought it'd take an eternity to talk about his own meager twenty-four years, but Corbet lost himself in the proffered affection. They rolled around in the sheets like children, softening the intense air between them with kisses and caresses that fell like downy snow.

Just as Corbet was about to propose they go again, the want and affection kindling in his veins like the makings of a forest fire, Ruari broke away with a sudden jolt. He rolled heavily onto his shoulder, falling to the bed with a muted grunt.

Unease trickled down him like rain through a forest canopy, collecting in heavy, cold drops somewhere deep in his stomach. Corbet pulled back and sat up, catching a look of pain pass over the fae's eyes. It was sharp enough to cut the mood to pieces.

Tensing, he reached for him. "What's wrong?" he asked, cupping Ruari's cheek. "Are you alright?"

The cold sweat from before had returned with a

vengeance. His lover paled. "Do you feel that?" Ruari murmured, his voice as shaky as his trembling body.

Corbet felt a spike of fear jab him in the spine. "Feel what? What's going on?" he pressed, keeping himself calm though his body longed to do otherwise.

Ruari closed his eyes and spat something in the fae language, the cadence of swearing the same in any tongue. "Something isn't right," he finally said after another bout of heated cursing. "This certainly doesn't bode well."

He reached out and stroked down his lover's shoulder, threading his fingers through his hair in hopes of helping alleviate whatever it was happening to him. "Ruari—"

Both of them startled when a knock sounded on the door, loud and insistent. Corbet looked at the door and then to Ruari, and Ruari buried his head in his hands. "This is the worst way for this day to begin," he managed to say, muffled a bit though his exhausted tone was all too clear.

Was it just a page with another list of things for Ruari to do? Corbet could see how Ruari looked, how absolutely drained he was of energy. Was it just some residual exhaustion from the night before? The questions built in his mind, but Ruari answered nothing, dragging his hands down his face to stare resolutely at Corbet lying below him.

Corbet didn't know what to do besides kiss back when

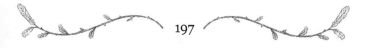

Ruari surged forward. He let the man dominate the move, losing himself in the skillful kiss until Ruari broke away and rose from the bed. Panting a little, he watched him dress himself with a snap of his fingers.

It was insane to think that Ruari, after all he had been through and as lousy as he looked and felt, was still going to answer the door and do his duty.

"Can't you tell them to go away?" he asked, inching towards the edge of the spacious bed. "You aren't feeling well. You're in no state to be up and about."

"Kings don't get the luxury of respite, even when ill," he sighed, holding Corbet's cheek in his hand for a moment.

For one fevered second, Corbet felt the undeniable urge to grab the hand and hold him there. He held tight when Ruari made to pull away, dread heavy and thick in the pit of his stomach. The knock sounded again, louder this time, and it only made the weight increase.

"I think you should ignore it," Corbet found himself saying. "Stay with me. Answer it after you feel better." He brought the hand to his lips, kissing it as if to tempt him back to the soft, easy intimacy they had just shared.

"It'll be alright, my lost one," Ruari promised, easing free of the panicked grip. "I'm not so hard up that I can't do my duty. And if I gave into my want for you too much, I might find myself too addicted to ever leave your embrace."

"Please," he murmured, staring up into gold eyes. "I have a bad feeling about this."

A hand stroked his cheek, the soothing nature of it ruined by the incessant pounding. "I'm sure it's just some servant or advisor needing approval for some document," Ruari said, though with the disquieting look on his face, Corbet could tell he didn't even believe that himself.

But it was too late for Corbet to insist. Ruari pressed a kiss to his hand and let go, moving to the door before Corbet could say more to dissuade him from answering.

The door was opened and Corbet held his breath.

He hadn't known what he was expecting. The way his stomach felt, tied in knots and churning with dread, he half expected a monster to be waiting on the other side of the threshold. But nothing reached out to grab his lover. Voices were heard, not in any language he could understand, and for a moment, Corbet relaxed.

It was probably just the page again, happy that this time she wasn't privy to their intimate acts while she read off her missive.

Or maybe not.

His eyes widened when Ruari's shoulders grew tight, his stance defensive and still shaky from the ghostly pall passing over him. Ruari rattled something off in the fae tongue and Corbet crawled to the foot of the bed, concerned enough to try and see who had come calling.

From this angle, he could barely see past Ruari and into the hall. Even with his limited view though, he made out a troop of what he assumed to be royal guards, at least six of them standing at attention just beyond the doorway.

A few gem-like eyes flickered their attention from Ruari to Corbet, and he leaned back out of sight, remembering his state of undress. He covered himself with the blankets and shifted to the edge of the bed, searching for his clothes from the night before.

What did that many guards need Ruari for? It must be serious if so many came. Corbet took up the pants and slipped them on, doing his best to pay attention to the words being spoken. For as long as he'd been here, the language still eluded him, as incomprehensible as shifting smoke rising in the air.

Was there some sort of attack? Did the Court even have enemies? He hated how little he knew. With the pants on, Corbet looked back over his shoulder to see Ruari gesticulating. He wondered if his presence might calm whatever argument was being fought, or at least give Ruari a cooler head.

The voices grew more heated and he jumped when Ruari began to shout.

The words were unintelligible but he knew panic when he heard it. He made a grab for a discarded shirt and threw it on, turning just in time to see Ruari be forced into the hall by the fae at the door.

"Ruari!" he called, forcing his arms into the sleeves and sprinting to the door as he settled the long léine over himself haphazardly. "Ruari, what the hell is going on?"

There were no answers to be found over the fae chatter rising into a noisy din. Corbet held tight to the doorframe and watched, sure that his lover would shout some command, use his magic, do something to resist the guards holding him. But something was said, some clipped, accusatory barb and Corbet's heart stalled when Ruari recoiled, almost like he had been physically struck.

Ruari fought the hands for all of a minute before going lax after that, letting his wrists be bound by thick, cruel vines.

Corbet was shoved to the side when he surged forward, knocked nearly to the floor by some bulky, massive fae who didn't want him intervening.

"Hey!" he said, shoving back and making another grab for Ruari. There was no way he was letting them take him. "What the hell is happening? Ruari! Why aren't you doing something?"

"Corbet, I-"

A fae snapped at him and Ruari grimaced, turning his attention to that guard instead of Corbet. The idea of him deferring to someone so far below him sent another burst of anger through him, making him fight all the harder to reach the bound king.

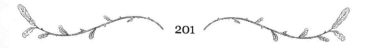

Corbet managed to force his way through the mass of guards to grab his lover by the sleeve, forcing his attention back to him.

"Why aren't you fighting them?" he hissed, wrapping himself around Ruari, hopeful that it would keep him from being taken away. A guard tried to grab him by the shoulder and he turned his head, glaring with so much heat that they backed off as if burned.

Ruari was silent, his eyes glued to the floor. His skin still held its dull pallor, growing more pronounced the longer he stood there. He needed to rest, Corbet thought frantically. Couldn't these fae see that? The king was unwell. He was in no condition to be treated like this. Why couldn't any of them see?

For a moment, he thought Ruari would agree, but the look of resignation won out. Dread churned angrily in his stomach. He knew before he even spoke what the words would be.

"I have to go with them," Ruari said, his voice pained. "You need to let this happen."

"You're a king, you don't have to do anything and neither do I," Corbet insisted, refusing to let go, even as the guards began to bark more orders and shift behind him. He could tell that they were gearing up to remove him by force. "Use your magic, order them to leave—"

"Corbet!" Ruari interjected, his voice taking on that quality it held when he demanded his subjects' attention

and their complete compliance. It made Corbet flinch. It'd never been used on him before.

Ruari had never spoken to him with anything but ardor in his voice.

His expression softened the moment Corbet stopped yanking at him, meeting his golden eyes. "Corbet, listen to me," he said, his voice low but even. "They're going to take me and you're going to let them."

He tightened his hands in his lover's shirt and grit his teeth. His entire body rejected the very idea. "But why?" he repeated, shoulders tensing as the guards began to move. "Ruari, why is this happening?"

Instead of answers, Ruari leaned down and kissed him silent. Corbet went lax, too conditioned to not. His eyes widened and he suddenly held tighter, knowing that something was very, very wrong. There was nothing of the previous comfort in this kiss. It held a desperate charge to it, one more painful than comforting.

It felt like a goodbye.

"What?" Corbet breathed the moment Ruari pulled away. "What was that? What did you do?"

"You're so clever, Corbet. You have to be careful," Ruari pushed, his voice muted. "Never stop fighting. Don't let them keep you."

Before he could demand more answers, his confusion edging him towards outright panic, Ruari dipped in for

another kiss just as the fae guards saw fit to separate them.

Corbet had only an instant of warm lips against his own before they were forced apart. The cold resettled like a jealous, spurned lover, and Corbet lost the grip he had on Ruari's clothing. He fought wildly, desperate for Ruari's heat.

He had to be restrained when they began to drag Ruari away.

The king didn't even fight. With his head down and his shoulders slumped, he let himself be marched away in bondage. The king's blood dripped from his wrists, the vine's thorns stabbing into his skin to keep him from struggling. It was superfluous; there was no fight to be found in the fae.

"Let me go!" he snarled, but the guard was as unmoving as stone, quelling every kick and bid for freedom with a harsh shake. "Ruari!"

He watched, powerless, as Ruari's back disappeared around a corner.

If this is what forever would feel like, Corbet regretted it already.

# CHAPTER 10

The worst thing, Corbet found, was that no one cared to tell him what was happening.

He threw off the arms holding him back and instead made a grab for the nearest remaining guard.

"Where are you taking him?" he asked, holding on when they tried to shake him off. The fae was short and squat, looking more like a toad than the humanoid type he was used to seeing. Green and grey muddied their skin and it flushed an angry teal the longer he held on.

The guard grimaced and yanked back their arm, trying to pull free. "No concern of yours, mortal," they croaked, spitting the word like a slur. Corbet grit his

teeth, the anger rising into a dull roar.

"What do you mean, no concern of mine?" he nearly hissed, digging his nails into the fae's arm. "That's my lover. Tell me where you're taking him or so help me—"

"The king's pet mortal?" the guard interrupted, their huge, amphibious eyes wide. They grinned. "And it thinks it's the king's lover. How cute. The Monarch gave word of you."

Something in their voice sounded aggressive. Appraising. Corbet backed away.

"Did they? How polite of them to think of me," he spat, only now realizing how the remaining fae watched him. With Ruari gone, their attention fell to him in spades.

Chatter broke out amongst the gathered guards, their eyes flickering to him with something that sent his instincts on edge. None of them were kind enough to keep it in a language he could actually understand.

Despite their tones, they made no move to reach for him. His back met the wall and he let it guide him as he built up distance between himself and the guards. If they laughed at him and his caution, he ignored it for the thoughts pounding in his skull.

Why on earth had the creature brought up the Unseelie ruler? Ruari was the king here, not them. His mind raced to process and disseminate the information, and he realized then that the style of armor worn by the

remaining guards looked nothing like the dress Gali or Corin wore.

Avenir had only met him briefly, and from how the encounter went he couldn't imagine them retaining a high opinion of him. If the Unseelie Monarch were behind this, he couldn't trust that he too wouldn't be arrested.

If that happened, there would be no one left to help Ruari.

The toad-like guard grinned at him and began to follow, ignoring the chatter of their fellow guards. "Running away already?" they asked, and Corbet was brought back to his first encounter with malicious fae. "Stay awhile. I'm certain we'll learn what to do with you soon enough."

Corbet returned the look steadily, letting no ounce of his panic show through. He had no idea if they were under orders to apprehend him, but even if they weren't, he wasn't going to stand around until one of them took the initiative to do it anyway.

"Go fuck yourself," he replied, putting on his most dangerous smile when the toad balked. It flushed a muddled green. The gathered guards laughed, no doubt joking about how mouthy the mortal was.

He didn't care what they thought. The toad stopped following him and that was all that mattered.

He kept up eye contact until he turned a corner, and then he refused to look back again.

It was easy to disappear in the hustle and bustle of the halls. The entire palace teemed with unfamiliar fae, their armor and weapons rattling as they moved through the halls in groups of four or five. His head throbbed with the loudness of his thoughts and rang with the marching stamp of feet. For every look he garnered, he gave back a glare.

None called out to him, but plenty whispered as he passed. He couldn't bring himself to care, so long as none tried to grab him. He didn't have a plan for that, and he doubted he could fight a guard off if it came down to it.

He kicked himself for not carrying his knife on him like he had before. It was obvious now that he'd grown complacent and trusting the longer he stayed, and now, with Ruari gone and the palace up in arms, the weight of that mistake settled around his shoulders like a suffocating yoke.

He wouldn't make that mistake again.

The sleeves of his shirt covered his hands, hiding his clenched fists. It was then, belatedly, that he realized he had taken Ruari's léine instead of his own. Corbet stuttered in his dogged stride, a wave of emotion crashing through him.

Now that he was paying attention to it, he could feel the hints of damp still clinging to the collar, to the

thicker hems. Wrapping his arms around himself, he tried to ignore the sickening panic burrowing a hole in his heart. Anger rose up to lick at the hurt.

He brought his wrist to his nose and let the woodsy scent calm him, pretending the saffron color was half as comforting as Ruari's golden eyes.

Being angry right now wouldn't help him. Being paralyzed with fear wouldn't either.

None of that would help Ruari.

Corbet's mind raced. What could he even do? His pace increased as his thoughts thundered in his skull.

Was it possible to trail after the guards that had taken him? There was no telling where they were headed or what he could possibly do if he caught up to them. Ruari's calm expression had seemed meant for Corbet more than for himself. Beneath it, he had read the tension in his shoulders, the unease in his eyes. Ruari was worried, be it from the capture or what he had felt in the moments before the knocking had begun.

He had to wonder if chasing after the king would only make things worse.

Worrying his bottom lip with his teeth, Corbet walked faster, the faces of the guards blurry in his peripheral vision. With his uncertainty mounting, he almost missed the shout entirely.

"Mortal! Halt!" a high-pitched voice commanded,

echoing off the stone walls.

Freezing in place, he turned his head, looking through the many present faeries for the one who had yelled. A few moments passed before he found them, and by then, the rest of the troops had fixed their eyes on him.

The one who shouted was an armored guard, her stare hard and intent. The tunic she wore was emblazoned with a symbol far from the type commonly seen on Ruari's subjects. Confused, he glanced at the others only to find the same symbol on them. The emblem was a diamond shaped sign, cut to look like falling leaves.

He knew the Seelie one to be circular, engraved with blooming flowers.

Realization came quickly after that: these weren't Ruari's subjects.

The guard's voice sounded again, her shout anything but benign. Soon enough, all attention locked on Corbet. An entire hall's worth of foot soldiers turned towards him, their eyes and intent aggressive.

Instinct rung like a bell between his ears and he broke into a sprint, turning a corner before the guard could shout for someone to grab him. He heard the cacophony of them giving chase beneath the sound of his ragged breath and slapping footfalls.

He darted down another hall and struggled to get his bearings. It would be suicide to run blindly, especially if

the palace were teeming with these enemy troops.

Where was he at? The halls all looked the same, especially with this veneer of growing panic overlaying his vision. Corbet had to get to his room. If nothing else, he had his knife in there, and even if it was useless against fae, it was still a weapon all the same.

He picked a direction and ran, tearing past clusters of fae who realized belatedly that they should be catching him, not watching him. There weren't many landmarks to tell him his location, but he kept on until he saw something familiar.

Roses and thorns decorated an entryway and it was enough to give him back his bearings.

Whatever relief that bought him promptly disappeared when he risked a look back and saw that he had somehow amassed what looked to be an entire army, all hell-bent on apprehending him. Corbet let out a noise, some desperate, disbelieving groan, and he put on another burst of speed, his vision blurring at the edges as he tore through the stone halls.

It all came to a stop though when Corbet was grabbed on either side, snatched from his frantic run like a mouse plucked up by a swooping hawk. Corbet hardly had the time to yelp before he found himself yanked down a side hall.

Corbet went instinctively for the knife he knew was absent from his hip, only belatedly recognizing the

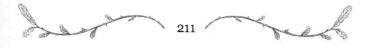

familiar forms of Corin and Gali. Eyes wide, they shoved him hurriedly into the hard wall, hissing to each other in their strange language while Corbet stared, confused.

"What's going on?" he tried asking, but a tawny hand clapped over his mouth.

Gali looked too frazzled to answer him, and he didn't try to fight off her hand. She held her finger to her lips and watched as Corin peeked around the corner.

"I think we're clear," he whispered, barely more than a breath, and Gali uncovered his mouth.

He was so relieved to see them both that he rested his hands on their shoulders, hardly resisting the urge to bury his face in Gali's shoulder. "What is going on?" he asked again, this time whispering. "What happened to Ruari? They took him and I-"

It was Corin this time who covered his mouth. "Corbet, we need you to stay calm," he said, and Gali took up position by the corner, watching for approaching fae.

If they were going to do that every time he opened his mouth, he might reevaluate his relief at seeing them. Corbet took Corin's thin wrist and moved it from his lips. "Then tell me what the hell is going on," he hissed, growing angry. "No one will talk. You're the first I've seen who even looks at me with anything but disdain."

"That's because we're the only ones who haven't been replaced yet and have even a modicum of fondness for

you," Corin hissed right back, and for the first time since he had woken, Corbet realized that maybe he wasn't the only one stressed out by the current situation.

"Replaced?" he asked, looking between the two fae. "Replaced by whom?" though he had a feeling he already knew.

Gali sighed and looked back at them, her autumn leaf hair rustling bleakly. She looked tired. Run down. "The Unseelie. Tis a coup, or whatever the justified version of that is. Those of the Seelie are being stripped of their ranks and sent elsewhere to prevent a possible uprising." She looked back at the hall and went stiff, pressing herself flat against the wall.

Corbet went willingly when Corin shoved him to do the same. A guard patrol marched past, none even sparing them a glance, be it by luck or some magic cast by his companions. He didn't breathe until Gali moved, again peering around to check that they were indeed alone.

He looked at Corin before speaking, just to be sure it was safe. "What do you mean?" he asked, trying his best to understand. "What do you mean by justified?" How could anything like this be justified when Ruari was the king?

"The Solstice was broken, and the barrier too," he sighed, rubbing tiredly at his eyes. "The king weakened us all. The Monarch felt it necessary to take control, since the king has erred so badly."

Corbet struggled to keep up. "The Solstice?" The dread heavy in his stomach turned to lead. His eyes met the fae's, comprehension dawning. "When Ruari went above for me?"

Their mirrored expressions of pity and exhaustion were answer enough.

"But how can they do this?!" he pressed. "Ruari did what he did for me, and to save another. The Monarch has no right to do this!"

"They have every right, tis the way of the two Courts. If one threatens the whole, the other steps in to right the balance," Corin explained. He bit his lip. "Tis not safe for you. You need to get to your room and stop this wandering. With the Monarch's guards patrolling, there is no telling what might become of you."

Corbet grit his teeth and dug his fingers into the stone at his side, furious. "Then what am I supposed to do? Just sit in my room and wait? I need Ruari back. I can't leave him."

When he saw them look like they were about to say yes, he took Corin by the shoulder. "Where did they take him?" he interjected, unwilling to even hear them suggest that he should sit on his hands. "What are they going to do with Ruari?"

It was Gali who intervened, her gentle touch calming in its own right. She pulled him off her friend and looked as apologetic as she could. "We don't know, Corbet. He

has probably been taken to the catacombs, imprisoned."

She didn't need to go into detail. From her voice alone, Corbet could tell that that was anything but good.

He sagged to the floor and the dread rose in his throat, tasting like bile. Burying his face in his arms, he took a deep, shaky breath. He was an adult, but all he wanted to do was cry like a child until the nightmare ended.

This couldn't be happening. The softness of the morning had been ripped away, leaving just this in its place. Corbet rubbed furiously at his eyes with his knuckles, trying to breathe. Ruari needed him right now, he told himself. There was no time to be acting like a pathetic child.

"What do I have to do to see him?" he asked, a bit muffled.

There was silence. He could tell the two fae were looking at each other, communicating without words.

"Appeal to the Monarch," Gali said gently, stroking her twig like fingers through his messy hair. They caught on knots and he swallowed to keep the pain down. He hadn't noticed that Ruari had tied more. He wondered if he did it without thinking again, or if he had wanted to help him untangle them, like Corbet had asked.

Gali went on. "There is not much else to be done. They are in control now," she told him, sounding so painfully accepting of the situation.

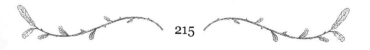

Corbet wasn't going to accept anything until he had Ruari back. He looked up. "What about you two?" he demanded. "What are you going to do? Help me get him back."

This time, he caught them sharing a look. Corin grimaced and then tensed, going to the corner to check for the approaching patrol. It left Gali to answer, and she looked anything but eager to do so.

"We can't do anything, Corbet," she leveled, tugging him up and onto his feet. Corbet let her yank at him for a minute before he let himself be dragged up, his knee jerk urge to resist exacerbated from her straight refusal. "And you need to go. There is no one to protect you here." Gali gestured between herself and Corin. "We too are to be replaced with the Unseelie and sent away from the Court. If you wish to return above, you cannot linger. We can get you to the entrance, but we have to do so now."

He didn't need time to think about it.

"I can't leave him."

Gali looked pained, but not surprised, and Corin gestured for them to hide as another set of guards stamped past, their intricate leather armor whispering as they moved. "Do you understand what you're saying and what it means?" she whispered, her lips close to his ear. "There's no guarantee you'll see him again. This is no time to be stubborn. If you have anything at all on the surface, you are throwing it away for something that may fail."

Corbet reached for her slender, delicate hand. "I have to try," he whispered back. "I don't have anything left for me up there. I can't abandon him. Not like this."

The guards' footfalls faded into the distance and Corin gave Gali a look, one that said they couldn't stay here much longer. Corin's ruddy forehead was beaded with sweat and his breathing was labored, as if from exertion.

Something like cool water trickled down Corbet's neck, and he realized belatedly that it was the sensation of a spell weakening. They were casting something to avert the eyes of the guards, but it wasn't going to last much longer. Ruari had weakened them all, Gali had said. If it were true, then they were wasting what little power they had left to warn him.

And to think, he mused, that even here he had friends that cared. It was still a novel feeling.

Novel, but gratifying.

He swallowed, resolute. "Go," Corbet told them, squeezing Gali's hand before letting it go. "Thank you. Both of you. For all you've done for me."

Corin rested his hand on his shoulder, his childlike face solemn. Gali caught up his hand one last time and pressed a small object into his palm. "Hang this from your door," she said. "It will turn their sight from it, for at least a little while." She waited until Corbet pocketed it before she turned away, her hair obscuring her eyes like leaves on a branch.

He watched them disappear and with them, his resolve grew stronger. There really was no turning back now, Corbet thought. Not after all they had risked for him and what he still had yet to risk himself.

It felt like he held his breath the entire way back to his room. Every turn he made, he felt his heart stutter, half expecting the guards littering the palace to leap out of the ornate wood and stone, to grab him and take him to God knows where. Corbet bit his lip and hid when he had to, a hand shoved deep in his pocket to hold the trinket close.

He wasn't going to ruin his chances to save Ruari for something as stupid as failing to get back to his room.

When he finally made it, at least an hour had passed him by in stifled breaths and close calls.

With Ruari gone, the absence of his guards at his door was far too conspicuous. It was obvious that the new authority in charge didn't know the location of his room. Corbet locked the door as soon as he entered, double checking it before he took out the small charm. He hadn't had a chance to look at it closely for fear of interruptions, and he most certainly didn't want them now.

It was round and spanned his palm, its thickness less than that of a coin. He thumbed the raised etching on the front, tracing the lines of the carved tree. Even with his lackluster senses, he could feel the thrum of magic resonating within the wood. He looped the attached leather thong around the handle of the door, tying it twice to be sure it hung firmly.

There was no discernable change in the door and Corbet bit his lip, wondering if it only worked from the outside. It would be a risk to open the door again, the wood too thick to hear through. If he had the bad luck of opening the door as a patrol marched by, no amount of magical amulets would be enough to help him.

He didn't think it would be worth the risk, especially if it potentially did work from within as well.

After a bit of internal debate, he left it alone and settled on pushing the heavy wardrobe in front of the door, just to be safe. When it came to those who could command magic to varying degrees, it was only prudent to take his security into his own hands. Another layer between him and the outside wouldn't hurt anything.

The animals stared at him as he huffed and pushed, and he only felt a little silly showing off his paranoia in front of them.

The moment the door was blocked, he leaned against the wardrobe and panted. "At least I can trust you guys," he breathed, looking to them as the trio of birds fluttered around his head, landing on his shoulders. "You'd tell me if you heard anyone coming, wouldn't you?"

The birds chirped and he took it as a yes, letting them peck and tug his messy locks. He winced as they pulled at a knot. Ruari had definitely been tying more of them, and with the abrupt end of their idyllic morning, there

had been no time to untangle them together.

His face fell at the thought.

He needed to get Ruari back, for that if nothing else.

"They took him away from me," he let out when the birds noticed his mood shift, their small eyes confused and concerned. Crossing the room, he sat on the bed, his head heavy in his hands. "They won't let me see him and it's my fault he's even there, wherever there is." Furry snouts nuzzled him close but even the warmth they brought wasn't enough to help.

A small weight fell into his lap and he dragged his hands down his face to take in Tailan. Tiny, bead-black eyes stared up at him sheepishly, and Corbet's heart broke a little.

He picked up the small hedgehog and kissed his head. "It's not your fault, Tai. I'd do it again if it meant making sure you were safe," he sighed, laying back to let the animals cuddle him. The hare flopped onto his stomach, his long ears twitching. "I just didn't expect for it to have such drastic repercussions."

Corbet grimaced as he recalled that night.

Ruari had told him he couldn't do it. He had said, quite plainly, that crossing the barrier wasn't as easy as it seemed on a night like the Solstice. He had been told all of that but he hadn't listened, and now he'd lost everything they had built together just as he'd finally

gotten it.

Not even the tiny kisses from the animals were enough to help.

The question of what would help eluded him. He had no idea where the Monarch was and any allies he had, minus the animals, were no doubt either detained or gone. It simply wasn't safe for him to wander the halls now to check.

Looking down at the assortment of creatures on the bed, he supposed he could use them as scouts if it came down to it. But, even with their support, even if they managed to find someone sympathetic to him, to meet with them was still so dangerous. Opening the door at all left him defenseless to any who happened to pass by at the moment.

That wasn't even factoring the potential danger of betrayal or the typical fae trickery. The risk to his freedom was far too great to try moving around right now. He had trusted all he could, and the only ones he could rely on at this point were the ones here, gathered in his bed. He tensed his jaw and closed his eyes to think.

Any move he made would have to be done from within this room.

After a moment of thought and some mindless play with the birds hopping along his chest, he came up with an idea.

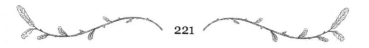

"Can you get a message to the Unseelie Monarch?" he asked the birds, stroking the butter yellow canary gently along her breast. Her little beak snipped at the gem of his ring. The color reminded him so much of Ruari, so he swallowed down the pain and stopped looking.

"If I appeal to them directly, they might not be able to ignore me," he explained, looking to the birds with soft eyes.

The more he thought about it, verbalizing it, the more sense it made as a course of action. Wasn't that how kingdoms did their business? People appealing to the monarchs through letters and missives until they were granted an audience? He didn't pretend to know how royalty conducted these sorts of things, but it made sense to him, and given the way his hands were tied, it allowed him to argue his case in a way that wouldn't get himself killed for being rude. And, with his own messenger provided, there was little risk to giving away his location.

The songbirds tweeted and chirped, hopping around on the bedspread. Their tiny black eyes shifted and he waited as they conferred amongst themselves. The hare rubbed his ears against Corbet's lax hand and for want of something to do, he pet the creature until he was asleep in his lap.

When the conference of birds had made their decision, they let him know by fluttering to his shoulders and tugging at his earrings.

A smile, the first one since that morning, broke across his face.

"Thank you," he breathed, rewarding them with some attention. "Excuse me, Phren," he addressed to the rabbit, nudging the bleary-eyed animal onto a pile of blankets, "but I have a letter to write."

He didn't have much paper, and Corbet steeled himself as he ripped out a blank page from a book. It was simply a spare page, just a folio between the cover and content, but even that much felt like defacement. It had been a gift from Ruari, a book he could actually read, and, for all he knew, it came from the fae's own personal library. Corbet whispered an apology to the tome and grabbed for a quill nib, his lip worried between his teeth.

If this worked, he'd make it up to him by putting him back on his throne where he belonged.

Tailan crawled over to watch him write, and Corbet looked down at the hedgehog indecisively. "What do I even say?" he asked the small face. "How do I even address them?"

It wasn't like he came from a background that dealt with nobility. Pejoratives and vicious anger threatened to cloud his speech. It was the Monarch who ordered Ruari arrested. It was their fault he was hiding like this, holed up in his room and hiding behind some amulet while troops stormed the halls in search of him.

Unsurprisingly, his small friend was no help. The

hedgehog simply shrugged his spines and gave an apologetic snuffle. The soft kiss to his hand was sweet though. It reminded him he had support here, as small as they all might be.

Corbet turned back to the blank page and put the nib to the parchment. This was no time to be at a loss for words. He chewed the inside of his cheek, writing as neatly as he could. Succinct and terse, it came out far more polite than he had any right to expect, given his current mood.

He fell back against the bedding the moment the letter was done and he couldn't bring himself to read back over it lest he rip it to pieces, unsatisfied with any attempt made at articulating his anger in a way that would prove conducive to the current situation.

"I think that's as good as it's going to get," he sighed, looking to the birds. Corbet snatched up the page and folded it carefully, tying it to the largest bird's leg with a bit of string taken from the drawstring of his knapsack. He cradled the blackbird in his hands, staring at her solemnly.

It was she who had brought Ruari to him before, when he had been cornered by Blisk and Avery. Hopefully she'd do the same this time, bringing him back to Corbet with the message near her claws.

"Please," he begged softly, "do all you can to get this to them."

The bird, Shetna, blinked and cawed gently, fluttering into the air the moment he released her. She made a circle around the room to test the new weight on her leg, and then disappeared through whatever opening they used as a door. No matter how many times he tried to watch their comings and goings, Corbet never could tell where the animals entered.

With nothing left to do, Corbet crumpled into the bed, his stress coalescing into pointed exhaustion. He threw a glance at the barricaded door. If he closed his eyes, he could almost hear the tramping of feet in the hall beyond, the endless array of guards and soldiers and strange, foreign fae filling the palace of the former king.

He wondered how many of the Seelie still remained. He wondered what had become of Gali and Corin. Did they make it to wherever they were going? Given the state of their waning magic, he hoped so.

How much of their energy did they waste on helping him?

He grit his teeth and buried his face in the pillows.

His missive flew on black wings. Corbet prayed they carried him through this.

# CHAPTER 11

When he didn't get a response that day, Corbet swallowed his panic and wrote another letter.

When a second day passed similarly, he set another.

On the third day, Corbet ran out of water.

All that Ruari had given him had been kept pristine in his room, high up on the desk and away from the perpetually hungry animals. Ruari had taken to apparating the meals daily, even when Corbet chose to spend his time in the king's bedroom. The meals from the past few days had accumulated, untouched by the servants or magic that kept his room cleaned. Corbet stared at the small pile, knowing in his gut that with

Ruari imprisoned, no more would appear while he slept.

Thankfully, there was no more begging from the animals that had taken up residence in his room. Something in their eyes told him that they knew the severity of the situation made it impossible for him to spare a single bite. He didn't know where they went for their meals now, but they didn't ask for handouts so he assumed they were faring well enough even without his food in their diets.

Corbet bit into an apple and tried to pretend it eased his thirst when it didn't.

He kept himself calm and wrote another letter.

They all said the same thing: Free Ruari. This was unjust and cruel, beyond the purview of the Monarch's authority; Corbet tried everything he could think to evoke any kind of emotional response that might allow him some sort of boon.

When he ran out of logical reasons, he fell to purely need. He was a human mortal stranded in the kingdom of the fae. If not for Ruari's sake, at least allow him to soothe his own anxieties. He was lonely, he said. He didn't understand. Let him see the king, please, Corbet wrote. What could a mortal do in a situation like this?

It took nearly a week for his endless messages to convince the Unseelie Monarch to grant him access to the prison.

A pounding knock roused him from his troubled sleep, nearly sending him into a heap on the floor from his fright. Corbet threw off the blankets and eased away from the animals around him, sprinting to the door with his heart in his throat.

"Who is it?" he called through the wood, his hand wrapping around the handle of his knife.

"A messenger from the Monarch," came the reply. "I have been commanded to take you to the former King. Your...friend brought me here."

And if that didn't sound like a trick, he didn't know what did.

"My friend?" he asked, leaning against the wooden door. He could hear the fae sigh exasperatedly.

"This bird? This incessant bird who won't stop shrieking at me?"

Corbet chuckled, rubbing at his eyes. "That certainly sounds like a friend of mine," he said quietly, before dragging his hand down his face to cover his mouth. Shetna wouldn't have led the messenger back to him if it were anything else but good news for him. But he was still too distrusting to simply accept good news at face value.

"How do I know you won't apprehend me the moment I open the door?" he called out, his hand tightening around the knife.

There was another exasperated sigh. "We have been given orders to leave you be," she said, the sharpness of her voice not dulled a bit through the door. "So long as you are with me or within your room, you will be left alone. The Monarch does not suffer rudeness on the part of guests."

He could tell she was upset by the verdict, and her voice carried the cadence of repetition. "How can I trust what you say?" Corbet demanded. She didn't sound like she was lying, but when it came to fae, he trusted nothing to be as it seemed.

"Because while it is in our nature to lie, we still uphold our duty," she replied with a bit of a hiss. She was getting fed up. "Now do you wish to see your king, or should I simply inform the Monarch that your continual demands were made in jest?"

Corbet's tired eyes went wide and he was moving before he really processed the threat. "Don't you even dare," he snarled, shoved with all his might at the heavy piece blocking the door. His throat burned when he pushed back the heavy wardrobe, but the shouted declaration, muted as it was through the thick door, was enough to give him the strength to move it back into place.

He tossed the wooden charm back onto the bed, taking the fae outside as indication enough that its power had long worn off. Even if this were a trick to flush him out, it wouldn't matter any longer. Corbet had enough

humility to admit to himself that he was nearing the end of his rope.

Whether the wait meant that it simply took that long to reach Avenir, or that they ignored him until he proved too tenacious to deter, he didn't know or care. No matter the case, Corbet was grateful, and he wasted no more time in demanding to be taken to Ruari.

"You're really going to take me to him?" he asked, noting how desperate he sounded and hating it.

The messenger balked a little, taking in his bedclothes and gaunt state. Shetna flew past her to return to the others still on the bed. "Yes," she replied, eyeing him like one would do to an animal that might be potentially rabid. "Are you fit to leave now?"

Corbet glared at her judgemental look and she jumped to attention the second she noticed. Even without Ruari, Corbet still seemed to hold the authority of his pseudo-position well enough. He wouldn't let them bully him. He hadn't before and he sure as hell wasn't going to start letting them now.

"Give me a moment, I'm not dressed." She made a huff as if to say that at least that much was obvious, but he ignored her. "Stay here."

Under the guise of changing, she missed him taking up Tai from the piles of blankets and hiding him inside his sleeve. The sleepy hedgehog didn't so much as fuss and Corbet felt a wave of affection flow through him. So

much trust. He appreciated every drop. He laced up his boots and grabbed a small leather pouch as well, tucking it around his neck to hide beneath the tunic.

With that done, he turned back to the door, looking up at the messenger who was quite obviously pretending that she hadn't been watching intently. "I'm ready now," he called, pulling her attention away from the no doubt fascinating wall molding. "If you'd be so kind?"

She frowned, turned on her heel, and made off without another look back. He wrinkled his nose and sneaked a look at Tailan, raising his brow. Her attitude was as sour as bad wine, and he wondered if it really had been that difficult to locate his room.

Corbet followed the tall fae through the halls, his own quick pace fueling hers to go faster. He did his best to memorize the path there, though she seemed intent on making the trip as convoluted as possible. He wasn't completely disenchanted with the idea of staging a prison break just yet, and any information was better than none, no matter how difficult the messenger was making this.

Given the state of his remaining food, any plan would have to be carried out within a day or two. He couldn't last much longer than that.

"Has there been any more news on Ruari's sentence?" he probed, leveling the messenger with a soft look, doing his best to play up his lost, lonely mortal angle.

She was unfamiliar to him, her coloring light and

delicate compared to the fae he was used to seeing. He wondered if that meant she came from the Unseelie Court like all the rest. He hadn't seen any fae along the way that looked Seelie, though that wasn't saying much since they seemed to command all manner of appearances.

She appeared uncomfortable talking to him, which told him at the very least that she was unaccustomed to conversing with mortals. Shuffling her bow, she forced herself to make eye contact. It looked like it took considerable effort, and the distaste she obviously held rankled.

"The king is to be kept in his cell until our Monarch has come to a ruling." She had the decency to at least try to look apologetic, though it still fell a bit flat. Her nose wrinkled when she saw him twisting at the ring on his hand, her eyes judgmental and cool. "It is not my place to say what ruling it might be."

His spirits were already too low to drop any further at the news. He held Tailan closer, masking the motion in the crossing of his arms. "Is the barrier really so damaged that it warrants this sort of reaction?" he muttered, his shoulders slumping. "I can't see any difference. Nothing seems like it's been affected."

The fae stopped in her tracks and glared at him, forcing Corbet to a stop as well.

"It figures that you wouldn't notice," she nearly hissed, her frustration manifesting in a discordant shift in her

voice. It echoed in the stone hall and Corbet flinched at the harsh, dichotomous sound. "You mortals are all so blissfully unaware of anything you can't see."

Her arm was forced into Corbet's line of sight, her sleeve angrily shoved back. Glaring, she went on with fire in her eyes and acid dripping from her clashing, two-toned voice.

"I can't even keep up my glamor," and even as she spoke, Corbet watched her skin change. Where before sat smooth, unblemished cream, now there rose scales. The textured, reptilian pattern fluttered along her forearm, flickering in and out of existence and dancing between grass green and peach pale.

Even in her eyes he could see the fight being fought between the two extremes. "Do you know how bad things have gotten to make us unable to even do this much?" she implored, her voice pained as her previously blue eyes morphed into that of a goat's.

Corbet didn't know what to say. He hadn't noticed. He hadn't seen enough fae to know what was intentional and what was a product of whatever it was that Ruari had supposedly done.

If the messenger recognized his shock, it didn't stop her from laying into him more.

"You may be the king's pet, but don't act like you know the extent of what's been done," she said, shoving past him to continue on their way. "Staying in on the Solstice

is a law for a reason. There is no telling how long this could take to mend, or what could potentially shatter while the Monarch fixes what the king so carelessly demolished with his selfishness."

"There's been no precedent?" Corbet asked, following behind to show he wasn't cowed by her temper. He grit his teeth through the barbs, unwilling to argue with her about this when he was dependent on her direction to guide him to Ruari.

"Not in the time I have been alive. I fear most for the forest. When magic breaks and dies, it seeps." She looked over her shoulder at him, her expression unreadable. "I wouldn't be surprised if you start to feel the effects soon."

He let out a huff.

"Well, that's ominous," Corbet said flatly.

She didn't bother sparing him another look.

Tailan scratched at his arm in support and Corbet didn't let her words phase him, not when he had Ruari to worry about. If things really were as bad as she said, then it made more sense to him to have Ruari helping to mitigate the fallout as well. Putting him behind bars did nothing but illustrate Avenir's distaste.

The temperature dropped dramatically when they descended a set of stairs, and he didn't need the cold stone or dark shadows to tell him they had arrived at the cells. He'd visited enough on his own adventures aboveground to recognize the stench of misery and damp that came endemic to imprisonment. He clung tighter to the hedgehog in his arms and kept close to the messenger.

Above, Corbet could attest to any who'd listen that he was no saint. Towns rarely loved travelers, and Corbet didn't do much to endear himself to strangers when his money ran out and hunger set in. The damp and dankness of a prison smelled the same even miles below the Earth and Corbet shuddered, recalling the sick fear he had felt seeing the iron bars close in front of him. Escape never took him long, but that didn't do much to erase the stink from his clothes and hair.

It made him sick to think of Ruari locked up in a place like this. He had to imagine escape to be significantly harder when magic was thrown into the equation.

They came to a barred door and the fae pounded on the heavy wood until it creaked open, armored guards standing at attention just beyond the threshold. Corbet bit his lip. Perhaps it wouldn't be so simple, breaking Ruari out.

"The Monarch has granted him permission to speak to the king," his guide explained.

He could tell just from their coloring and the design of their garb that they too were subjects of the Unseelie Court. The two guards shared a look and opened the door wider, gesturing Corbet in. The messenger turned on her heel and left for the stairs, probably happy to be rid of

him.

"Well, come on then," the wider of them said, his tone almost friendly in a way that Corbet wasn't expecting. "You must be the king's mortal."

Corbet hid his grimace in a smile and nodded. "I suppose I am," he said, peering up at the taller one who walked on his other side. They were massive, a few heads taller than him at least, and lumbered like giants. "Where is he?"

He couldn't see any sign of his lover, though he peered into every cell they passed. They were all dark, and only a handful were filled. Those inside were clad in shadows and despair, their appearances ragged and unkempt. Corbet wondered what they had done to deserve this. He wondered if they were Unseelie or Seelie.

The quiet guard didn't bother answering him. Instead, they walked faster and unlocked a thick barred door at the end of the cellblock, their long strides leaving Corbet struggling to keep up. Corbet held his breath as he passed through, the stench of musty suffering thick enough to choke.

As soon as he entered, he saw Ruari.

It took everything in him not to run to the cell door.

Corbet breathed in a shaky breath and instead, looked to the guards. "Can I have some time alone with him?" he asked, wanting nothing more than to grab the bars, rip

236

them down, and hold his lover to him until reality faded away.

The two shared a look. The chatty one let out a sigh, shaking his head. "It's not permitted for security reasons," he explained.

Corbet rolled his eyes. "What would I even be able to do?" he asked, gesturing to himself. "I'm a mortal. I hardly think I command the power to open locked doors with nothing but my mind." He put on his most hurt expression, crossing his arms to make himself appear as small and defenseless as he could.

"Please," he pleaded. "Just a few minutes."

The wider of the two huffed out what he took to be a laugh. He nudged his companion and gestured towards the door. "Felk, let's give the little human some time. It just misses its owner," he chuckled.

He bristled at the patronizing tone, but since it got him what he wanted, Corbet swallowed it down and tried to look sad but hopeful.

Felk stared at him and, just before Corbet was convinced he was going to have to force himself to shed some tears, the fae sighed. "Fine," they said, giving Corbet one last piercing look. "I guess it'd be cruel not to."

"Thank you," Corbet breathed, making his eyes shine. "You both are so kind."

The first fae smiled brightly at him the way one would

smile at a particularly adorable animal and took Felk by the arm, guiding them through the door and back to the entrance.

The moment he heard their footsteps fade, Corbet dropped the act and grimaced. These fae really did hold such a low opinion of mortals. He didn't remember it being like this around Ruari's Court, but then again, Ruari had done much to keep his Court respectful towards him.

Evidently Avenir didn't hold the same consideration.

"Can you keep watch?" Corbet whispered to the hedgehog in his arms, and he felt himself smile despite the surroundings when Tailan gave a little chirp. "Thank you, Tai," he said, kissing the small head before gently putting the creature on the rough stone.

He watched Tailan waddle over to the door, his bristles at the ready should anyone try to disturb them unannounced. Turning back to Ruari, Corbet's face fell into a pained frown.

There was nothing of him that reminded him of the cocky, handsome stranger who had come upon him in the woods so long ago. Ruari sagged against the filthy cell wall, his arms chained above his head in heavy manacles. His clothing was torn, his chest only covered by a thin shirt that might have once been white.

There was no sign of water or food with the enclosure, but blood speckled the wall and Ruari's exposed skin. He

could tell from simply looking that Ruari's status as king allowed him little in the way of better treatment.

Corbet grimaced and leaned against the bars separating them. "Ruari?" he called out quietly. "Ruari, please wake up."

The fae stirred and opened his eyes, the gold the brightest thing in the dingy surroundings. "Good morning, love," he answered slowly, and Corbet bit his lip, ecstatic to find him coherent.

"Are you okay?" he asked, testing the door for any give. Ruari was too far back in the cell to reach, and seeing him move and hearing him speak, Corbet wouldn't settle for anything less than physical contact.

Ruari seemed to ponder the question, looking down at the state he was in. "Well," he winced, sitting up a little straighter, "I certainly think I prefer my own bed. You would think they'd treat their king better, but I suppose given the circumstances, I can understand their anger with me."

He pulled out his lock picks and set to opening it, thankful that despite their propensity towards magic and farcical embellishments, the fae still left their locks as simple as any mortal's. "If you're able to joke, I guess you're in better shape than you look at least." The lock clicked open with a muted sound and Corbet sighed, letting it fall to the ground.

"Now where on earth did you learn to do that?" Ruari

said, his voice worn and tired.

Corbet threw open the cell door and fell to his knees in front of his lover, reaching for his battered face. "Did I never tell you?" he whispered, stroking through his hair to move it from his eyes. "I'm not a very reputable mortal. You kidnapped a lost criminal, but now you're the one behind bars."

"How funny." If it surprised Ruari, he was too exhausted to show it. "You probably shouldn't be in here," he gave instead, leaning into the proffered kiss like a man dying of thirst. "I don't think Avenir is as fond of you as I am."

"Fuck them," Corbet growled, reaching for the chains holding Ruari to the wall. He could pick these. He knew he could. They'd escape somehow, some way, but for the moment all he cared to do was see Ruari free.

He wasn't ready for Ruari to groan, his body jerking with pain. "You're far too pretty to be using such foul language," he wheezed, anguish coloring his voice weak.

Corbet let go of the manacle with alarm. "What is it? Are you hurt?" he asked, leaning up to look at the metal where it touched Ruari's skin. His mouth fell open when he saw the flesh mangled, red and bloody and shiny, as if it had been scorched. There was no way that the thorn bindings could have done all of this.

Ruari managed a strained laugh, determined to grin through the pain. "Cold iron," he grunted, wincing when

Corbet's gentle examination brushed his skin against the cuff. "Can't say Avenir likes me all that much either. I think this is cathartic for them, given all I've done to earn their ire over the centuries."

As confused as he was, he could tell that the metal burned the more it touched. "What do you mean, 'cold iron?'" he probed, ripping the bottom of his shirt into strips. Carefully, he wedged the fabric through the metal cuff, working it around until it shielded all of Ruari's wrist from the surface of the cuff.

"It's deadly to us. Burns. Like salt on a slug." He grit his teeth while Corbet worked, but the moment the cloth was in place, his relief was obvious. "You really shouldn't be in here."

"Since when have you cared about what should and shouldn't be done?"

Ruari laughed wryly. "About the same time I got thrown in here for doing something I knew I shouldn't have done," he answered.

Corbet grit his teeth. "You only did it because I asked."

"I think you'll find that in our laws and dusty rulebooks, the reasons behind our misdeeds rarely get remembered. If it were me in Avenir's pointy shoes, I would have done the same." He sighed, leaning into the hand on his cheek. "I endangered my sovereignty, Corbet. Avenir is well within their rights as my counterpart to take control like this."

"But I don't care about that. I only care about you," Corbet insisted. "I won't let you rot in here. You're mine no matter what you do. Don't pick now to start being the type to listen to reason."

Ruari laughed and it almost transported him back to that morning together, where they kissed and held each other with no thought to what might transpire outside their room. His look was so fond, as beaten and hurt as he was.

"You are so surprising," the fae gave. "Can't say any moment with you is a bore. Are you alright, my love?" he asked suddenly, his golden eyes still sharp. They widened a moment later. "What have you been eating? You must be so hungry."

Soft hair curled slightly in his fingers. "I'm going to get you out of here and then let you worry about me," Corbet decided, moving for the lock again, his pick ready. "I'm going to get you out and we're going to set this right."

"You didn't answer me, and no, you're not," Ruari chuckled. "You're going to leave me here and go back. You know where the tapestry is. Get to the main hall and return to the surface. There's no helping me now, so you should just get out while you can." He managed a wry smile. "Preferably before Avenir decides they like the idea of trying out a mortal pet. If you stay much longer, you won't have much of a choice if it comes to that."

There were no words to articulate properly how abhorrent the idea of leaving was to him.

Tailan began to chirp and squeak, and Corbet swore under his breath, not even through half of the tumblers on the first manacle.

"Someone's coming," Ruari sighed, picking up on the signs. "You need to get out of here before they see you in here with me."

Corbet grimaced, wanting nothing more than to break the damn locks and drag Ruari away with him. He could see it in his mind's eye: them running, fighting off any who tried to hold them down. Anger flared in his stomach.

There really wasn't much he wouldn't do to keep them together.

But he knew well enough what would happen if he were caught, and Ruari couldn't go through more pain on his account. He settled for one last, painfully short kiss and then pulled away, snatching up the lock and threading it through the cell door. It shut with a click and a whispered 'I love you' just as the guards turned the corner.

"It's time you left," the brute of a fae hissed, something reptilian in the sound. His glamor must be failing as well.

Corbet put on his most winsome smile and picked up Tai, letting the tiny hedgehog burrow his cold nose into his sleeve. He felt a pang of guilt rise up. It must have been rather chilly sitting on the floor for so long, but Tai hadn't complained once.

"Of course," he said, holding the small animal closer to his chest. "Anything you say."

There was no chance in hell that he was leaving things as they were.

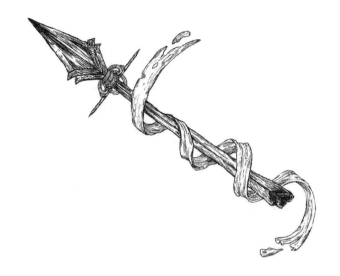

# CHAPTER 12

"It's worse than I thought," Corbet said the moment he and Tai returned to his room. He settled the hedgehog down on the sheets and went to go barricade the door. The messenger had assured him he would be left to his own devices so long as he remained inside, but if there had been one thing he had learned in the faerie realm, it was to never disregard the capricious nature of the creatures around him.

The regular assortment of animals were gathered on his bed and watched him huff and puff, all of them curled up among the pillows and sheets. Tailan was eager to join them, warming his small body in the pile of fur and feathers when he finished shoving the wardrobe back into place.

Corbet went over to sit beside them and gave the hedgehog a grateful stroke along his spines. The poor thing had done so much for him, suffering the cold and damp just to give him time with Ruari. He deserved far more attention than he could give at the moment.

Phren popped his head out of the mass of messy blankets and animals, staring at him to ask him to continue. The birds tweeted and chirped. Corbet dragged a hand down his face, the phantom image of his lover chained and bloody stamped in the black of his closed eyes. He kept them open, unwilling to let the sight haunt him.

He was motivated and enraged enough as it was.

"We need to help Ruari," he began, grabbing the charm from beneath the pile of bodies to tie around the door handle. Even if it were truly depleted, it gave him some measure of false comfort regardless.

The moment it was situated, he turned, joining them all on the bed. "He's only where he is now because he saved Tailan when I asked. I can't just leave him in a cell to rot." He couldn't, but he didn't know what else he could do. Keeping himself out of the Unseelie's grasp was a challenge in itself, not to mention simply keeping himself functioning.

Corbet looked over to the desk and saw how little food remained. He had only a few more apples, their brilliant

red skin softening more and more as the days passed. They'd have to be eaten soon lest they rot away, and he already knew how poor a substitute they made for a cup of water.

"I don't have much time," he admitted, looking back at the little faces listening with complete attention. "If we can't make this work, I'll have no choice but to trap myself here." And as much as Ruari had tried to get him to do exactly that, he still had no idea what all it would entail. He couldn't risk it while Avenir held the power.

"I'm going to talk to them," he decided, and immediately the council before him broke out in frantic chatter, the animals puffing out their feathers and bristling their fur and quills in vehement opposition. "I have to," Corbet frowned, holding his hands out, placating. "There's no other option. I can write letters until I run out of books, but they'll just ignore them until I've nothing left to eat. They want to force me into a corner, like trapping a rabbit at the end of a hunt."

Phren made a doleful look and Corbet grimaced, scratching his ears apologetically for the analogy.

Desperate times call for desperate measures, he thought. It would be hard for them to ignore him in person. He knew he had a tendency to make his voice heard, no matter how obstinate the listener. And if he had to get himself caught, then so be it. He had his lock picks. He'd manage to escape eventually.

The animals were anything but happy. Tailan crawled

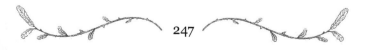

into his lap and kept on bristling, chuffing out little sounds to show his displeasure. Corbet carefully stroked down his spines. He wondered if they'd be alright without him. It wasn't as if he was all that helpful to them now, trapped and foodless as he was.

"Don't worry so much," he tried, hoping to soothe the small hedgehog of the fear he felt too. "I'm not completely defenseless. I've plenty left to barter with, so long as I get my way in the end."

He could tell just by the way his nose twitched that Tailan wasn't convinced. He glared up at Corbet before turning towards his friends, prompting them into motion with a little squeak. The birds twittered and the hare thumped his hind leg on the bed, but whatever discussion they were having, Corbet had a feeling Tailan would end up getting his way. He was too stubborn not to.

After a moment more of their argument, the birds took to the air in a huff, flying over to the corner of the room to prod and peck at his long forgotten pack. Corbet furrowed his brow and set Tailan back on the bed, standing to go see what they were doing. He hadn't needed to delve into its depths since Ruari had taken to feeding and clothing him.

Something metallic clattered on the floor, the birds succeeding in yanking whatever it was they wanted from the unfastened bag.

He moved a little faster, crossing the room in a few strides. Were they hungry? He knew he hadn't been

feeding them, but he hadn't thought they were so dependent on his scraps that they would take to rooting through his pack for any forgotten morsels.

Kneeling down, he gently brushed the songbirds to the side to see for himself the object they had found.

Corbet's heart clenched in his chest. It certainly wasn't food.

"I had completely forgotten about this," he said, taking the gift in hand. The metal was a cool weight between his fingers and he couldn't believe he'd forgotten the piece of church fence given to him by that blood-stained butcher back in the village. How had they known it was inside?

He turned back to Tailan and saw the hedgehog watching him, his tiny black eyes looking smug. Corbet smiled and turned the piece in his hand, the comfortable weight settling like his favorite blade in his palm.

On a whim, he pressed his finger to the jagged edge and immediately winced. He sucked on his bleeding finger. Cold and sharp. He definitely wasn't going into the lion's den unarmed now.

The animals stared down at him from the bed and he wasted no more time ruminating. He'd managed to keep this from the fae by hiding it, and he needed to make sure it came with him to meet Avenir. It needed to be covered, and it needed to be concealed until he found a need to use it.

He made a sweep of the desk from below, swiping along the surface until he found the spare bit of leather used to cover the utensils that always came with his meals. He wrapped the piece up, covering it completely, and slipped it up his sleeve.

"Thank you. All of you," Corbet imparted, moving back to the bed and petting them all in turn. "I'll do this and be back before you know it, right as rain." And with Ruari in tow, he hoped. "I promise."

The animals still seemed uneasy, but at least Tailan had calmed his defensive curl. His nose kissed Corbet's hand, his tiny foot resting on his thumb for a moment. Corbet's heart warmed at the sight. How could he fail with such support cheering him on? He reluctantly pulled away after one last pet to the hare's long ears, resolute and ready.

With that settled, it was as simple as leaving the room and waiting for the next patrol to happen along.

It didn't take long, not with the palace still under strict watch. Corbet wandered down the hall and listened intently for the heavy footfalls. He had to time this right to make it appear accidental.

He waited until the tromping of boots and rattle of armor was nearly on top of him before turning the corner, running straight into the front guard hard enough to fall to the ground. "Ow!" he exclaimed, his hand going instinctively to his shoulder to rub at the bruise he could feel forming.

The pain only grew sharper when the fae he hit grabbed him by the shoulder, jerking him to his feet with preternatural strength. "You are the mortal," the fae grinned, his shiny, sharp teeth visible through the opening in his helmet. "You've been hiding from us."

Corbet struggled against the iron hold and put an expression of fear on his face. Beneath it though, he was pleased. The messenger must have been truthful when she said that they weren't permitted to hunt him in his room.

"Let me go," he hissed, swinging out with his other hand. It barely made it an inch through the air before he was flanked by another guard, his wrist seized and held in place by a hand that looked more bestial than human.

Hot, fetid breath hit his ear and Corbet froze, feeling more than seeing the razor sharp teeth decorating the mouth on the guard. "The Monarch has orders to capture you," he said, snuffling and chewing the words like an animal before spitting them out. "But you must have known that. The little mortal, flushed from its burrow. The Monarch will be pleased to have you, even as scrawny as you are."

"Well I have no wish to go," he shot back, yelping a little as both of his hands were seized, held together in one massive paw.

"How cute," the first guard crooned, shoving at Corbet's back until he began to walk. "It thinks it has a choice."

"The king coddled it too much," the beastly one replied, yanking Corbet along when he deemed his pace too slow.

"It is right here and it can hear everything you say," Corbet hissed, his voice venomous. "Where are you taking me?"

Cold eyes barely spared him a glance. The beastly one even went as far as to chuff at him, as if he were being entertaining. "Is it scared? It really is cute." The hand that wasn't holding Corbet's reached towards his face. "Do you think the Monarch will let us have it once they're bored of it?"

There was no way to mistake the meaning behind that and Corbet snapped at the fingers before they could touch him, snarling like the animal dragging him down the hall. "You'd better hope for your sake they don't," he spat, baring his teeth until the hand was pulled back.

Something in his voice or posture seemed to dissuade the fae from further jeering, and Corbet spent the rest of the walk in relative silence broken only by the shifting of armor and the loud, boorish grunts of the one fae's breathing. They passed countless other guard patrols and each turned to watch them go, their gossip obvious and excited.

"They finally caught the mortal," one twittered.

"The Monarch will be pleased," another replied, their voice as dry as an autumn leaf. "It was only a matter of

time, after all."

Corbet shrugged the words off and kept his eyes focused on the fae leading him. Their opinions meant little anyway.

The doors rose above their heads to nearly scrape the vaulted ceiling. Were he in any other situation, Corbet might have found it impressive, maybe even awe inspiring. But with his wrists held in a bruising grip and the fae serving him up to their Monarch on a platter, it only managed to look imposing. The guards knocked on the thick oaken door three times before entering, dragging Corbet over the threshold.

The first thing to greet him wasn't the sanctimonious face of the Unseelie Court Monarch, but the immense size of the room itself. It rose far higher than the ceilings in the halls or even the banquet spaces, high enough that when Corbet tried to look upwards, his head spun and vertigo struck. Crystal so clear it seemed more liquid than mineral dripped from the hanging fixtures and faerie lights flit to and fro, lighting the room with their gentle glow. Their petals sang gently as they danced, but it did little to relax the tight knot in his stomach.

The sight of them brought him back hard to the underground garden his first night there, where the lights had danced between his fingers and Ruari had held him close, whispering to him of his devotion. Corbet swallowed and turned his attention to eye level, the memories less of a boon in the moment than they might

have been otherwise.

The rest of the room was almost enough to distract him from his thoughts. Every available surface was decorated just as lavishly as what lay above, the walls inlaid with reliefs that danced with figures along every border. He wondered what they represented and whether they told the history of the Court or some similar tale.

If Ruari were here, he knew he'd tell him every story, sparing no details.

The guards cut his thoughts short with a shove, forcing him forward where the seated figure lay in wait.

Corbet squared his shoulders and prepared himself for an experience he was already regretting.

Avenir was waiting for him in what could only be Ruari's throne room. He'd never been there before himself, Ruari having kept him at arm's length from his official work with a dogged determination, but seeing the tall, willowy fae occupying the gilt throne aggravated him nevertheless. They didn't belong there, but they certainly made it seem like they did.

The addition of Ruari's crown interlocked with their own only added to the insult.

Clearing his throat, Corbet smiled as diplomatically as he knew how. He knew all too well how personal this must be to the Monarch, and one wrong move could seal his and Ruari's fate permanently.

"I'm told you wished to see me," he said, swallowing his frustration and bowing low, like one would before the royalty aboveground. "Your guards were rather insistent."

The Monarch gave a graceful wave of their hand, their lips quirked in a prideful smile. "You were very persistent in entreating us. It was difficult for us to ignore you." Avenir gave him a thorough once-over, enjoying the situation far too much as they took in his no doubt ragged state. "We are...intrigued."

Curiosity nagged him like an insistent fly, and he couldn't help but ask. "Why didn't you come to me in my room, then, if you were so intrigued?" he probed, watching the fae for any minute expressions that might betray their intent. "You must have learned of my location from your messenger."

A small smile betrayed nothing. "Is it not more entertaining to flush quarry from it's nest by means of hunger, rather than force?" they asked in return, and Corbet bit the inside of his cheek to keep his expression in place. Avenir's head cocked, considering him the way one would muse at a particularly interesting beast on display. "You may have held out for longer than we anticipated, but the wait was fruitful in the end."

Corbet smiled brightly and the mask only slightly itched. "I apologize for any inconveniences I may have caused, but I'm sure you can imagine my anxiety at the current state of things." He moved closer when the

Monarch gestured him in, and it was almost deafening, the closing of the large door and the retreating footfalls of the entire guard leaving him alone with the royal fae.

It was abundantly clear from their retreat that Avenir didn't fear him at all.

"Can we?" they asked, the billowy fabric of their opulent robe shifting as they crossed their ankles atop the throne. "We would think this would grant you some measure of peace. You are far better off away from that braggart, and he better away from you."

"How do you suppose that?" Corbet nearly bit, his polite smile cracking at the edges.

"Is it not obvious? You have proven to be a terrible influence on the former king," they said, their orange eyes dancing as they emphasized former. "With you away from him, perhaps he may one day find penance for his crimes."

Corbet could tell they meant far more than what damage he had done to the barrier.

They paused, looking him up and down. Avenir's lips quirked into a malicious smile at whatever they saw in him. "And you. An unbound mortal in a realm of constancy. If you truly wished to stay, you would have long eaten of our food." Their teeth shone sharp in the unnatural magical light. "Perhaps now you may return above, your thoughts unclouded by the king's wiles."

Orange eyes flared bright, so inhuman it stung.

"Or perhaps you will choose to stay," Avenir posed. "You certainly do look hungry."

Corbet ground his teeth and schooled his expression into one of abject passivity. He couldn't let his anger guide him.

At least, not yet.

"You speak as if Ruari's punishment is absolute. What exactly has he done?" Corbet asked, dragging the conversation away from himself for fear of exacerbating the appraising look in Avenir's eye. They obviously didn't hold a high opinion of mortals, but they didn't have to like him to want to keep him for their own.

The Monarch raised a thin brow, their head resting on a thin hand. "What hasn't he done?" they replied, looking far too entertained. "He broke the Solstice, Mortal. He willfully disregarded a sacred law and now, as you've no doubt paid witness to, the barrier is weakened. Our magic is in disarray. Those fae who hold lesser power can no longer maintain a simple glamor and are no longer able to venture above. This realm is built upon balance. Ours is a sacred duty to protect this balance."

Avenir paused for a moment, letting their words ring in the voluminous hall.

"Your king has abandoned this duty, and as a leader who lets his people suffer, we have come to grant what

succor we can to the Summer Court," they intoned, pinning Corbet in place as if he alone were to blame for the calamity befalling the realm. "Imprisonment is a kindness given to him based on rank alone. Were he any other, he would be dead for such a crime."

Corbet breathed through his nose and clasped his hands behind his back so Avenir wouldn't see how they clenched. "That's..." he tried, but his voice died as the words reverberated in his skull. The fae from before hadn't given him the idea that it was as bad as that. He hardly believed the punishment fit the crime, but then again, he knew Avenir had their own reasons for wanting Ruari to suffer.

The burning, flickering, ever-changing orb that had crowned the Solstice festivities burned in his mind's eye. He recalled how it had dimmed as they walked back to his room. Was that the barrier, weakened by Ruari's absence? He felt the Monarch's eyes on him and he glanced up, tearing his gaze from the floor.

They looked at Corbet with nothing but pitied scorn and, for a moment, he wondered if they were capable of feeling anything more.

"You say that Ruari has earned this for abandoning his duty," Corbet said finally, fixing the Monarch with a calculated calm he only half felt. "I say he has fulfilled one duty at the sake of another."

They arched a brow but said nothing, waiting for him to proceed. He could tell just by looking in their

eyes that they hardly cared about what he had to say. The judgement was already given, the fate a forgone conclusion.

Corbet bit the inside of his cheek. "Ruari went out to save the life of one of his subjects. Is protecting one's subjects not the duty of a king?" he asked.

"You act like the life of one subject is equal to that of an entire kingdom. Mortal, you do not understand the extent to which Ruari has threatened us. You have no right to even offer your thoughts on the matter."

Burnt orange eyes narrowed and a graceful wave of their slender hand forced him down into a conjured seat. Dark lips curled into an inhuman smile, the impassiveness replaced by something unreadable.

Corbet struggled minutely against the invisible force holding him down, but he refused to drop his placid smile. "I'm sorry you feel that way," he grit through his bared teeth, "because you're going to get my thoughts regardless."

"You would presume as much?" Avenir intoned, their voice erring on the edge of hostility as they stood from their throne, as tall as a willow. "You, a mortal who has refused even to eat of the realm? What right have you to speak of our affairs when you so rigidly stand apart from us?" A cool hand reached out to cup his chin, tilting his face up to meet their relentless gaze.

"Maybe I'm saving that for marriage," he sniped,

wanting nothing more than to yank his face away from the creature hovering over him. "Wouldn't want to rush into anything, you know how it is."

He didn't register the slap until his cheek began to sting, the heat of it building like a growing fire. Corbet blinked slowly, the speed of the strike too fast to process. A trickle of blood rolled down his chin. Inside his mouth, his tongue ached as iron sluggishly pooled across his taste buds.

"You will speak to us with respect, Mortal," the Monarch said in a dangerous whisper. "We are not Ruari with his trifling fancies. We will not tolerate as he has done."

Corbet spat out the blood in his mouth and grinned, hoping it covered his teeth like an animal. "Oh, you're nothing like Ruari. You don't need to tell me that," he said, grimacing a little as the words aggravated the tender flesh of his cheek.

It'd been awhile since he last felt such pointed hatred for any person or thing. He'd almost forgotten the taste of it. Cold and thick; like swallowing an acrid poison.

"Such loyalty towards someone so undeserving," Avenir observed, their tone pensive and dark with what sounded like envy. "What could he have done to instill such behavior in you? We know all too well the loose chain he keeps you upon, so it cannot be simple training."

Corbet tried to not let anything show on his face. He

bit the inside of his cheek and it stung.

Avenir raised a brow and took him by the chin, forcing his eyes up. "Do you think he loves you?" they asked, curiosity and pity warring it out on their face. "If he does, think of it as the way the cat loves the mouse. Simple distraction is all you afford him, no matter how prettily he says otherwise. He has never been anything other than a creature bent on satisfying his whims however he may."

His eyes widened and then he clenched them shut, pulling away from the hand. "So you won't grant Ruari mercy?" Corbet whispered, cracking open his eyes.

The Monarch's lips curled into a pitying grin. They spared him a derisive laugh when they turned, making their way back to their throne as dismissively as they could.

It was answer enough.

"What of me then?" he called out, halting the fae with his voice trembling. "Without Ruari, I have nothing here. Will you send me back to my realm?"

Avenir stood still, slowly turning their head to meet his eyes. The look on their face was anything but kind. "What of you, indeed," they crooned. Their slender, reed-like fingers traced their lips as they slowly doubled back to him. "You have a way of insinuating yourself into places you fit not. It would be charming were it not so indicative of your lack of discipline."

Corbet licked at the split in his lip and blew a lock of hair from his eyes. "I like it here," he admitted, his gaze flickering between the fae and the floor. "I feel wanted here. I don't want to lose that."

Cool fingers fell to his cheek again, pressing cruelly on the hot, sensitive bruise. "What an interesting mortal. You fall in love with this place, but we assure you, it does not love you in return." Avenir stroked through his hair like one would a pet, smiling that indifferent, contemplative smile.

He nuzzled into the hand, letting his eyes fall to half-mast. "Maybe I'm not looking for love," Corbet breathed, sagging into the chair, tired of fighting. "Maybe I'm just looking for a place to belong. For someone to belong to."

Holding his breath, he watched the idea turn over in the fae's eyes. The nut brown fingers trailed down his neck and settled on his chest, assessing him. "You really aren't loyal at all, are you?" they asked, walking a circle around his back to settle both hands on his shoulders.

He pouted, letting his head rest against a slim arm. "I can be," he said, "so long as I know I'm wanted. If I've no one, then what's the point?" Corbet asked.

"Poor pet," Avenir crooned, cupping his neck. "And you would be loyal to us, and only us? Loyal to the one who sates your hunger?"

It was so hard to tell if the tone were sincere and whether the hunger they referred to was literal or

innuendo, but Corbet closed his eyes and pressed a kiss to the fae's smooth skin, taking it as what it was; an offer.

"I would, I would," he promised, and the moment he felt the magic pinning his wrists lessen, he reached for Avenir. "Please, I'm so hungry."

His job was made easier when the fae came around to his front and sat on his lap, their cold, orange eyes dancing with victory. "We expect perfect obedience, pet. We won't let you run wild like Ruari did." The fae spat the king's name like a curse. "He shall rot and suffer with the thought of you in our grasp, eating from our hand."

Though every fae he had encountered had spoken of the magic of the land being depleted, Avenir still summoned a morsel of food with no visible strain. Whether those claims were hyperbole, or simply a testament to the Monarch's considerable strength, he couldn't tell.

Corbet recoiled slightly when the hand drifted closer, the fae-food held gently between a thumb and forefinger. Hatred flared hot and bright so he hid it in a sigh, so very angry at the fae treating this all as a game.

In their hand was a morsel of fruit: dark, perfect, and formed in the shape of a blackberry.

Avenir followed his eyes and glanced at the candy with a knowing smile. "What is it, pet? Does this not suit your tastes?" they asked, pressing it to his lips regardless.

Gritting his teeth into a placid smile, Corbet let the fae trace the shape of his lips with the cool treat. It smelled as good as it had when Ruari had done the same, but, as hungry as he was, he felt no desire to eat. Not from this hand at least.

"No," he sighed, and he closed his eyes. "It's perfect."

Textured flesh met his tongue, followed by a burst of juice as the ripe berry surrendered for him, and Corbet, for all that he hadn't eaten in the last week, couldn't help but think he'd rather go hungry than swallow it down. Avenir was no doubt grinning above him, so victorious it stung, but Corbet chewed obediently, noting the hints of sour and sweet that played subtly beneath the taste of failure.

The moment he swallowed, Avenir laughed. "You're mine now, pet," they said, stroking through his hair with spindly fingers. "Oh, how you shall make that wretched king weep."

Corbet palmed the makeshift knife hidden in his sleeve and wasted no more time on a lost cause.

The cold iron burned like fire in his hand the moment it tasted the fae's flesh. Avenir screamed and convulsed, their hand grabbing for the protruding metal lodged in their ribs. Corbet shoved the Monarch to the floor and watched their fingers burn on the naked handle, the pain so horrific that there was little chance of it being removed.

264

Blood bathed his hands when he reached down to push theirs away from it, giving the knife a vicious twist to kill the fight still raging in orange eyes.

"You look really surprised," he observed, glancing down to see that his ring glimmered brightly, even covered as it was in gore. He turned it this way and that, admiring it for a moment. "Ruari told me that this was common, royals being deposed when they've angered their subjects. You of all people should know that." The flickering fae lights made it burn like an ember on his finger. He had never felt so cruel, and he couldn't say he hated the feeling.

"You will...regret this, you filthy creature," Avenir mangled, their voice ragged and ruined. "How could you? You lying, rotten toy..." They trailed off, their desperate attempt to stand up thwarted when Corbet forced them back down with his boot.

"That's something you failed to realize about mortals," Corbet crooned, brushing the fae's hair from their eyes. "You treat us as animals but look so shocked when we bite."

Avenir spat blood, their violent orange eyes horrified. "You're a monster," they gurgled, the blood on their lips foaming. He must have punctured a lung, if faeries had lungs.

Corbet smiled. "No more than you are," he said. "It's funny, isn't it? The things we do for love and duty. Just think, you'd depose a king simply for saving one subject.

I'd kill a Monarch to put him back on his throne. What a funny world."

"You won't...get away with this-"

He pulled the shard of metal from their ribs and examined the fae blood still sizzling on the blade. "But won't I?" he reasoned, standing up. "After all, you said it yourself. What's the life of one compared to that of an entire kingdom? Ruari will be freed and you will die knowing that he's the one with both kingdoms' best intentions at heart."

Avenir made a grab for his ankle, some weak, pitiful move that barely snagged his trouser leg. Blood drained all the faster, pooling around the prone fae. In the unnatural light of the room, it almost appeared black.

"You know not...what you do," they choked, their eyes losing focus. "Mortal!" they spat, their hand falling to the floor, strength gone. "You lose your humanity with this—" but they were cut off when he slit their throat.

Corbet flicked the blood off his makeshift blade and grinned. "So long as I have Ruari, I really couldn't give a damn," he said to the stilling corpse. He sheathed the fence piece in its leather thong and pocketed it, turning his attention towards the room at large.

For some reason, the death of a Monarch went surprisingly unnoticed by the world. He didn't know if he expected something cataclysmic to occur, like the roof caving in or the door being stormed by guards, but for

the faerie lights above to keep twinkling as they did; well, it just seemed rather dull.

He toed at Avenir's body, just to make sure they were in fact expired. Blood seeped slowly out in a growing pool, staining the tips of his boots. He smiled at the ruby red. With Avenir out of the way, there really was nothing left between getting Ruari back and the return to normalcy that he felt was long overdue.

The thought alone was enough to make his heart sing.

Corbet didn't spare Avenir another look. He turned on his heel and made for the door, playing back through his mind the path he had taken with the messenger. How far was he from the catacombs? Could Ruari feel the shift in power? Was he close enough to feel the death of a Monarch? It made him smile to think so. He wanted Ruari to know he was coming. He wanted him to know they were nearing their happy ending.

The door rose above him and Corbet took a deep breath, preparing himself for the challenges that still lay ahead. Guards outside the door, guards in the halls, guards standing at attention outside of the cells; the iron blade rested heavily on his thigh. He definitely had his work cut out for him, no matter how close he was to the end. He ran his bloody fingers through his hair absentmindedly, ready for whatever it was to come.

Everything came to a screeching halt when the pain hit.

Sweat prickled his brow, the discomfort starting in his throat, his fingers, the side of his temple. Corbet shrugged and stopped moving, leaning over to catch his breath. It was unlike anything he had ever felt before, ebbing and flowing in time to his heartbeat.

He pushed himself upright again. He didn't have time for this, whatever it might be. Gritting his teeth, Corbet steeled himself and made again for the door.

And then, the pain pushed inwards, doubling in its intensity. He managed to take two more steps before he crumpled to his knees, clutching his chest. "What?" he gasped, a spear of pure ice stabbing into him viciously, mercilessly.

The blood still tacky on his fingers stained his shirt and seemed to exacerbate the agony, burning wherever it managed to soak through his clothing.

His eyes went wide and he tore at the cloth, scrubbing frantically to try and rid himself of the gore staining his skin. Something was happening. He didn't know what, but something was happening and it was the blood doing it.

Energy sparked. His heart stuttered. He fell to the floor in a crumpled heap, overcome for a moment. Corbet cried out, throwing his arm down to leverage himself back up. He didn't have time for this! His mind screamed for him to stand, to go, to get to Ruari, but something compelled him to look back though his path lay just ahead.

The still body of the fae greeted him when he gave in to the urge, and for a moment, he was horrified by the possibility that they had somehow survived. Nausea and fear roiled angrily in his stomach.

The pain only doubled and he forced himself to look away from the corpse.

Avenir lay as dead as winter. They weren't the one doing this to him. They couldn't be.

But, if not them, then who?

Panicking, Corbet reached for the knife in his belt. They were dead and gone but it wouldn't hurt to make sure, the pain growing with every second he spent fumbling. His chest seized and his heart gave another stuttering pound, as if it were fighting off some invisible force. Why hadn't he brought Tailan with him? He didn't think he could handle this alone.

Fear rose in his throat like bile and he grew frantic, nearly dropping the knife as a wave of pure agony washed over him. The leather fell from the blade and to the floor. He reached for it with shaking hands only to drop it again.

His skin burned the instant he touched, as if he had thrust his hand into a roaring fire.

His eyes widened in horror. What was happening to him?

Fingers blistered, Corbet curled into himself, cradling his heart with his hands, as if the radiating burn could warm the cold collecting in his ribcage. What was happening to him? The question pounded in his head like a mantra. His skin prickled and his heart...his heart pounded so hard, beating against his ribcage like a hammer to an anvil. Tears poured down his cheeks and stained the floor below.

He felt so cold. So very, very cold.

Black burst across his vision like smoke, and for a moment, he was sure he was about to die. Ruari's voice whispered in his ear, a calming phantom just out of reach. Corbet's mind filled with pain, with the cold.

It wasn't until it faded away, like fog dissipating in sunlight, that he realized the pain was dulling with it, receding in time to his slowing, aching heartbeats.

He stared down at his burned hands and Corbet fell still, silent; he was so very, very cold. His chest, his fingers, his head: ice flowed through his veins. It felt like his very blood had been frozen. The knife lay at his side and he edged away from it, instinct telling him to keep his distance.

Cold iron burns, it crooned. It's deadly to us.

What was this? What voice was this in his head? Was it a memory, or his own? Corbet stared at the loathed blade but it sounded no more.

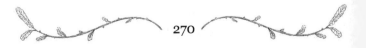

He couldn't remember, he realized quite suddenly, why he was here. What he had done. His thoughts echoed so slowly in his mind, like listening to the reverberations sound against a cave wall. The questions returned nothing, no matter how loud he screamed into the dark.

Corbet furrowed his brow. There was a ring on his hand, shining dully through the blackened blood. It was lovely, but was it his?

He couldn't remember. He just couldn't remember.

He turned to take in the room instead, his memories yielding nothing. A body rested on the ground behind him, thin and desiccated like a rotten leaf. He stared at it but it didn't move or speak. Thoughts swam in his head, drifting aimless and intangible the more he stared. He knew he must have killed this creature, their blood still staining his hands.

Corbet looked down at it and watched it flake off. It was so black, more soot and char than liquid blood.

Did they deserve it? They must have. Every time he looked into their ruined face, his cold heart burned.

Regardless of whatever this monster had done, he had killed it. But why did something still feel off? If he killed the monster, shouldn't the world feel right? The air hummed like an irksome insect flitting too close to his ear. Within his very bones, he felt an ache that resonated in time to it.

*The balance is off,* that same voice supplied in the back of his mind. *Right it. Right it before it all comes crashing down.*

Without pausing to think, he crawled to the corpse and reached for the crowns upon its husk of a head. They came free with no effort, glimmering dully in the heat haze of the room. He broke the two apart, holding braided vine in a hand and woven ivy in the other. The thrum grew louder, so much more incessant, and Corbet closed his eyes, shoving the former on his head.

And all at once, the pressure stopped. Corbet sighed and then gasped, warmth pouring through him from his head down to his feet. He looked at his hand and watched the black blood melt away, leaving his skin as clear and white as snow.

Wiping at his messy face, he trembled under the weight of the power teeming through him. Curious and inquisitive, it searched every inch of him until it felt like home. It slumbered beneath the surface, curled up like a sleeping snake that could be woken at the slightest of sounds.

This was magic, Corbet realized. This was magic and it was tenuously holding him, seeping into his marrow as it fought to equalize.

It needed more.

It wasn't content with just him. He wasn't big enough or strong enough to take it all alone.

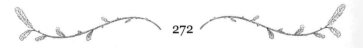

Maintain the balance.

Corbet knew what he had to do. Forcing himself to his feet, he sprinted to the heavy door. It opened before him with just a thought and the fae outside stared at him, passivity turning to horror in an instant.

"Get me the king," Corbet commanded, the crown burning like fire on his head and ice in his hand. "You've a new Monarch now."

# CHAPTER 13

When Ruari heard the clanging of the cell door opening, he didn't deign to look up.

There really was no point to doing so. Nothing good would come of it. Those who guarded him weren't of his Court, and they made that more than abundantly clear with their treatment.

Even given that, he still couldn't smother the burst of curiosity that made him crack an eye.

The fae lurking by the door seemed to struggle with the heavy lock. Ruari chuckled, closing his eyes again. So, he thought, he'd have to wait a little for this beating to come. With that on the docket for the day, he made sure to feign sleep. He couldn't say he felt like inviting more pain, especially when he knew how fond these jailers were of hearing him break.

More clanging and rattling echoed in the small cell, followed by some muted cursing. It made him smile a little. They must be new to have such a hard time with it. None of the regulars seemed to struggle this much. Shifting a bit to buy himself a better angle to peek, he choked on the pained gasp that followed, gritting his teeth to keep it from slipping out.

As much as he enjoyed seeing whoever this was suffer with the door, he knew well enough he'd have it far worse the moment they managed to get inside.

Ruari chewed the inside of his cheek, already knowing he had it pretty bad as it was. Everything ached. Every bit of his exposed skin burned and stung, and his wrists were the worst by far. What little Corbet had been able to do to spare him exposure to the iron had long since been found and removed.

The thought made him grimace. He had a motley assortment of bruises and gashes from when the guards had discovered it. Even now, he couldn't tell if the momentary reprieve had been worth the fallout.

The bloodied strips of fabric were still with him though, tattered and stained on the ground near his knees. They reminded him of that reprieve. They reminded him of his lost one. He would stare at them

sometimes and imagine warm hands, a soft voice, and eyes as dark as night.

Ruari sighed. He longed for the relief the fabric had brought.

He longed for Corbet.

How long had it been at this point? Ruari grimaced and rolled his head so his fevered cheek brushed the cold stone wall. For the life of him, he didn't know. The passage of time was immeasurable here. The lights never dimmed or brightened to signify the changing of day. The guards never gave him any indication of how much time had gone by.

Corbet had looked so thin when he had come calling. It was foolish to think he hadn't succumbed and eaten the fae food by now. It would only be human, and even if it wasn't what he wanted, he'd rather Corbet eat than starve.

The corners of his mouth turned downwards. To just give in and eat...that wasn't the Corbet he knew. He couldn't help but think of how doggedly he had avoided all the attempts Ruari had made to get him to eat, and that was when he was still around to protect him. Bitterness coated his tongue.

Maybe he had just left for the surface before it came to that. Cold and tight, his stomach clenched into a knot. The thought shouldn't sicken him as much as it did. He should want him safe and far from Avenir, even if it took

him far from Ruari too.

He should, but he knew he was too possessive to ever be so selfless. He didn't know which of the two options he preferred, not when neither ended with Corbet in his bed.

He'd read him a thousand books until his voice dried up if it only meant that he would stay.

It hurt more than all he'd experienced down here, how much he wanted him back.

"...ur majesty? Your majesty, can you hear me?"

Ruari looked up at that, broken from his thoughts and worry. "Haven't been called that in a while," he croaked, his throat as dry as sand. "Nearly forgot the feeling of being something other than a traitor."

The fae looming over him had somehow managed to unlock the cell door and enter while he mused, something almost surprising given her rather loud confrontation with the obstinate lock. Her face looked so uncomfortable, like she half expected to be killed simply for breathing in his space. The thought made him almost quirk a smile. If only he had that kind of strength left.

"Can you stand, your majesty? You've been summoned by the Monarch. I'm to take you." She wrung her hands as she hovered, the key dangling from her hip.

He managed a worn smile, hiding his despondence. "Take these off me and I'll fly," he laughed, regretting

it immediately as the movement jostled his burning, throbbing wrists.

It would be better to ignore the pain, he told himself. If Avenir was sending for him, he couldn't really afford to look as miserable as he felt. If he had learned anything from his centuries of interactions with them, it was that it wouldn't do to give them something else to celebrate.

They'd had enough fun at his expense.

And speaking of fun, it was obvious this new fae wasn't having an ounce. His liberator didn't so much as crack a smile at his attempt at humor, which Ruari thought was rather disappointing. He didn't get to make many jokes down here, not with the guards ordered to treat him like refuse.

"You don't talk much, do you?" he observed, and he was surprised when she startled, looking up like a terrified deer. "You hardly look to be the usual guards I'm familiar with."

She struggled a bit under with his watching, fumbling the key in her small hands. "Everyone else was relocated," she mumbled, finally fitting the key into the lock. He winced as the iron burned him the more she shifted the metal. It wasn't her fault, he told himself, breathing harshly through the fire. There was no easy way to do this while avoiding the iron herself.

Patiently, he waited as she unlocked the manacles, his arms falling numbly into his lap the moment they were

free. Relief washed over him in waves, followed quickly by pain. "Relocated? Now that sounds interesting. I wonder what could be happening." The blood flow stung like needles, but he rubbed life back into his hands, savoring it over the burn of the iron.

"A lot," she said, looking unsure of what to do next. "I'm only a messenger. They don't tell me much, but I know a lot has happened."

Curiosity prickled his skin like a cold chill. Now what could she mean by that? This was no time to be lazing about on the floor, that was for sure. Ruari braced his ruined hands on his knees, steeling himself.

He quickly found out that he was in no state to stand, let alone fly.

No matter how he pushed himself, he couldn't summon the strength to even rise more than a few inches. He fell forward onto his knees with a muted groan and everything erupted into a dull ache. His vision swam, black spotting like mold on the dingy stone, and he heard the small fae make a noise of concern.

"your majesty!" she squeaked, looking around for help though they both knew perfectly well that there was no one else to call upon. "Are you alright? Tell me what to do, please!" she said, her frightened concern a balm compared to the pain he was used to receiving.

He schooled his breathing, doing his best to be composed for her sake, if not his own. "I'll be alright,

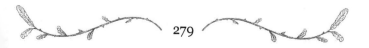

little one. Give me a hand up though," he wheezed, holding out his hand. "Avoid the wrists, if you'd be so kind."

"Of course," she rushed, taking his forearm into her tiny hands with as much care as she could. Given her diminutive body, she wasn't able to do much beyond offer some support for him as he dragged himself to his feet.

It was enough though, and she huffed and puffed along with him when they managed to get him standing.

"Thank you," he exhaled, leaning against the dingy wall to catch his breath for a moment. Now that he was at eye level with her, or well, perhaps looking down on her was more accurate, he could look at her properly.

The first thing he noticed of the short fae was her delicate coloring. Those of the Seelie tended to care little for maintaining the looks of mortals, and it would show in their natural appearances. There was no sign of her glamor, but without it, her skin was still light, freckled. She wasn't one of his, and it made his curiosity grow.

"What are you called?" he asked, dragging a hand through his filthy hair to get it out of his eyes. He felt disgusting but he doubted there was time for a bath. "I'm not familiar with you Unseelie."

She wet her lips and looked like he had asked her to give him her eyes instead of her name. "It's uh," she stammered, trying to square her jaw and look confident. It must be hard for her, Ruari thought, to look

intimidating when she had all the presence of a fawn. "It's Breena, your majesty."

"Breena," he repeated. "Pleasure to meet you, Breena." With some effort, Ruari pushed off the wall and towards the door. "You'll have to explain to me why Avenir wants me now of all times," he chuckled, grateful when the petite messenger-turned-guard ducked under his arm to help him walk. He hadn't needed to ask, sparing him from admitting another moment of weakness. "I wonder if they've finally had their fun. I didn't expect this to end so soon."

He figured he'd have at least a century of torture before they grew bored of rubbing their victory in his face.

Breena blew her green hair from her eyes before she looked up at him, carefully easing him up the stone stairs. "Your majesty, I believe you are uninformed," she spoke, her voice far too light for the dark of the dungeon around them. "They are no longer the Monarch."

Ruari froze mid-step, nearly unbalancing them both on the crumbling staircase. He pinned her with a look and she shrunk beneath his gaze. "What do you mean?" he asked, his voice hard. "Who is it, if not Avenir?"

Her lips trembled as she spoke. "They are no longer the Monarch," Breena repeated, her eyes fixed to the floor, unable to meet his stare. "I know not who replaced them, but they are no longer my Monarch."

This wasn't possible, for many reasons, the least of which was the state of the barrier. There was no way a shift in power could occur with things so precarious. No force would be stupid enough to organize a coup with things as they were, and if there was one thing Ruari knew, it was in orchestrating coups.

It would mean the ruin of them all. He surged forward under his own strength, dragging the small fae behind him.

"Take me to them. Now," he commanded, letting his position tinge his voice.

She managed a nod and a scared gulp, unlocking the door to the hall with shaking hands. The moment it was open, Ruari stormed through, his energy swelling with the scent of fresh air and light. Breena had to run to keep up, her tiny voice cracking as she tried to guide him verbally, if not physically.

"The throne room!" she shouted, falling behind as her breath grew ragged. "Go to the throne room, please!"

Ruari didn't even spare her a look, already gone.

There were far more pressing matters at hand.

The barrier was a delicate thing and was almost alive in its own right. Balance was key. Without it, the whole thing would come tumbling down. He remembered all too clearly the tremor that had tore through it all those centuries ago when he forced the old queen to abdicate.

That was done in a peaceful time, when the barrier hadn't been on the verge of disintegrating. He couldn't imagine what another displacement would feel like now, if they'd have time to feel it at all before it collapsed over their heads.

Ruari allowed himself only a fraction of a second to assess the current state of the magic teeming across his skin, and he found it to be as damaged as it had been before; no worse or better for the time he had spent in the dungeon.

His eyes widened and he slowed for a split second. Nothing had changed, but given the new Monarch, it made no sense for it to be anything but in tatters. The only thing that could have preserved the tenuous balance would be his and Avenir's magic. It took time to accept a new source. Decades, if not a full century. Any foreign entity would be rejected outright unless properly inundated.

If Avenir was no longer in power, he couldn't imagine what might have occurred to allow a new fae to take control with no discernable change in the balance.

The uncertainty only pushed him to move faster.

Ruari knew his palace like the back of his hand and he was at the door of his throne room within minutes. Guards bracketed the heavy oak entrance on both sides, both wearing the Unseelie emblem. His pace faltered a bit as he came closer.

At the base of the door sat Corbet's collection of animals. The birds flapped their wings and screeched, the hare pounding his foot to the floor like a drum. Tailan, Corbet's hedgehog friend, led the charge, hissing and spitting at the guards who were too unsettled to try and pick him up while the spikes stood at attention.

"What do you think you're doing?" Ruari called out, cutting in with an extra burst of speed before the braver guard drew back his boot to kick the small creature.

It was obvious they weren't expecting him to have arrived this early. They saluted him as their station demanded and Ruari walked up, barely registering the respect he had been denied since his imprisonment.

"Your majesty," one of the guards sputtered, fumbling with his weapon while the birds flitted closer to box him in. "We were just trying to rid the entrance of these pests before your arrival."

After all that he had been through, the thought of these guards hurting the last kind faces Corbet had in his absence stung like a punch to the gut. "Leave them be," he ordered, forcing his voice to reflect every bit of command his appearance lacked. "Open the doors."

The two fae shared a look and hurried to do as he had said. In the moment it took them, Ruari looked down to meet eyes with Tailan. The creature had never liked him, but with their shared interest conspicuously absent, he hoped the hedgehog would put aside his distaste for long enough to fill him in.

Tailan looked frightened, panicked, and he twitched his nose and squeaked rapidly. Corbet is inside, he said. I felt something change.

Ruari furrowed his brow, the question on his lips, but there was no time to ask before the door finally swung open and the animals took off. The birds took to the air and the hare bounded inside, Tailan moving as fast as he could to get inside. Running a hand over his face, Ruari prepared himself before he followed in after.

He had been in countless conflicts during his reign. Wars, coups, uprisings, betrayals-- the list was as endless as the stars in the sky. This was not the first time he had been thrown off his throne and found someone else seated in it, and he doubted it would be the last.

Ruari was no stranger to hardship, but even with his long history behind him, he was still struck to a standstill the moment he entered and looked to the one who had summoned him from his perdition.

Nothing in his long life could have prepared him for what he saw. He doubted anything could compare to the pain that hit only a moment later, once his mind had processed it. The agony of his body faded to the background, playing second fiddle to the cold, constricting vice fixed around his unbeating heart.

Even from across the room, he could still see the preternatural shine in Corbet's eyes.

Even from across the room, he could tell that Corbet

was no longer human.

Ruari's mouth went dry. Centuries of conflict and strife kept him from showing his horror, the habit of keeping everything inside too ingrained after a millennia of dealing with Avenir. Ice flooded his veins and he forced himself to keep walking.

He was used to this, he told himself. He'd done this before.

But this wasn't Avenir. His lover sat high and regal on Ruari's throne, his legs crossed demurely at the knee: beautiful, detached, and ultimately, untouchable.

"So," Corbet spoke in perfect, unaccented Fae'l. The sound made him flinch. It held nothing of the softness or affection Ruari had come to associate with him. "You're the Seelie king, knocked from his throne. Captivity hasn't treated you kindly."

There wasn't a drop of familiarity in his voice at all. Ruari stared at his lost one, his mind racing to keep up and process what was obviously happening. He watched the animals reach the base of the throne, Corbet staring down at them cooly with no hint of recognition in his eyes. The exhaustion hit him all at once, coalescing with his distress in a way that he knew was painted on his face like a mask of weakness.

If he were before Avenir, he would have slit his own throat for the disservice it did him.

"I suppose I am and I suppose it hasn't, though that's of no fault of my own," he managed to reply when he saw Corbet raise a brow, impatient for a reply.

Tailan scratched at the throne's leg, trying his best to climb the smooth surface. Corbet broke eye contact with him to look down pensively. Ruari held his breath, watching his lover pick up the hedgehog in his hand.

"What are all of these creatures doing here?" he asked, examining the hedgehog with curious eyes. The birds landed lightly on his shoulders, nipping affectionately at his earrings. "This is certainly a warmer welcome than I've received from anyone else so far."

His heart sunk like a stone, cold and dead in an icy sea. "They must like you," Ruari said, watching Tailan huddle up into a ball in Corbet's hand. "Have you ever met them before?"

Gray eyes flicked up to meet his, a brow raised. "No, I haven't." He settled the sad creature into his lap, looking down at the hare curled up by his feet. "It must be a good sign if I'm able to incite such devotion into them upon a first meeting. It speaks well of my reign."

Ruari waited a beat, unable to bite his tongue. "Do you know me?" he asked, sounding so disgustingly hopeful that he hardly recognized himself.

The distance on Corbet's face was painful. Ruari knew the answer before it came.

"I've never met you," he answered, furrowing his brow. He crossed his arms and frowned, his expressions the same even with his memories gone. Tailan peeked out his head from his defensive curl, and Ruari read pity in his small black eyes.

Ruari knew it was pointless, but hearing it said still hurt regardless. "Come now," he tried, mindful of the weakness in his voice. "Nothing at all?"

Corbet curled his lip in something like annoyance. "Do I know you?" he parroted. "I know that you're the reason the barrier is the way it is. I know that you're the one who sacrificed the law for his own whims."

He flinched and felt his stomach turn to lead. Despite it all, he tried to put up a smile. "Oh, is that all?" he said. "What a horrible way to make a first impression, if that's the case."

Aloof and indifferent, there was no sign that Corbet recalled anything. He must have been briefed by Avenir's advisors and guards. Not much else explained the acerbic, scathing reception.

"You sound strained. Should we continue this after you've rested, or are you willing to help me fix the mistake you made sooner rather than later?"

Ruari didn't let the pain show. "I think I'm duty bound to solve this as soon as possible," he gave, standing up straight so as not to seem cowed. "But tell me, how is this to work? How do you fix what Avenir couldn't?" Avenir

was far older than Ruari, and had been reigning when the barrier had been put into place. If they of all people couldn't fix it, how was a mortal-turned-fae to do it?

How do you know anything about the barrier at all, he longed to ask, a question in a field of hundreds. They grew like weeds in his mind, all battling for the sun's attention.

He'd only heard tell of something like this happening. It made his stomach sink to think about. What sat before him looked like Corbet, but he was as good as a stranger now. Perhaps even worse.

"My predecessor was blinded by envy and spite. They didn't see the obvious in front of them, focused as they were on making you suffer." Corbet looked so comfortable in Ruari's throne, wearing the title of Monarch like a well-tailored suit.

He interjected there, too curious to let all of his questions go without saying. "What did become of your... predecessor?" Ruari asked. Corbet wore the regalia of the Unseelie Court, but there was no sign of Avenir. "I hardly know them to be the type to step down from anything." Especially when they had won his Court and so thoroughly beaten him.

Corbet tilted his head, resting it on his propped up hand. His other stroked the breast of the blackbird softly. "I killed them, I suppose. I can't really seem to recall why or how."

"You can't remember at all?" Ruari pressed. "Aren't you at all curious?" The Corbet he knew was voraciously inquisitive, not this apathetic creature resting atop his throne.

He noticed immediately Ruari's look of shock. It made him smile, something cold and jovial. "Why should I be? I did what I did and I don't feel that the details are all that important, and these fae are very helpful in filling in the blanks. What use are the reasons if they're meaningless?"

Ruari didn't know what to say to that.

Corbet noticed. He leaned forward a bit, his head cocked. At least that was the same, his unabashed nature peeking through the gaps of this hard exterior. "Oh, are you surprised?"

He really couldn't say he was surprised. At least, not when it came to the murder. Corbet had always been calculating. Quick with his knife and even quicker with his tongue. His mind went back to his first encounter with him, in that forest clearing so very long ago. If he felt threatened, he fought. If he felt cornered, he lashed out.

So no, he wasn't surprised. But he was beginning to understand. Corbet had gone from mortal to fae, and as shocking as that in itself was, he knew it wasn't unheard of. Ruari wished he had been there to see it, if only to have helped to mitigate the unfamiliarity now assaulting his lover.

"Does your heart hold a beat?" he asked, wanting to confirm his suspicions.

Corbet looked thrown at the change in topic. He furrowed his brow. "What kind of question is that?" he asked.

"One to which I'd like to know the answer," he replied gently, and he watched as Corbet reluctantly placed his hand to his chest, his expression one of annoyance.

That annoyance quickly shifted to alarm. His eyes widened. His hand moved on his chest, his eyes looking down to check by sight what he couldn't feel by touch alone. Corbet looked up, a bit fearful with the question heavy on his lips. The hare nuzzled his ankle before going back to sleep.

Ruari sighed before he could ask. "I thought as much. I can probably guess why and how you did it," he gave, looking up at his lover with something that could only be fondness.

No wonder the barrier remained as it had. Avenir's magic had to go somewhere, and Corbet still held traces of blood on his boots. It must have been so frightening, he thought, to have felt himself die. Ruari swallowed painfully. Corbet had been all alone as his victim's magic-tinged blood seeped into his body.

"You've really done your best without me, haven't you?" he mused fondly.

"My best?" Corbet shot, irritation evident and enough to distract him from the realization that his heart was as frozen in his chest as Ruari's. As any fae's. "You have nothing to do with what I have done, your majesty. I would expect some gratitude on your part. Without me, you'd still be rotting in that cell."

Before today, he never knew he had missed being on the receiving end of that temper. Tailan perked up, watching with interest.

"Of course," he smiled, lowering his eyes and head in a small bow. "My gratitude is endless. Please, tell me what you came up with," Ruari pressed, unable to wipe away the lovesick look no doubt at home on his face. If nothing else, Corbet's frustration was still the same. "If I am able to right the wrongs I have committed, then my hands are yours to guide."

Corbet resettled into the throne, for all the world looking like a pleased cat on the verge of purring. He stroked Tailan's spiky back, and for a moment, it was as if nothing had changed at all. "That's a better attitude," he grinned. "These guards told me you'd be tricky and treacherous, but you're rather obedient, aren't you?"

Only for you, he longed to say, but he knew well enough not to present himself like that in front of his counterpart, even if it was his forgetful lover. Instead, he just smiled. "I merely want what is best for my subjects," he replied.

Humming, Corbet rubbed his foot against the rabbit

curled up at the base of the carved throne. Phren rubbed back, scent marking him. "Spoken like a true king. Maybe there's hope for you yet." He sat up a bit straighter, leaning forward in a way that drew Ruari in like a moth to flame.

A smile broke across his perfect face, his eyes so dark and deep. "What I propose is simple. Have another Solstice."

"Another?" Ruari questioned, confused. "My dea—" and he had to stop himself, swallowing back the pet name. "Your majesty," he corrected, "do you know what a Solstice is? It occurs only once a year. We simply can't have another one."

Corbet frowned, crossing his arms. Though he was doing his best to appear aloof, the birds hopping and dancing along his shoulders softened the look considerably. "Well, why not? You broke the seal by interrupting the feast. Just have another one, and recreate what went unfinished. It can't be that complicated." He slumped in his throne and kicked the base with his heel. "Life is rarely as convoluted as you make it out to be."

"It doesn't work like that," he began to say. "The moon has to be in position, the earth keyed to its movement. There is something special in the air at the time of Solstice that simply doesn't exist any other time of the year. Displaced magic becomes polarized in the moonlight, equalizing all that has been thrown into flux.

"To simply have another Solstice, well, it's just not possible. Not without yanking the moon from its path to force it back—"

And then his mind stuttered to a stop, the idea turning over, gaining traction on a single word. Why wouldn't it work? All he'd ever known of the Solstice came from Avenir. It was the shortest night of the year with the longest day, so to right the balance, wouldn't the reverse achieve the same result? If the fundamentals were there, in theory....

"The Winter Solstice," he muttered, his hand coming up to cover his mouth. He quickly brought it back down, his eyes widening.

"The what?" Corbet asked, his curiosity piquing like a cat coaxed into play.

"I said, I think you've found our solution." Ruari felt himself smile, and this time, it reached his eyes. "It's very clever of you to think of that," he continued, nothing but adoration in his voice. "You really never stop surprising, do you?"

Corbet gave him a look and then turned away a bit, a light dusting of pink on his high cheeks. "It's simple logic," he brushed off, gathering his detached mien from where it had momentarily scattered with the praise. "It'll be a long process to right that which was broken," Corbet warned, shifting in his seat, "regardless of whatever it is you've realized."

He looked more comfortable in the throne than Ruari ever had, and it pained him to think that Corbet would call the Unseelie Court his home now.

His home, but not his final destination. Not if Ruari had any say in the matter.

"I am prepared for what lay ahead, no matter what it may be," Ruari answered, coming up to the foot of the throne. "Let us work together until balance has been found and equilibrium restored." He said it like a pledge, like a treaty between the Courts.

Corbet stared up at him when he approached. In his hand, he held Ruari's own crown. "I suppose I should give this back then," he pondered, gesturing for Ruari to kneel. Were it anyone else, Ruari would have refused, but no matter how long he lived, he would never be able to refuse Corbet.

Ruari knelt before the new Monarch, taking his lover by the hand to press a kiss to the ruby red ring still at home on his finger. He still wore it, and be it by chance or by some small measure of recognition, Ruari took it for what he saw it as; hope.

"Welcome to the throne, your majesty," he offered, looking up into dark, dark eyes as the crown was returned to his head. "I look forward to our eternal dance. May you move swiftly and act with conviction."

And fall back into his arms, never to leave them again.

Be it in this life or the next,

he would have his lost one returned.

RUARI AND CORBET
WILL RETURN IN DELUGE...

For more information, please visit:
tdcloud.tumblr.com

Made in the USA
Charleston, SC
06 February 2017